That Ain't The Whole Plan

Skeeter & Bil Stories

By Bil Lepp

Halfdollar Press

leppstorytelling.com

To my wife and kids, the toughest and best critics in the world.
I love you guys!

Cover Photo: Bil Lepp
Back Cover Photo: SAM PAYNE!
Edited by Katelyn Cooney- but any mistakes are mine.

First Edition

10 9 8 7 6 5 4 3 2 1

Table of Contents

A Quick Word 4
Being Civic-Minded Young Men 5
Making it Mine 6
Worst Christmas Ever 9
Skeeter and Bil Break the Ocean 19
Vacation Bible School 33
You're Out! 40
Pinewood Derby: Hand's Off, Dad! 45
The Teacher in the Patriotic Bathing Suit 47
Corn Maze 58
Wally! Come Down Right Now! 67
Ice Sledding 76
Over-Solving 81
The Inflated Easter Bunnies of Halfdollar 86
Strike Anywhere Matches & Anything Can Stretch 93
Church Organ 104
Geomorphology & the Rope Swing 110
Egg Babies 123
Fortune Cookies 140
Mayhem Dressed as an Eight-Point Buck 146
Not Like a Sexy Centaur 150
Love Song to David Bowie 157
Washing Machine Rodeo 162
The Nickel 169
Christmas Artificial Trees 176
Book Reports 182
Bored Gourd 198
Silent Letters 207
Skunks 216
Tunaball 221
Montina the Divine Bovine 226
Raised on Hose Water 235

A Quick Word

I wrote the very first Skeeter story, which in this book is divided into *Making It Mine* and *Mayhem Dressed as an Eight-Point Buck* in 1998, I think. A bunch more followed. There are over thirty Skeet stories in this collection, written over a period of two decades. These stories are arranged in chronological order, more or less, by the age of Skeeter and Bil. Not all of these have been told on stage. If you are familiar with my stories you will recognize parts of some of these tales from where they have crept into other stories. Hopefully your favorite is in here. And hopefully something new will entertain you.

Please note that my full-time job is telling these stories on stage. If you have somehow found this book and have never heard of me, or heard me tell any of these stories, don't fret. Lots of people haven't heard of me. I write most of my own material. When I write, I write things I am going to say out loud and so I write in the spoken language. I have tried very hard to translate this collection from the spoken word into the written word. Also, I'm terrible with commas. I sent a few of these stories to my favorite English professor to edit. He told me commas just slow things down. Get rid of them. I deleted so many commas from this book that it is, I kid you not, an entire page shorter sans commas. Please just read the book and don't fuss over the mistakes. I'm sure there are plenty. There is no need to point them out to me.

Being Civic-Minded Young Men

If you were ever a teenager in a small town
then you know
that the cops are bored, too.
So, they come looking for you
to see what you are doing.
Being civic-minded young men,
Skeeter and I endeavored to participate
in activities
which allowed local law enforcement the opportunity
to practice the skills
they had learned at the academy.

Making it Mine

There are things a father will teach a child that, if the mother knew, would kill her.

We had a dog named Deacon when I was five years old. Every night, my dad took Deacon for a walk. It was during my fifth year that I was deemed old enough to go on that walk with Dad and Deacon. Right away, I started learning things I know my mother didn't want me to know.

Deacon stopped at every tree, lamppost, and fire hydrant along the way. He'd sniff all around the base of the object, lift his leg, and do his thing. I asked Dad what that was about.

"That's the way Deacon marks his territory," Dad explained. "He leaves his mark on those things, and if another dog comes into this neighborhood, he'll smell the scent and know this land belongs to Deacon."

"What if that dog wants the land?"

"Then that dog leaves his mark. The next time Deacon and that dog get together they'll talk about it or fight about it to see who gets the land."

I was five. It didn't make that much sense to me. But it did give me a whole new respect for what real estate agents did all day long.

Mrs. Crankberry lived next door to us. She was the meanest woman I ever met. She was the chairwoman down at the church for the Committee of Little Old Ladies Who Want to be Angry About Something. She had her hair done religiously twice a year. She had it put up into a cone then sealed with all-weather concrete sealant so that it wouldn't move for six months.

Through some twist of the universal irony, the great Yin-Yang, Mrs. Crankberry had the most beautiful yard I had ever seen. It had a slope in the back that was perfect for sledding in the winter. On the other side of her yard was Skitter creek. Right in the middle of her yard was a giant oak tree that rained acorns all summer. But I could not step foot in that yard. Even if one of those acorns were to drop out of that tree and roll into my yard, if Mrs. Crankberry saw me pick it up, she would lower that spike of hair and chase me like a rabid rhinoceros. And this was back in the 1970s when it was still perfectly legal to hurt your neighbors' children.

I'm the last of five children. When you are the last of a long line of children you learn that your parents just don't care that much anymore. My parents' attitude was: "We tried everything with the other four. Nothing worked. Let him figure it out on his own. He can't do any worse than we did."

My mom was more like a jailhouse guard than a maternal figure. She'd look out the window about every eight minutes to check on me and then I had seven minutes and fifty-five seconds to do whatever I wanted to do.

I was sitting in my backyard one day when Mrs. Crankberry came out of her house, got in her enormous car, and drove away. I had an idea. I got up out of my yard and walked into Mrs. Crankberry's yard. I went straight to that big oak tree, got down on my hands and knees, and sniffed all the way around the base of the tree. I didn't know what I was sniffing for but I knew it was part of the process. Then I stood up, dropped my pants, and made that tree mine.

It occurred to me that I had never seen Mrs. Crankberry pee on that tree so maybe it didn't even belong to her. I was five, but she was like a hundred and five, so I figured I could take her in a fight.

Every couple of days, I'd sneak over there and make something else mine.

And then she died.

I don't think it had anything to do with me peeing in her yard.

Within two weeks of her death everything eighteen inches and below in that yard belonged to me.

You can see how it came as quite a surprise when I came home from the grocery store with my mother one day and there was a moving van parked out in front of that house, which I had rightfully claimed. People moving stuff in! Didn't they sniff?

In the backyard there was a kid about my age putting toys out all over the place. That was the last straw. I knew what I had to do. I walked into that yard in front of God and everyone. I went straight up to that oak tree, dropped my pants, and made that tree mine, yet again.

The kid thought that was funny. He came over, dropped his pants, and started going. I knew what I had to do. I slugged him as hard as I could. He slugged me back. Soon, there were two five-year-old boys with their pants around their ankles fighting to the death.

Our mothers saw us and came over to break us up. They made us pull up our pants, apologize to each other, and introduce ourselves.

I felt like I knew that kid pretty well by that point.

His name was Skeeter Barth and after that we became fast friends. But having Skeeter for your best friend is like having a head-cold for a best friend. I never feel right, and he won't go away.

Skeeter was always coming up with ideas that were barely legal, even at the tender age of five.

We'd been in kindergarten for about ten minutes when Skeeter nudged me and said, "Don't you think we ought to make this classroom ours?"

Next thing we knew we were in the nurse's office. We had to stand over the toilet and prove that we knew what to do. It was taking a while because we were tapped out.

Skeeter went pale.

I said, "What's the matter, Buddy?"

He said, "My older brother had a squirt gun. He squirted somebody with it, and they took it away from him. What do you suppose they're going to do to us?"

We made it through that, intact, and embarked on a life-long friendship.

Worst Christmas Ever

My Worst Christmas Ever started the year before.

The world can be a very confusing place when you're a small child because you have a limited vocabulary, and you have to filter everything you hear through that limited vocabulary.

When my youngest daughter was two or three years old, and was just beginning to assemble a vocabulary, and had only recently nailed her first shaky piton into the wall of understanding time, she figured out that not everything happens Today, but the only other day that she could both understand and articulate was Yesterday. She would ask me questions like, “Are we going to Grandma's house Today or Yesterday?”

I would say, “We're going Yesterday,” and we would both be happy because she thinks she's a Time Lord, and I think I'm funny.

So, my worst Christmas Ever actually started the year before. It was just after Christmas. I was four years old. I noticed for the first time that my dad had a bald spot on the back of his head. I asked him how he got it. He said, “On Christmas Eve, I heard a noise on the roof so I went out to see what it was. When I stepped out from underneath the carport something licked the back of my head. I turned around and saw that it was Rudolph. Rudolph licked the hair right off the back of my head.” Then Dad said, “I swore right then and there that if I ever saw Rudolph again, I was going to shoo him away.”

That was not an expression with which I was familiar. When I filtered ‘Shoo him away’ through my limited vocabulary, I came up with ‘Shoot him anyway.’ I thought, “Oh no! Dad is going to kill Rudolph. That could put a damper on next Christmas.”

I worried about that for a few days, but I was four, so I forgot about it soon thereafter. I didn't think of it again until the holiday season started to roll around again.

When you are an adult, and are jaded and have lost all hope, when you hear the phrase ‘the holiday season,’ you think, “Dear Lord, that incredibly stressful period of time between Thanksgiving and New Year's.” But when you are a child, and still have joy in your heart, you rejoice. Kids know that the first holiday in the holiday season is not Thanksgiving. The first, and possibly second most important holiday in the holiday season, is Halloween because that is the other day you get free stuff.

I wondered if Dad remembered his vendetta. I didn't want to remind him, but I had to know. I began asking a series of surreptitious questions. I asked, "Dad, do you even own a gun?"

He said, "No, but I could get one."

I said, "Do you hunt?"

"No. But sometimes I read Field & Stream."

And then I asked a question so veiled that he could never possibly see through it. I said, "Dad, is it even legal to shoot a deer on your roof?"

I don't know what the urban deer population is like where you live but in Halfdollar, West Virginia, yes, if that deer is on your roof, that's your deer.

Dad was going to shoot Rudolph.

To make matters worse there was a national election coming up. I heard my neighbor say, "If Jimmy Carter gets elected president the entire country is going to Hell."

I was five. I had a very narrow, very theological understanding of Hell.

I told my buddy Skeeter about it and he said, "You mean, right away? Or when we die?"

I said, "I think it means right away. If Jimmy Carter gets elected, the people in Canada and the people in Mexico are going to pull out the pins. The entire continental United States is going to fall into the sulfuric pits!"

"Geez," muttered Skeet. "That sounds bad."

Jimmy Carter got elected.

Dad was going to shoot Rudolph. Jimmy Carter was taking us down. I wasn't even sure we would make it to Christmas.

The only thing I had going for me was kindergarten. Our kindergarten teacher was teaching us about world religions, and I was excited. You may think that that is a heady academic curriculum for a bunch of five-year-olds but rest assured, there was going to be plenty of glue, glitter, and macaroni involved.

Our little town of Halfdollar, West Virginia, had two streets. One was called Main Street, and the other was called, Nah, That Ain't Main Street. We were mostly white and mostly Christian. I'm not making excuses for it or apologizing. I'm simply illustrating that we had little or no knowledge about world religions. We had the Methodist church and your standard variety pack of Baptist churches. Our parents told us that there were some Catholics who lived over the hill but we didn't know if that was true or just something they told us so we would go to bed at night. Skeet's family attended the Methodist church where my father was the pastor, so we had similar theological views.

Our teacher was from our small town but she had gone off to Yale or Columbia and had gotten all full of liberal. This was the end of the Hippie era, and while she was not a full-blown hippy, she was certainly a carrier. She was going to teach us about Buddhism, Hinduism, Islam, Confucianism, Judaism, and whatever else she knew about.

The first thing she told us was that not everybody celebrated the birth of the Lord Jesus Christ. This blew us away. No one had ever told us that before. We thought, "Those poor children don't worship Jesus? Shocking." We were shocked, but not so much in a theological, "Oh my, what of their eternal souls," kind of way. It was more of a good ol' American capitalist "Oh boy. No Jesus means no Christmas. Which means no free stuff. Those poor kids."

We learned that Muslims fast from dawn to dusk for thirty days during Ramadan. To understand what it felt like to fast for thirty days, we skipped snack one day. Then we knew what a month of fasting was like.

We were also going to make a Menorah and a felt Santa Claus.

I very much wanted to make that felt Santa for several reasons. First, I thought if I did a really good job on it, it would be like a talisman, a positive Voodoo doll, and Santa would sense what a good job I had done on his image, and if Dad did shoot Rudolph, maybe Santa wouldn't visit the sins of the father on the son. Second, it was a Christmas tree ornament. If I did a good job on it, I could give it to my mother as a present and she would hang it on the tree where the best ornaments go, which is of course the back of the tree.

I had some friends over to my house during this period, and we were playing Hide and Seek. My oldest brother had the measles and was lying on the couch under a blanket. It seemed like the perfect place to hide. I thought, "What idiot would look under that blanket?" It never occurred to me to ask, "What moron would hide under that blanket?"

Nobody found me. In fact, I didn't see anybody but my mother and the doctor for the next ten days. They had already made the felt Santas when I went back to school. I asked the teacher if I could make one anyway and she said, "No. We've moved past that. But you can make a Menorah." I thought, "I had the measles, not my Bar Mitzvah." (Don't get too emotionally involved. Most of this is made up.)

I told my mother about it when I got home but I'm the last of five children. Maybe it's not that my mother didn't care; it's just that her Sympathy tank was empty. I had to lose a limb, and it not be my own fault, if I wanted any sympathy. When I told her I didn't get to make the Santa, she said, "Whatever doesn't kill you will put hair on your chest."

Dad was going to shoot Rudolph. Jimmy Carter was taking us down. And I didn't get to make the Santa.

Now the only thing I had going for me was when my mother said, "Oh, I'm so excited. Someone gave us tickets to go see Elephant Gerald at the symphony hall."

I loved elephants when I was a kid. I had elephant stuffed animals, elephant trinkets, elephant knick-knacks, posters of elephants, and elephant bed sheets. My favorite book was *Babar*.

I had no idea who Elephant Gerald was, but I did know that only important elephants had names. Babar, Dumbo, Jumbo, and Horton were the only elephants I knew by name. How many other elephants were important enough to have a name?

Mom said Elephant Gerald was a singer and that there would be music.

I told Skeet that mom said Elephant Gerald had played with Count Basie, Duke Ellington, and Louis Armstrong.

"Louis Armstrong?" he asked, amazed. "The first man on the moon?"

"Yep. And a Count and a Duke."

Skeet whistled. "Boy, you gotta be important to play with a Count and a Duke." He paused, then mused, "I wonder how elephants even play music?"

I didn't know much about music at the time. I thought trombone players were the greatest musicians in the world because I fully misunderstood the mechanics of the instrument. I thought they were swallowing the slide. I said, "I think elephants play their trunks like trumpets."

"Or maybe," said Skeet, "they stick their trunks out to the side, and another elephant plays it like a flute."

"Orrrrr!" I said excitedly, "Orrrr, an elephant comes on stage in a kilt, sticks his trunk in his own mouth, and then blows 'til he's full of air. Then, he holds is breath, squeezes himself like a bagpipe, and sound comes out his backside."

We were five years old. It was an intoxicating idea.

The big day arrived. My mother told me to go get dressed. She had laid out an outfit for me but I had a better idea. I had a three-piece suit. What more, I had assembled it myself. I knew that to have a three-piece suit, one needed pants, a vest, and a jacket all made of the same material. I had recently acquired a denim vest at a garage sale. This, along with a pair of Toughskin blue jeans and a blue jean jacket, completed the set.

I put on my three-piece suit and went upstairs. My mother pointed and said, "No!"

I went back downstairs and put on the boring outfit she had laid out for me.

We drove the hour and a half to the symphony hall and took our seats. I was excited. The lights dimmed, the music started, the curtains opened, and what I took for the opening act came on stage. She was a Rubenesque, middle-aged, African American woman. She sang a song about a knife named Mack. When she finished, I asked my mother, "Where's the elephant?"

She said, "Shh."

Every time the lady on stage finished a song I asked my mother, with increasing urgency, "Where's the elephant?" My mother's shushing became more and more insistent. Then the lady sang *A*

Tisket, A Tasket, and *Sleigh Bells* and left the stage. People stood and applauded. The lights came on. The show was over. We got in the car.

I was distraught. I began to sob like only a child can. I was wracked with tears, gasping for air.

"What is wrong with you?" asked my parents.

"I…wanted…to…see…the…elephant!" I said in a nearly un-understandable sob.

"What elephant?" my confused and exasperated mother asked.

"El…e…phant Ger…ald!"

And she burst out laughing in the way that adults do when a child has utterly misunderstood the world. "No, no, baby, not Ele*phant* Gerald," she howled, gasping almost as hard as I was. "Ella *Fitz*gerald."

Years later, when I first told my wife that story, she told me that when she was a child in Yazoo County, Mississippi, which is as flat as it can be for farther than you can see, her parents decided to take her and her sister to the Great Smokey Mountains to see what Not Flat looked like.

They were driving up the mountains and her sister said, "My ears just popped."

Her mother said, "Oh, my ears just popped."

My wife said, "My ears have not popped. What will happen if my ears don't pop?'

Her father said, "Your head will explode."

Five minutes later she was in the backseat sobbing: "My…head…is…going…to…EXPLODE!"

Hilarious. You can imagine the torments we put our children through.

Dad was going to shoot Rudolph. Jimmy Carter was taking us down. I didn't get to make the Santa. There was no elephant. And we had to go visit Aunt Lenore.

Aunt Lenore was not our aunt. She was a friend of my grandmother. Aunt Lenore had no family of her own so she adopted my grandmother's grandchildren as her own. Every year she knitted each cousin a pair of slippers. But I didn't know they were slippers for a long time because they were not foot shaped. They were football shaped. And the hole was in the middle so that there was room for foot in front of the hole and foot behind the hole. I don't know anybody with foot in front of the hole and foot behind the hole, except the Peanuts gang, and I'm not related to any of them. Except, of course, Snoopy (which we will discuss later). But Snoopy rarely wears slippers. To make matters worse, Aunt Lenore was legally blind, bless her heart. I think the ladies at the yarn store took advantage of her. She would ask for red and green colored yarn, but they would give her puke and vomit colored yarn.

Every Christmas we had to visit Aunt Lenore because, let's face it, Christmas is the time of year you go see people you don't really like. And you had to hug Aunt Lenore. Aunt Lenore had that particular old lady smell- not the general old lady smell, most old ladies smell like lilacs and Ben Gay- Aunt Lenore had that particular old lady smell which was equal parts mothballs and cat urine.

We had to hug Aunt Lenore. Hugging Aunt Lenore was like hugging an old Christmas tree. Chances were, you were going to get poked, come away sticky, and, if you weren't gentle, you'd break off a limb.

I found myself home alone three days before the culmination of my worst Christmas ever. I was five years old. It wasn't neglect. It was the Seventies.

When you are the last of five children nobody gets tired of telling you that you are 'everybody's responsibility.' That's code for 'nobody's responsibility.' Everyone assumes everyone else is teaching you things. I was nineteen years old when I finally figured out the difference between my elbow and my shoulder. (The previous joke is an oral joke, not a written joke, which is why you may not have laughed just now. Imagine, though, that I am SAYING this joke to you and when I say "elbow," I point at my shoulder, and when I say "shoulder," I point at my elbow. Get it? No? Try it in front of a mirror. I'll wait.)

I found myself home alone. The Christmas tree was up in the living room. There were presents under the tree. Some of those presents were for me. Dad was going to shoot Rudolph. Jimmy Carter was taking us down. I didn't even know if we were going to make it to Christmas. I figured I might as well open them and see what I would have gotten had events not transpired to send both Rudolph and me to the fiery pits of Hell.

I unwrapped them. I saw what they were. I rewrapped them. My mother is a meticulous wrapper. That is in no way a hip-hop reference. I rewrapped the presents as best I could.

Finally, it was Christmas Eve. I was lying in my bed with warring emotions raging in my head. I was anxious and excited.

I was anxious because Christmas was just a few hours away but so much could go wrong in those few hours. Dad could shoot Rudolph. Jimmy Carter could take us down.

I was excited because it was just a few hours to Christmas, and if we could make it through those few hours, everything would be okay.

I don't know if I dreamt it, imagined it, or if it happened, but I heard the screen door go *fump-fump*, which is the sound I think the screen door makes when it opens and closes, and then I heard, *BLAM*! I thought, "Oh no. He did it. Dad shot Rudolph."

I fell asleep eventually. I know I did because I woke up, and that is evidence that you fell asleep. I awoke and it was Christmas morning. We'd made it! My Christmas stocking was on the bed beside me. In our household the stocking did not remain hanging by the fire with care. Santa brought the stocking into your room and laid it beside you in the bed.

We got the same thing in our stockings every year. My parents, Santa, and my grandfather, whom we called Grosspapa- it's German for 'Great Papa' and has nothing to do with his hygiene- worked in conjunction to fill our stockings.

From our parents, we got two walnuts and an orange because they had lived through the Depression, and they wanted us to know how miserable their Christmases had been.

Grosspapa gave each of the cousins a prescription bottle full of coins. He saved all his prescription bottles throughout the year and filled them with coins. Grosspapa didn't care about equal pay, though. You got the coin that fit the diameter of the bottle.

He took one pill that must have been enormous because the bottle held Eisenhower dollars. One kid got twenty bucks in Eisenhower dollars, and one kid got a buck-twenty in dimes. Grosspapa was happy as long as each kid got a bottle of coins.

Oh, and he didn't wash the bottles. About halfway through Christmas Day Mom would look at your glazed eyes and scream, "Take that dime out of your mouth!"

"But it feels so good…"

From Santa, each of us got two packets of Quaker flavored oatmeal: one pack of Cinnamon & Apple, and one pack of Maple & Brown Sugar. That would be our Christmas breakfast. We only ever got flavored oatmeal at Christmas. We never saw flavored oatmeal except on Christmas day. I don't know why. It's not any more expensive than regular oatmeal. Maybe there were fewer arguments if we had no choices.

I wet the bed until I was eleven years old. Not continuously. I got some other things done. I'd wet the bed that night and so when I awoke my oatmeal had already begun. Which was awful because that meant I was going to have to swap it out with one of my siblings' oatmeal when nobody was looking.

I went upstairs and opened presents. Some of them were not what they were supposed to be. I knew what they were supposed to be because I had opened them three days ago. What was supposed to be a basketball was now a pillow duct-taped into a sphere. I may have given myself away when I opened another present and said, "Hey, this isn't supposed to be a sixteen ounce can of mixed vegetables."

It was explained to me that I got the vegetables so I could 'learn a very important lesson' about opening gifts early. Let me tell you, Christmas is no day to 'learn a very important lesson.'

I can tell you what I wasn't thinking that night as I lay in bed. I wasn't thinking that I should be thankful that I had educators who really wanted to expand my mind; a family that loved me (when they remembered me); a family that was willing to take in people like Aunt Lenore- marginalized people who had no one else in the world- and make sure they felt loved and wanted. I should have been thankful for a roof to sleep under, food to eat, and a nice, warm, safe bed to pee in. I should have been thinking of that, and how my worst Christmas was probably better than many people's best Christmas.

But I wasn't thinking that because I was five years old.

What I wish I had been thinking was "Almost all of these problems occurred because I misunderstood something." I bet ninety percent of the problems in the world happen because we misunderstand each other. And a lot of the time we deliberately misunderstand each other. We see someone coming toward us and we think, "I don't care what that person says or thinks. I don't like the color of their skin, or how they vote, or how they identify, who they worship, who they love… so I don't care what they say; I'm not listening." But if we took five minutes out of our day to really listen to other people, people we don't think we agree with, and try to understand, not agree with, but at least understand, what they are saying, I bet we could solve eighty-five percent of the problems in the world. But I wasn't thinking that. Because I was five.

What I was thinking was, "THIS IS THE WORST CHRISTMAS EVER!"

Skeeter and Bil Break the Ocean

Adults, if you are not lying to your children or grandchildren, you need to start.

Children, if you have adults who are not lying to you, you need to find better adults.

People ask me all the time how I learned to tell stories. I trace it back to my grandfather, whom we called Grosspapa.

The truth is fluid in our family. It is up to the listener to decide what is true. I had friends who loathed going to their grandparents' because "they always tell the same stories." Grosspapa never told the same story, at least not the same way. He would tell us, "Once, my buddy and I were riding our horses down the street, and we saw a woman being accosted by a man. My buddy jumped off his horse and saved the woman." The next time I heard the story it would be, "Once, my buddy and I were riding our horses down the street, and we saw a woman being accosted by ten men. My buddy *and I* jumped off our horses and saved the woman." Next time it would be, "Once, I was riding my horse down the street, and I saw a woman being attacked by the entire Red Army, and I jumped off my horse and saved the woman."

Grosspapa told me he rode with Lawrence of Arabia. It made sense. He was in that part of the world at that time, spoke some Arabic. I believed that story until I was about fourteen. I told it to a reporter, and she put in the paper that Grosspapa had ridden with Laurence Olivier. So now we have that going for us, too.

He told me ice cream trucks only played music when they were out of ice cream. He probably didn't invent that but it illustrates the kind of man he was.

He told me we were related to the man who shot down the Red Baron, and that that man's nickname was Snoopy, so I am also related to Snoopy.

I have never spent time verifying the veracity of Grosspapa's stories. I believe what I want, and that is who I am.

My mother-in-law thought she was interesting. She had heard that she was part Native American, part Black, part Romani, and part other ethnicities. She wanted to take one of those DNA tests. I told her not to, to just be satisfied with who she thought she was.

She took the test and found out she was 97.8% Northern European. No offense to Northern Europeans, but there is nothing less interesting than 97.8% Northern European. I told her, "Maybe you suffered ethnic leak."

My buddy, Andy Offutt Irwin's Aunt Marguerite is the same sort of person as Grosspapa. Andy caught a mess of tadpoles when he was a kid and put them in a five-gallon pickle jar. Every day he would come home from school and watch the tadpoles. Aunt Marguerite showed up one day and said, "What are you doing?"

"Watching my tadpoles."

"Watching for what?" asked Aunt Marguerite.

"Watching for them to turn into frogs," explained Andy.

"You know how you can speed that process up?" asked Aunt Marguerite, clearly headed down a Grosspapa-like path.

"No," said an attentive Andy.

Aunt Marguerite asked, "What does a tadpole have that a frog doesn't?"

"A tale."

"And what does a frog have that a tadpole doesn't?"

"Legs."

Aunt Marguerite said, "Right. If you push the tale in, the legs will pop out."

Advice like that doesn't do much for the tadpole, but it undoubtedly rouses a young person's interest in scientific experimentation.

My father-in-law practiced the same sort of 'insert what facts you will to enhance a story' policy. Thus, it was perfectly acceptable when I participated in the following conversation at his funeral:

"What did your father-in-law do?"

"He worked for the Forest Service for forty-some years."

"How old was he when he died?"

"We're not sure. But after everybody leaves we are going to cut him in half and count the rings."

I grew up in a family, and I associate with people from families, who told and tell stories to entertain both themselves and their listeners and who put the best polish on even the miserable times.

When I was a little kid, I was little. I didn't break six-feet tall or a hundred pounds until I was a freshman in high school. I was bad at everything. I didn't win much.

To make matters worse, Katie, my sibling closest in age, was good at everything. One wall of her room was nothing but blue ribbons from the swim team we were on, with a rare second place ribbon here and there from when she was forced to be on a relay team with some weak sister who was never heard from again. Another wall was nothing but trophies. And they were not 'Your Parents Paid $25 for You to be on the Team' trophies. They were 'Most Runs Batted In,' 'Most Baskets Scored,' 'Most Awards Won' trophies. Katie got good grades and had all the teachers I had, but a year ahead of me, thus setting up unachievable expectations for my academic abilities and leading to teachers saying things like, "You're not the same caliber of student as your sister are you?"

The year I was in the third grade I figured out in August what I wanted to be for Halloween. I was going to go as a Rice Krispies box. I started working on my costume right away. I got a big box and cut a hole out of the top. I painted Snap, Crackle, and Pop on the front. I painted educational yet entertaining games on the back. On one side I painted nutritional information. On the other side I painted the recipe for Rice Krispie treats.

It was announced that we were going to be able to wear our costumes to school for Halloween. We were going to have a contest. You could win 'Best in Class' and 'Best in School.' My sister asked if she could wear my costume to school for the contest. In a fit of generosity, I agreed. She won 'Best in Class' and 'Best in School.' And she would not give me the ribbons.

Her name is Katie. She lives in Dayton. If you see her, give her the stink eye.

We were learning about the Water Cycle in class at that time. We learned how the Sun evaporates water in the ocean. The evaporated water then rises into the air, condenses, collects itself into clouds, and those clouds eventually drift over the land, get heavy, and then return the water to the surface in the form of rain. The rain makes its way to the streams and rivers where it subsequently flows back into the oceans where it can evaporate and start the whole process over again.

I decided I would do my Science Fair project on the Water Cycle. I filled a brownie pan with water and rigged a hairdryer to blow hot air into the water, causing some of it to evaporate. I put a terrarium, which is a fancy word for an upside-down fish tank, over the brownie pan and hair dryer. I painted a seascape to put behind the terrarium. Condensation gathered on the top of the terrarium, and I could bump the table with my hip, and the condensation would fall down like rain, back into the pan. It was nifty, and I was hoping to win first place.

The judges came to my table. I read my report and then bumped the table. The hairdryer fell into the pan of water, and the lights went out. In the entire county.

I didn't win.

I went home and cried to my mother about how bad I was at everything, and how I would never be good at anything, and about how I would never be much use in the world. That I would never change the world.

I don't know why I thought I needed to change the world but I was upset about it.

She told me I was good at stuff (though now that I look back I realize she wasn't very specific about WHAT I was good at) and would, eventually, not only find my place in the world, but maybe change the world. She said most people who changed the world didn't set out to do that. Newton, George Washington, Rosa Parks, Chuck Yeager, Harvey Milk, Freddie Mercury (my mother said neither Harvey Milk nor Freddie Mercury but I know she meant them, too) were just doing what they liked to do, or needed to do, and their actions changed things, or inspired others, but they didn't mean to change the world. She said most people who changed the world were just living their lives as best they could.

I said I was too little and too powerless to change the world.

But what she said made me feel better, or at least it made me fall asleep.

My family vacationed on the island of Islesboro, Maine most summers when I was a kid. My father would put our eighteen-foot Grumman canoe in the driveway. He would pack all of the family's gear into heavy duty trash bags and then lash them into the canoe. Mr. Kosky would come over and help Dad lift the canoe onto the luggage rack of our Grand Safari Pontiac station wagon.

If you don't know what a station wagon is just imagine a mini-van, only lower, and cooler. A station wagon is called a station wagon because it was designed to take people and their steamer trunks to and from the station. That car was longer than the room you are sitting in. When Dad and Mr. Kosky put the eighteen-foot canoe atop the car, the canoe did not stick out over the windshield or the back of the car.

The reason Dad needed to put all the luggage on top of the car was because in that car, for the twenty-one-hour trip to Maine, was my father, my mother, Grosspapa, Ama, my brothers Paul and Kevin, my sisters Tammy and Katie, myself, my buddy Skeeter, and the dog.

Ten people and a dog in a car that had more cigarette lighters than seatbelts.

My dad drove, mom beside him, Grosspapa on the passenger side of the front bench seat. My brother Paul, Ama, and my brother Kevin rode in the middle bench seat. In the back of that car, in the wide-open area designed to transport steamer trunks were my sisters Tammy and Katie, myself, Skeeter, and the dog.

It was spacious back there. We could do anything we wanted because even if the adults had been inclined to look back to see what we were doing, and they were not inclined, they couldn't reach us.

The back of the car had a tailgate door. The window in the door was as wide as the door. Dad rolled that window all the way down.

My sisters, Skeeter, and I played a game we liked to call: *Who Can Be the Last Person to Leave a State?*

This involved stretching as far out that back window as possible. "Hold my belt! Hold my ankles!"

The people in the cars behind us thought it was hilarious.

We stopped at a rest stop somewhere in the vast wastelands of New England. When you are on a long trip, if one person has to go to the bathroom, everybody has to go to the bathroom. I was the last person to get back in the car. The easiest way for me to get in and out of the car was to climb through the back window. I made eye contact with Dad and Grosspapa in the rearview mirror. I was tired so I pulled a blanket over me.

My brother Kevin tended to get car sick so he had switched places with my sister Tammy. She was now in the middle seat, and Kevin was in the back because it was less of a mess for him to puke out the back window of the car than out of the side window. At least for us: not so much for the cars behind us.

Dad pulled out of the rest stop and headed down the highway. About twenty miles later, my sister Tammy shouted, "Where's Bil? I think we left Bil back at the rest stop!"

That's how it is when you're the fifth child. It takes twenty miles for someone to notice you're not there.

Grosspapa said, "Well, I told him we'd leave him if he didn't hurry."

Tammy burst into tears.

My dad said, "We'll pick him up on the way back."

My mom said, "JOHN!"

Dad said, "Oh, he'll be fine."

My mom said, "JOHN!"

I thought my dad's name was JOHN! instead of just John, for the first eleven years of my life.

My sister was wailing.

I stayed hidden for another five minutes.

Ah, good memories.

The final event of the in-motion portion of the trip was the ferry ride. We drove the car onto a big ferry boat that shuttled us, and others, from the mainland over to Islesboro. We got out of the car and leaned on the rails and watched the water as we crossed the bay. There were lots of colorful buoys in the water marking lobster traps, but I didn't know what they were. I asked Grosspapa. He pondered the brightly colored buoys dotting the bay and said, "Those mark the spots where all the other ferry boats sank."

You'd think I would've eventually learned not to ask Grosspapa questions but by the time I figured out he always lied, I had also figured out why his answers were the best answers.

Tempers were a little short when we finally arrived at the cabin, after two days in the car with ten people.

Skeeter and I were of an age where we were more helpful if we weren't involved.

Young people, if your parents want you to do the dishes, just break the dishes and they'll stop asking. (Legal Notice: Don't break the dishes. That's just a joke.)

The adults said what amounted to, "You two. You two, seven-year-old boys. Go play in the ocean. Go play unsupervised in the ocean. You'll probably be fine. If not, well, that's a shame."

Grosspapa was old enough, and wise enough, to get out of work whenever possible. He volunteered to babysit us which would have rankled us, except we knew he just meant he was going to take a nap. Skeet and I ran toward the ocean, and Grosspapa grabbed a lawn chair and followed.

In front of our little cabin was about twenty-feet of grass, then a path down a slight slope, and then it was maybe fifty-yards across a rock-covered beach to the ocean.

Skeet and I ran across the yard, down the beach, and straight into the North Atlantic Ocean, then straight out of the North Atlantic Ocean. Even in July the water was cold. Very cold. When you weigh fifty-three pounds and have about 3% body fat you can go hypothermic holding a lukewarm soda at noon in the Sahara.

That is the coldest water I have ever been in. By the end of that trip I was blue from my feet to my knees from wading in the water. I was pale white from my knees to my waist where my trunks covered me, and I was bright red from my waist to my forehead from sunburn. I looked like a patriotic rocket popsicle.

Skeet and I made our way over to Grosspapa. He took one look at our blue lips and shivering bodies and asked, "Is it cold?"

"Yes."

He said, "You need to acclimate yourselves to the water. Then you won't notice how cold it is."

"How do we do that?"

"The best way to do that is to run into the water as deep as you can, then submerge yourselves fully in the water."

Skeeter and I ran into the ocean and dove beneath the surface. We popped out of the water and ran back up the beach.

"Are you acclimated?" Grosspapa asked.

"I don't think so," I said.

"Did you open your eyes?" Grosspapa asked.

"No."

"You have to open your eyes to get acclimated."

Skeeter and I ran into the ocean and dove beneath the surface. We opened our eyes. We popped out of the water and ran back up the beach.

"Did you open your eyes?"

"Yes."

"What happened?" Grosspapa asked.

"It burned," I said.

"Yeah," said Grosspapa, "that's because it's saltwater."

"It was dark," Skeeter said.

Grosspapa nodded as if he already knew all these things. "It's dark because the sunlight can only penetrate so deep into the water. The deeper you go in the ocean the darker it gets. If you go deep enough there is no light at all."

"Wait," I said. That can't be true. I can see all the way to the bottom of the deep end of the swimming pool."

"That," said Grosspapa, "is because the pool is freshwater, but the ocean is saltwater. Saltwater is more buoyant than freshwater, so the light can't penetrate as deep."

"Why?"

"Because," he said, "it's light. So, it floats." He continued, "If you go deep enough, deep, deep, deep down into the ocean, where there is no light at all, there are bioluminescent creatures. Creatures who make their own light."

"Like lightening bugs?"

"Sorta. There's a fish, for example, called the anglerfish. It has a pole, like a light pole, sticking right out of its forehead, with a light on the end so it can see where it is going."

"How come it doesn't float to the surface if it has a light on its head?"

"It's a fish. It can swim."

"How deep down are the anglerfish?" Skeet asked.

"Deep. Six, maybe seven feet down."

Skeeter and I spent the next thirty minutes taking deep breaths, diving beneath the surface of the frigid North Atlantic, grabbing rocks so we wouldn't float, opening our eyes in the burning saltwater, and waiting for anglerfish to swim by.

This is why you should lie to children. A high-quality adult can almost always find a way to get kids to overcome discomfort and have fun despite circumstances.

Eventually, Skeet and I couldn't spend one more minute in the water. We returned to Grosspapa, who was sitting beside a stream that ran into the ocean. "You boys ever built a dam?" Grosspapa asked.

"Sure," we said. "Lots of 'em."

"If you build a dam in this creek," Grosspapa explained, "you can create a pool of water behind it. The sun will heat the pool. It'll be like a hot tub. You can go swim in the ocean, and when you get too cold you can come sit in your hot tub until you warm up." He looked at just me and said, "You're a natural born dam builder."

"I am?"

"You know what church our family belonged to when I was your age?"

There was no sense trying to figure out where Grosspapa was headed. It was best to just roll with him.

"Mennonite," I said.

"Do you know what Mennonites are famous for?"

Skeet and I shook our heads.

"Well, not to put too fine a point on it, but a lot of people didn't like the Mennonites. They were forced from their homes time and again and when there was no place left to go, the Mennonites invented dikes and dams, built them along the coast of western Europe, and invented Holland. Catharine the Great was so impressed she invited the Mennonites to move to Russia where they invented farming."

We set to work on the dam. Skeet and I worked for hours piling up rocks and sticks, shoveling sand to fill holes, and extending the sides. By the time my mother called us to supper our dam was four feet tall and maybe eight feet long. Not a drop of water made it through or around our dam.

We ate supper, played some board games, then we all went to bed.

Skeeter and I 'got to' sleep on the screened in porch.

Children people, if your adults start telling you how lucky you are that you 'get to' do something, beware! If they are making you think it's wonderful to 'get to' do something like sleep in a sleeping bag on the board floor of the screened in porch while they 'have to' sleep in a room, in a bed, in the house, you are being manipulated. If it was so great to do whatever they are telling you you 'get to' do, they'd just move you and do it themselves.

It was creepy out on the porch. In the 1970s, the little island of Islesboro, Maine had more, not per capita, just more werewolves and lunatic hordes of axe murderers roaming the woods than any other place in the world. The only thing that separated us from them was 0.4 millimeters of screen. Every noise we heard was an approaching hostile. But we weren't scared. We told each other ghost stories to prove we weren't scared. At about four AM we were too tired to not be scared anymore, so we fell asleep.

Grosspapa woke us at dawn. We heard his soft whisper saying quietly, but urgently, "Boys, boys?! Wake up. Look at this." He was pointing toward the ocean. We wiped sleep from our eyes and sat up.

"I think you have a problem," he whispered. "I think you broke the ocean."

My stomach sank. Sure enough. Whereas the water's edge had been maybe fifty yards down the beach when we had arrived yesterday, now the water's edge was at least seventy-five yards away.

"What? How? How did we break the ocean?" Skeet and I asked.

"Do you know anything about the Water Cycle?" Grosspapa asked.

"As a matter of fact, I do," I stated. "The Sun evaporates ocean water, that water turns to vapor, then it forms into clouds which blow out over the land. They get heavy. It rains. The rain falls on the Earth's surface and flows into creeks, which refill the ocean."

"Exactly," said Grosspapa. "That dam you built. It's stopping the flow of water back into the ocean. And that is bad. Boys, this is very serious. I'm not sure what to say about what you have done." He said this while shaking his head as though he weren't complicit. He went on, "Think of the destruction. If there is no water in the ocean all the whales and fishes and starfishes and mackerel and urchins and crabs and sharks and rays and jellyfish and dogfish and sea bass and seals and barnacles and otters and anglerfish will perish. Not to mention that all sea-going cargo will cease, probably bringing the world markets to a halt. And, of course, if you drain the ocean, then there's no water to evaporate. If there is no water, the water cycle will stop, and there'll be no more rain. There will be droughts and famine. Oh boys, you better work fast. Go tear that dam down!"

"No way," Skeet protested.

"'No way' what?" Grosspapa asked.

"No way human activity could possibly impact the environment that drastically."

"Go dig," Grosspapa said. "You boys run to the dam. Start tearing it down. Get the water flowing back into the ocean. I'll cover for you. Maybe if you hurry, and get the water flowing again, you can refill the ocean before anybody notices."

As Skeet and I attacked the dam Grosspapa strolled up with his lawn chair and a cup of coffee.

It didn't take long to tear the dam down.

"Okay," Grosspapa said, looking over from his chair. "Now, you two hide behind this log, and I'll go get us some breakfast. But you hide in case the ocean cops show up. They'll probably be undercover, disguised as small sail boats, or big freighters, or lobster boats, or motorboats. We just can't be sure."

He brought us a breakfast picnic which we ate behind our log.

There were plenty of undercover ocean police cruising offshore.

"Probably trying to triangulate our position," said Skeet.

Skeet and I lay down behind the log. The exertion of tearing down the dam, the food in our bellies, the lack of sleep, and the ebbing adrenaline lulled us into a deep, late morning nap.

From which Grosspapa woke us sometime later to say, "Boys, look. I think it's working."

We looked. Sure enough, the water was creeping up. It was about back to where it had been yesterday.

"Yesterday?" Grosspapa asked, "How high was the water? Do you think it was this high?"

"I don't know," Skeet said.

"I don't know either. I think it is higher today than it was yesterday." Grosspapa said. "I think you might have started letting too much water into the ocean. If too much water is flowing in, the ocean is going to flood Maine. And Maine is north. And north is up. And water flows downhill. If you flood Maine, all that water is going to bottleneck down through New England, flood the rest of the United States, and then Mexico and South America. You've got to get that creek flowing exactly like it was yesterday."

There we were, two seven-year-old boys with no knowledge of hydrology, trying to restore the creek to the proper flow.

Mom called us for supper. We ate supper, played some board games, then we all went to bed.

"Boys, boys," Grosspapa woke us the next morning. "Look! It's draining again. You slowed the flow of the creek too much."

Stupid ocean!

"All I can think to do," Grosspapa said, "well, I have one last idea. Displacement. Do you know what displacement is?"

"No," we yawned.

"Displacement is, uh, the idea that two bodies of mass can't occupy the same space. Like when you fill the tub halfway up and then get in. The water rises but not because there is more water in the tub. It's just that your mass pushes the water out of its way, so the water rises.

"I'm thinking," Grosspapa continued, "that if you can throw enough rocks into the ocean, you may displace enough water to make it look like the ocean is as full as it should be."

Off to the beach we went, to spend the day throwing stones into the surf. We threw rocks until we couldn't move our right arms anymore. Then we threw rocks until we couldn't move our left arms. Then we kicked rocks into the ocean.

It was working. The water was rising. In fact, the water rose so high that Grosspapa said, "Maybe you threw too many rocks. You better build a seawall in case there is a flood."

We were building the seawall when I heard my parents coming up behind us. You may be asking yourself, "Where have they been for two days?"

I don't know.

My mom said, "What are you guys doing?"

The emotion, the lack of sleep, the adrenaline, and the angst collided inside me. "We broke the ocean! We broke the ocean!"

My dad looked at his dad.

Then my dad said, "Goodness. I guess we better hide you in the basement."

"JOHN!" shouted my mother.

"What?" Dad said. "Only until after the ocean cops come. Then we can stow them away on a ship to Timbuktu."

"JOHN!" shouted my mother.

Dad and Grosspapa walked off giggling.

My mom knelt between me and Skeeter. "Look," she said, "there is no doubt that the two of you are good at breaking things. But I don't think even the two of you alone could break the ocean. Didn't anyone ever teach you about the tides?"

I'm from West Virginia. The freshest seafood I ever had as a kid said 'StarKist' on the can. I did not know about the tides.

Mom said, "The Moon and the Sun pull on the water in the ocean. In fact, their gravity pulls on everything on Earth, but because water is fluid it is the only thing that you can easily see move. The Sun is a star and is enormous, but the Moon is closer, and proximity is power. Tides are complicated, but suffice it to say, as the Earth spins beneath the Moon, the Moon's gravity pulls the ocean toward it in a bulge. As your part of the world spins into that bulge of water, you experience high tide. The water comes up the beach. As you spin out of the bulge, you get low tide. The water recedes. You generally get two high tides and two low tides a day.

"The ocean is huge," she continued. "It has enormous volume and is almost inexpressibly larger and more powerful than the two of you. The ocean has incredible potential energy.

"The ocean is pulled by the Moon and Sun, blown by hurricanes, frozen by frigid air, earthquakes on one side of the world can cause tsunamis on the other. The ocean can toss ships around or crush them in its ice. It can wash away bridges and roads. It can wipe out whole islands or cities. The ocean's power can be harnessed by all sorts of forces to change the world. But," my mother paused, putting her hands on our shoulders, "you two are more powerful than the ocean. The ocean can't do anything on its own. The ocean can't change the world unless another force acts on it. You two are smaller, way, way smaller than the ocean, but you are more powerful than the ocean because you can *decide* to change the world, and the ocean can't decide anything."

She stood and left us.

Skeet and I stared at the sea. I turned and walked toward the house.

"Where are you goin?" Skeet asked.

"To change the world."

"How?"

"I'm gonna get an extension cord and the world's biggest hairdryer."

Vacation Bible School

Skeeter and I loved the Halfdollar Baptist church. When I say we loved the Baptist church I mean we loved the *building* that was the Baptist church. We were indifferent to the institution because we were Methodist.

The reason we loved the building that was the Baptist church is because the attic was infested with bats. On spring, summer, and fall evenings you could sit behind the church and watch thousands and thousands of bats fly out from under the eaves, from the steeple, and the vents. It was a beautiful sight to see.

Skeeter and I were very excited when it was announced that because they were doing renovations at the Methodist church, we would have a joint Vacation Bible School at the Baptist church. We were excited for several reasons. First, we had lots of Baptist friends, but it was difficult to tell the Baptist kids from the Methodist kids on the playground because we all knew the same bad words. We were excited to have the opportunity to see the Baptist kids being Baptist in their natural Baptist habitat. Second, we understood they had a baptismal in the Baptist church.

Methodists get baptized as infants. You don't have much to do with it. Just a little water sprinkled on your head. Baptists get fully submerged in a thing kind of like a bathtub, which is called a baptismal.

I asked my dad why Methodists got a little water on the head, but the Baptists got a full-bore dunking. He said that is because Methodists just have dirty minds, but the Baptists are dirty all over.

Finally, there is no re-baptism in the Methodist church. It's a once and done event. We understood that there were Baptists who got baptized, like, once a week. We were hoping to see that happen.

When we got to the church on the first day of Vacation Bible School the little old ladies who were running the show put the boys on one side of the sanctuary and the girls on the other.

We sang some hymns and right away you could tell the Baptist kids from the Methodist kids because the Baptist kids knew the words, and the Methodist kids were looking for the hymnals. Somebody gave a goofy devotional, and then it was time to give the offering.

Instead of passing the plates in the traditional fashion, the boys were lined up along the wall on our side of the sanctuary, and the girls were lined up on their side. We progressed forward. Someone had built in front of the altar an offering-giving device the likes of which I had never seen before and have never seen since. It was a two-by-four, standing upright, maybe three feet tall. Bolted loosely across the top of it was another two-by-four, so that it formed a cross, or a scale. On our side of the crosspiece, hanging by binders twine, was a coffee can painted blue. On the girls' side, hanging by binders twine, was a coffee can painted pink. The boys put their money in the blue can; the girls put their money in the pink can. Whichever side, pink or blue, went down, that gender *won* the offering.

There is a lot wrong with that.

And it's not even all theological.

Part of the problem is that the simple weight of American money no longer has much to do with the value of American money. A nickel is twice the size of a dime but is only worth half as much. Ten pennies weigh more than a hundred-dollar bill.

Skeet and I knew that firsthand.

There had been a blizzard earlier that year and Skeet and I had decided to shovel snow to make a little money.

I'm the last of five children, as I may have pointed out once or twice before. That means I did not own a new article of clothing until I was seventeen years old. It was all hand-me-downs. The worst part of that was that my two closest siblings, in age and size, were my sisters. I would say to my mother: "I don't want to wear girl's pants. I don't want to wear a girl's shirt."

My mother would say, "There is no such thing as girl's pants. There is no such thing as a girl's shirt."

And I would say, "Then why does my shirt stick out right here?"

"Hush. There are children in Biafra," was her response.

I was born after the inventions of rubber and wool, but before the inventions of Gor-tex and Thinsulate. My snow boots were thin rubber rain boots with metal clasps to tighten them. They were one size fits all, which means my oldest brother. They had four siblings' worth of holes worn through the soles and burned through the uppers by the time they got to me. My mother put two wool socks on each of my feet and then, to render the boots winter-proof, she would take space-age, state-of-the-art, arctic-rated Wonder Bread bags and put two on each foot. She would work a rubber band up my calf and snap it tight. My feet would be numb within fifteen minutes. I didn't know if it was from frostbite or lack of circulation.

Thusly clad we headed out. "Goodbye, boys," my mother called. "Go. Knock on strangers' doors. If they invite you in, by all means, go. If they offer you food and drink, say 'please' and 'thank you.' See you when you get home…or not. You're the last of five. We may not notice."

Our outing turned out to be not just an exercise in occupation but also sort of a sociology experiment. If the man of the house opened the door, we would say, "Hello, can we shovel your driveway?"

He would ask: 'How much?"

We would say: "Five bucks."

He would say: "Have at it."

If the woman of the house opened the door we would say, "Hello, can we shovel your driveway?"

She would say, "Oh, no. My husband is going to do that," and shut the door.

We would walk away and, thirty seconds later, the door of the house would open and there would be the man of the house saying, "Boys, boys, boys! Come back!"

We learned to simply stay on the porch after the woman shut the door. The door would open shortly thereafter, and there would be the man of the house looking for us. But he wouldn't see us because we were thigh-high, and he was looking down the street. When he couldn't locate us, we would learn a new word. Then we would make a noise. That would startle him. And we would learn another new word.

Skeeter and I each had twenty-five or thirty bucks, cash money, in our pockets by the end of the day. The last house we did was that of a little old lady who invited us in for cookies and cocoa when we were done. We said "please" and "thank you."

She paid us each $5. But she paid us in pennies.

Skeeter and I had to sit there and count out five hundred pennies apiece. The only vessel I had large enough to carry five hundred pennies was a Wonder Bread bag. You can walk about a hundred yards with five hundred pennies in a Wonder Bread bag before the bag gives out.

Skeet divided his pennies into two, two-hundred-and-fifty penny piles, then double bagged them. His pennies made it home fine.

All of that to say, Skeeter and I were well aware that the weight of American money has very little to do with the value of American money.

So, back to the Vacation Bible School.

What me and Skeet wanted most was to get in the baptismal. I don't know why exactly, except that we were seven, and it seemed like the right thing to do. We went to the baptismal whenever we could sneak away from class, and the sanctuary was empty. We didn't have quite enough courage to get in. We'd just look. I don't know what we thought we'd see. I guess we thought we'd see Baptist sin swimming around, like koi.

"Look, there goes avarice."

"Ohhh, there goes gluttony."

The Baptist pastor would appear behind us. We didn't go to that church, but it was a small town so we knew him. He was a cranky, old guy. Well, I say he was old. Now I realize he was probably thirty. He had a wonderful attitude. He really did not care whether you agreed with him or not because he knew he was right. He knew that you would either someday come to agree with him or that you would go to Hell. He was fine with either outcome.

He'd materialized behind us at the baptismal time after time and say, "Boys, boys, boys. I know you want to get in there. But that's not a toy. When a man does things purely for his own enjoyment, and not for the benefit of others, or the glory of God, he will be tainted and stained, that others may know."

It was powerful stuff. It didn't change our minds about getting in the baptismal, but there was no denying it was powerful stuff.

That pastor hated the way we were doing the offering, but any pastor worth his or her salt knows that there are only so many battles you can win. Taking on the little old ladies who run the Vacation Bible School is not a wise career move. He held his tongue for three days, but by Thursday he couldn't take it anymore. He got up to do the devotional that day, rather than one of the little old ladies. He didn't read a goofy little poem, either. He got up in the pulpit and gave a full sermon.

He started by telling us the story of Jesus and the Disciples watching people in the Temple give their offerings. The rich guys are throwing in tons and tons of cash, then a little old lady comes up and she puts in her two mites, or two pennies. Jesus turns to the Disciples and says, "Who gave the greater offering?"

One of the Disciples pipes up and gives one of those answers that make me think Jesus chose those twelve guys because he knew they were morons--- before you get angry or self-righteous, I mean, Jesus knew he could ask those guys questions that you and I needed to know the answers to, and that they would say the first stupid thing that popped into their minds, just like we would do, and then Jesus could explain the correct answer without us having to sound like idiots. See? He was already looking out for you.

Jesus says, "Who gave the greater offering?"

And one of the Disciples says, "Clearly the rich guys gave the greater offering."

Jesus says, "The rich men gave from their abundance, but the little old lady gave from her poverty."

The pastor explained that when you give an offering you are supposed to put yourself in a position where-in you become dependent upon God. The rich gave from their abundance, and abundance means 'more than you need.' So, the rich men didn't give anything of value, but the little old lady gave all she had and there-by became completely dependent upon God, and thus she gave the greater offering.

Parenthetically, that is in no way a Prosperity verse. Also, I will say on behalf of any church treasurers reading this, if you are giving out of your abundance, don't stop. It's not doing you any good but the rest of us are benefiting.

The pastor continued, "The rich men gave from their perfidy."

We didn't know what it meant either, but it seemed like a weird place to keep your money.

The pastor pointed at the scale we were using for the offering and he said, "If you continue giving in this perfidious way the demons of Hell will descend upon you! Snatch your souls! And drag them down to the sulfuric pits of HELL!"

The sulfuric pits of Hell came up surprisingly often in my childhood.

We were moved by the pastor's words. I admit it. But not in the way the pastor intended. We were Methodists. Methodists don't have demons of Hell. We have covered dish dinners. Demons of Hell sounded neat. Furthermore, the pastor's words reminded us of the little old lady who had given us one thousand pennies earlier that year.

That night we went home and collected every penny in both of our houses. We didn't put them in a Wonder Bread bag. We got an old wool sock and filled it up. I bet we had that sock stretched eighteen inches long, probably a foot in diameter. Pounds and pounds of pre-1983 pennies.
One hundred and seventy-four pennies to the pound.

Skeeter kept the tube of pennies behind his back when we got to the church the next day. You are likely familiar with the idea that even the observation of an experiment can change the outcome of the experiment? The same can certainly be said of a prank in church. The observation of the prank increases the consequences.

Skeeter made sure he was last in line when it came time to do the offering. He kept the sock of pennies hidden between his back and the wall. He did not gently introduce the pennies into the blue can when it was finally his turn. He held the tube of pennies about twelve inches above the blue can and dropped it. When those pennies landed in that can, that side of the scale dropped dramatically, causing the other side to rise precipitously. The scale stopped when the blue can hit the floor. But the pink can didn't stop. It kept going until it reached the end of the binders twine lashing it to the scale. The binders twine broke, and every eye in that church watched as that pink can flew through the sanctuary.

It hit the ceiling but it still did not stop. It punched a hole right through the ceiling.

We all stood, staring at that hole.

And then the demons of Hell began to pour forth.

Bats. Thousands and thousands of bats roiled out of the hole and swarmed into the little sanctuary.

Everybody screamed and ran for the exits, holding their souls tightly to their chests lest they be ripped away and drug down to the sulfuric pits. Everybody ran. Everybody. But Skeeter and me.

We knew this was our chance. We headed straight for the baptismal. We didn't stop to look. We put our hands on the side and vaulted over. When we had gone just far enough that we were no longer anything but slaves to physics, when all we could do was fly a little farther, and fall, we looked down.

Someone, some unknown person, had dyed the water red.

When we joined the rest of the kids on the lawn of the church, we were limping, and dripping. And dyed pink. We heard a voice from behind that said, "Boys, boys, boys. When a man does things purely for his own enjoyment, and not for the benefit of others, or the glory of God, he will be tainted and stained, that others may know."

You're Out!

I hate baseball. I know it is not nice to say, but I hate baseball. Let me correct that a little. I hate to play baseball. I love to listen to baseball on the radio. And I love the stats in baseball. Only in baseball will you hear something like, "He's only the third player in history to hit a homerun in his initial at-bat after being reacquired by a team that traded him earlier in the season." But I hate playing baseball.

I was on a Little League baseball team when I was a kid, but I was in the annual team photo more often than I was on first base. What I loved most about being on the team was when games were rained out. That was as liberating as a snow day from school.

I was inexplicably signed up for baseball each year. It was like going to church. It just happened and there was no way to prevent it. I would go to the first practice of the season, recollect that I hate baseball, go home, tell my mother I wanted to quit, and she would say, "Then you shouldn't have signed up for it. We don't quit things we've already started."

"But I didn't sign up for it," I would plead.

"You must of or you wouldn't be on the team. Besides, it's good for you."

The second-best day I had at the ballfield I made it to first base. 'Second-best' may lead you to believe that there is a long list of days I enjoyed at the ballfield. There isn't. Instead of 'second-best,' perhaps I should say, 'The day I made it to first base was one of two days I enjoyed at the ballfield.'

I'd made it to first base but I'm pretty sure it wasn't my fault. There are at least seven ways to get to first base and only one of them is the batter getting a base-hit. I did not get a hit. I think I must've gotten hit. By a pitch. Which is the most miserable and humiliating way to make it to first base. It hurts physically and emotionally.

This was Little League. I was eight years old. The pitcher was eight years old. The pitcher's mound was forty-six feet from home plate. The pitcher's fastball probably clocked in at twenty-five miles per hour, tops. That would provide more than an entire second to step out of the way of the ball. If you saw a car forty-six feet away headed toward you at twenty-five miles per hour, you could probably dodge it. A baseball is way smaller than a car so it ought to be easier to dodge a ball than a car. It's embarrassing. And it hurt.

I batted last in the line-up and there were generally already two outs by the time I got to the plate. I usually ended the at-bat for our team. The number of times I got the third out is almost certainly a record but the Hall of Fame hasn't called yet.

Umpire Judge Tally was the umpire for all our home games. That man had only ever said four things to me: "Strike One," "Strike Two," "Strike Three," and, "You're Out." I knew he could say other words because I'd heard him speak things, beautiful things, to other players. Words like: "Ball Four," "Take Your Base," and "Safe!"

But to me, it was always strikes and "You're Out." I think he enjoyed calling me out. He always followed it with a laugh that went, "Heheheheheh." The laugh sounded like a mirthful smoker's cough.

The ump was a full-time umpire, and, as I understood it, moonlighted as the county judge. I would occasionally have nightmares of becoming a criminal. Well, I didn't have nightmares about becoming a criminal; I had dreams of becoming a criminal. My nightmares revolved around appearing before Judge Tally in court and hearing him say, over the course of several years; "Strike One!" "Strike Two!" "Strike Three!" Then I would encounter him on the street fifteen to twenty years later and he would ask dubiously, "You're out?"

But this time I wasn't the third out. At least not yet. I had made it to first base, and Skeeter batted first, at the top of the line-up. Skeeter was a reliable batter and he put the ball into right field. The first base coach screamed at me to run toward second. When I got to second I stopped. More coaches were screaming. So many coaches screaming. I turned back toward first and saw Skeeter running toward second. I was comfortable on second base. However, some nagging, silent, reminder in my brain was warning me that Skeet and I could not both occupy second. He and the first base coach were telling me to go to third.

I turned toward third. The third base coach was yelling and motioning me to run. I took off. I had never been to third. I had never been to second, except maybe in practice. I had never slid into a base. I decided to slide into third. Nobody was telling me to; I just figured I may never have the chance again. But I didn't slide four feet away from third base. I slid at about four feet away from second base. I stopped sliding at the shortstop. I didn't want to get up and run though, since I'd already committed to sliding, so I propelled myself with my hands all the way to third..

The third base coach told me to run for home. It was Little League. Lord knows where the ball was. I jumped up and ran, Skeet hot on my heels. I slid into home. Why not? Skeet slid, too. The ball arrived in the catcher's mitt, and the catcher touched my leg. Umpire Judge Tally looked down at me and said, "You're out! Heheheheheh."

It was glorious.

Skeet and I walked to the dugout giggling.

And thus ended my second-best day at the ballfield.

My best day at the ballfield was a cloudy, rainy day. Dad had driven me and Skeet. Dad was not an athlete. I had no pressure to be good at sports from my parents. They had no hope of scholarships for me, athletic or academic. I come from a long line of bad ball players: my sister Katie is a great athlete, but she is adopted. My wife was so disappointed when we got married. I mean, my wife was disappointed when we had kids. Hold on, I mean, my wife was disappointed to learn that our children inherited my sports genes and not hers.

Dad drove through town on the way to the game and pointed out all the landmarks, like he did every time we drove through town. He was proud of our little town. He would point at different people on the street and tell us what they did for a living. How smart they were. How tough they were. How much hardship they had overcome. He would say with a note of pride, "Boys, there are a lot of benefits to growing up in a small town. These are the smartest people you have ever known." In truth, they were the only people I had ever known, but he was proud of them, and how smart they were.

It had been raining all night and the infield was a swamp. I was elated. No game today! But the coaches of both teams, and a bunch of the parents, were adamant that we play.

I don't know why. It was as if they enjoyed baseball. Maybe it was an important make-up game. Maybe it was a playoff game. Maybe it was game seven of the World Series. All I know is the adults started hashing out ideas of ways to dry the infield.

Mind you, this was not a modern, brick-dust infield, or a diamond with rubber pellets under artificial turf with a high-tech drainage system. This was a 1970s Halfdollar, West Virginia, sponsored by the Lions Club, bare patches where the outfielders whiled away hours of their lives, faded 'Thank You for Your Business' banners from long-shuttered businesses blowing in shreds on the outfield fence, graffiti-covered, cinderblock dugouts from whose walls I learned a great deal about the mothers and daughters of Dry County, tattered American flag, and a completely, all-natural, hard as pavement on a hot day, lose a shoe on a wet day, regular, old fashioned, dirt infield.

Most of the dads and some of the moms started walking toward the parking lot. Skeet, Dad, and I went too, assuming the game was called. But the adults didn't leave. They went to their cars and opened their trunks, or reached into the backs of their pick-ups, or went to the storage shed where the mower was, and produced one, two, and five-gallon containers of gasoline.

Men began walking back and forth pouring gasoline all over the infield.

My dad was not one of them. He took Skeet's and my hands and started backing us away from the field.

It took several minutes to douse the whole infield with gasoline. The explosive fumes had filled the dugouts, seeped into the concession stand, and gathered beneath the weather-beaten wooden bleachers by the time the men finished pouring and someone struck a match. I felt the wind concuss as the baseball field exploded.

The concession stand and bleachers burning was neat, but of little consequence to me. But watching the dugouts burn, with their trove of graffiti, was what it must have been like witnessing the Library of Alexandria burn.

The adults had removed the bases so they wouldn't burn. But they had left home plate in place. Home plate had a stem, or pipe, centered on its underside. The stem went into a metal tube embedded in the ground. This kept home plate from moving. Gasoline fumes had seeped into the metal tube and when the ballfield lit, the explosion went down the tube. It was like a mortar tube, and home plate launched into the air.

Fortunately, the entire Dry County volunteer fire department was at the Little League field because they were the dads and moms of the players. Unfortunately, none of their equipment was there because they had come for a ballgame, not an arson.

My father was standing between me and Skeeter. He had not taken part in the conflagration. He held our hands as we watched everything burn. He shook his head and muttered, "Boys, there are a lot of benefits to growing up in a small town, but in a moment like this, I realize that these are the smartest people you've ever known." There was no pride in the statement this time.

Umpire Judge Tally was walking toward us. He opened his mouth to say something to my dad, and home plate plummeted out of the sky and hit Umpire Judge Tally smack on top of his little umpire hat. He dropped like a stone.

My father gasped, but before Dad could do anything, I stepped over to Umpire Judge Tally's prone form, and said, maybe too enthusiastically, "You're out! Heheheheheh."

Pinewood Derby: Hand's Off, Dad!

Cub Scouts have a Pinewood Derby every year. Each Cub gets an officially sanctioned block of pine about seven inches long, an inch tall, and two inches wide. The block comes with four plastic wheels and nails for axels. The theory is that each boy will take his block of wood, a pocketknife, a saw, sandpaper, and some paint to create a racecar to compete against cars made by other boys. Adults are supposed to help and to be prepared to administer first-aid, but the adults are not supposed to build the cars.

Yeah. Right.

Each January, I received my kit. My eyes glazed over and ideas raced through my brain. I could make an Indy car. Or a wedge. Or a 1950s hot rod. I contemplated how I was going to saw it, where I was going to place the wheels, and how I was going to paint it. I'd sketch my car with little lines coming off the back to depict great speed as it blazed by the other boys' cars. Each year I received that hunk of pine and, like Michelangelo, I could see the speedy David locked in the wood.

Then I would go home and give the hunk to my dad. His eyes glazed over and ideas for cars raced through his brain. He sketched his car with little lines coming off the back to depict great speed as it blazed by the other dads' cars.

I had two older brothers so my dad had already 'helped' build six Derby cars. He'd never had a winner. I was his last chance. I'd watch as he measured, jig-sawed, power-sanded, graphited, smoothed, carved, and crafted "my" car. Sometimes, he let me sand the car- but only on the back or the bottom.

My mom would call down, "JOHN! He's supposed to be building it."

My dad would call up, "He is. He's sanding it right now."

I also got to help ensure the car was the proper weight. Each car was supposed to weigh five ounces. Dad would drill holes in the bottom of the car and fill the holes with molten lead. We got the molten lead by melting fishing weights with a propane torch. Dad let me hold the torch.

Dad worked hard on those cars. And year after year his cars failed to take home the Gold.

My final race came when I was ten. This was Dad's last chance, too. I watched Dad put the finishing touches on 'my' car. It was about 10:30, the night before the race. The phone rang.

Dad said, "What? Oh, hello Christian." Christian was a kid in our Cub Scout Den. "Well, why didn't you call last week?"

Dad hung up. "Christian needs a car."

Dad went to pick up Christian and his hunk of pine. Christian sat beside me while Dad did what he could. He'd spent weeks making my car but he had mere hours to build Christian's. My dad rounded the edges with his knife, touched the wood with the sander and let Christian apply a coat of paint. Dad slapped the wheels on without adjusting or balancing them.

You guessed it. Dad had his winner. Christian's hastily carved, barely sanded, poorly painted car won the whole competition.

My car didn't even place

You may think the moral of this story is: "If you leave things to the last minute, you'll probably win the whole race," but that is not the moral. In fact, it's not even moral time because that isn't the end of the story.

I grew up. I had a child who joined the Cub Scouts. Hunks of pine were handed out in January. My kid stared at that piece of wood, dreaming of how the car would look, how to cut it....

And I remembered how much, when I was a kid, I'd wanted to make my own Pinewood Derby car.

I said to my child, "Let me help you with that." And I cut, and I sawed, and I sanded, and I chiseled, and I painted, and I balanced, and I graphited- and you know what? We won second place.

I got home from the race and called my dad. "See? You should have let me build my own cars. You might'a won."

So, kids, wrestle that block of wood from your dad's hand and do it yourself. But don't be selfish. He really wants to help. Maybe let him sand the bottom or the back.

The Teacher in the Patriotic Bathing Suit

No offense to any teachers reading this now, but Mrs. Baird, my fourth grade teacher, was one of the two greatest teachers who ever lived- and this is why.

Our entire fourth grade year, Mrs. Baird never yelled at us. She never raised her voice. She never screamed.

We had two chalkboards in our classroom- one in the front of the class and one in the back. Mrs. Baird came into the classroom on the first day of school, went to the back chalkboard, and wrote each student's name on the board with yellow chalk. Mrs. Baird wouldn't holler when a student misbehaved. She would simply walk to the back of the class, pick up a piece of purple chalk, and make a mark by that student's name. If you could go all week without getting more than three marks beside your name you got a lollipop at the end of the week. It was an uphill struggle for most of us. I got three lollipops my entire fourth grade career. I was at home, sick for four days, the week I got one of them.

The only person who consistently got a lollipop was a little girl named Alicia Snitch. It was a very unfortunate name. Alicia got so many lollipops our fourth grade year that she was going to need dentures long before she needed braces.

We loved and respected Mrs. Baird but we had one problem with her, one sneaking suspicion.

When I was in the fourth grade there was a television show called *Wonder Woman*, and the actress who played Wonder Woman was named Lynda Carter. Mrs. Baird looked exactly like Lynda Carter. We were not as sophisticated as fourth graders are today. We didn't know where to draw the line between fact and fantasy. We figured that if Mrs. Baird looked like Lynda Carter, and Lynda Carter played Wonder Woman on television, then it was logical to conclude that Mrs. Baird *was* Wonder Woman. Everybody in our class thought that Mrs. Baird was Wonder Woman, except Alicia Snitch. Many lunchroom discussions revolved around the subject of Mrs. Baird's identity.

Alicia would adamantly declare, "Wonder Woman isn't real!

She's a made-up character!"

"Is too!" the rest of us would insist.

"Is not," and so on.

One day Wally said to Alicia, "Think about this: Jimmy Carter is the President of the United States of America. Lynda Carter is Wonder Woman. They have the same last name."

"So?" Alicia asked.

"So?" Wally retorted, "they must be related."

"Maybe," Skeeter suggested, "Wonder Woman is the president's mother."

"Maybe she's his daughter," I said.

"Maybe," Wally said, "Wonder Woman is the president's wife! Think about it. If the president was married to a superhero, we wouldn't even need an army anymore. If there was trouble in the Middle East, or South America, the president could just send his wife to take care of it!"

One kid, who came from a predominantly Republican family, said, "So *that's* how Jimmy Carter got elected president!"

That stopped Alicia in her tracks. She said, "Boys are so dumb! What would the wife of the President of the United States of America be doing teaching fourth grade at Halfdollar Elementary School?"

"Maybe," Skeet said, "to protect her identity."

"Maybe there's some evil afoot," I said.

"Maybe," Wally said, "the third graders are an alien army!"

We all turned, wide-eyed, to look at the third-grader lunch table. We had long suspected that they were aliens. Half the boys were making baboon arms, with carrots up their noses.

"Well," I said, "there's only one thing to do. We have to find out if Mrs. Baird is Wonder Woman. One of us has to put themself in great peril. If one of us is about to die, Mrs. Baird will have to spin around and turn herself into Wonder Woman."

Skeeter volunteered. At recess he climbed the monkey bars, crossed halfway, and then, he let go… with one hand. Skeeter was hanging there, with his shoes a full two feet off the ground! If he fell from that height he would surely sprain an ankle or skin a knee. Mortal peril!

We yelled, "Help! Help! Help!"

We all knew that to turn herself into Wonder Woman, Mrs. Baird would have to throw her arms out, spin around in circles, then there would be a bright light. When the light faded she would be standing there wearing that, that, well, you know what Wonder Woman wears. It's a sort of modest, one-piece patriotic bathing suit. There's a golden WW on her chest, calf-high boots, a golden rope, and a tiara, like Ms. America wears. It doesn't seem like very practical crime- fighting wear to me, but what do I know?

Parenthetically, one of my buddy's older brothers told us that if you watched really close while she was spinning around, there was a brief moment when she had removed her street clothes but had not yet put on her Wonder Woman clothes. It's not really germane to the story but some people find it interesting.

We watched Mrs. Baird closely. She had turned to speak to another teacher, but when we began yelling "Help!," she threw out her arms, and, as if in slow motion, began to spin around. We were sure she was going to keep spinning, do a full 1440, shed her teacher clothes, and leap to Skeet's rescue, clad only as Wonder Woman.

Mrs. Baird spun halfway around. She looked over the situation, and said, "Well Lordy, Skeeter; just let go." There was no bright light, no rope, no patriotic bathing suit.

We had to come up with another plan.

We tried everything. Six of the girls in our class had Wonder Woman lunch boxes. Those girls would walk to Mrs. Baird's desk, and oh-so sneakily hold the lunch boxes next to Mrs. Baird's head to compare and contrast the punched tin icons of Wonder Woman with Mrs. Baird. *It was her*! There, seated behind the maple desk, with the apples and the crocheted gifts, was clearly Wonder Woman herself, in deep, deep cover. But could we out her?

We were in the lunchroom having our 'Is-too-Is-not' argument with Alicia when Wally ran in saying, "I got it. I know it. I figured it out."

"Lay it on me," I said.

"Think about this," he began. "Halfdollar, West Virginia, is a long way from Metropolis, where the Hall of Justice is located, and where the DC superheroes hangout. Wonder Woman has to be able to get there quickly in a crisis. So, she can't just drive a car to school every day; she'd never be able to get to Metropolis quick enough. Therefore, she must come to school every day in her invisible jet. And if she does come in the invisible jet, she must park it in the teachers' parking lot."

We figured that since the invisible jet was invisible, it must be made of really clean glass. If we could hit it with a pebble it would go, *tink*. If we could hit it with a large enough stone it would shatter. If we could shatter the invisible jet Mrs. Baird would be forced to assume that the Legion of Doom was rising out of the woods. She would spin around, turn into Wonder Woman, and come save us.

The teachers' parking lot was right beside the playground. During recess we would walk to the edge of the playground nonchalantly. We'd whistle. If you whistle, nobody knows you're up to anything. We would surreptitiously pick up pebbles at the edge of the parking lot. Then we would pretend to yawn and stretch, then throw the stones into empty-looking spaces in the teachers' parking lot.

Wally, one sunny morning, tossed a rock into a deserted portion of the parking lot. It was a fine throw which bounced off the asphalt and flew into the woods. We heard the slight *tink* of a rock hitting glass. A collective, "OOOOOOOOHHHHHHHH," went up from the crowd.

Wally said, "I think I just hit Wonder Woman's jet with a rock!"

"I think you hit a bottle," Alicia said.

"What would a bottle be doing in the woods?" asked Skeeter.

"What would Wonder Woman's jet be doing in the woods?" asked Alicia.

"Maybe she's hiding it there," I said.

"Why," pressed Alicia, "would Wonder Woman need to *hide* an invisible jet? It's self-hiding. That's why it's invisible."

"But," Skeet said, "since it is invisible, she can't just leave it laying around because someone might accidentally run into it."

Wally, unbeknownst to us, had found a rock about the size

and shape of an English muffin. He was in the process of gripping the stone like a discus and spinning around in preparation to toss it. As we became aware of him, and what he was doing, a slow-motion scream of "Wally! Noooooo!" arose from us.

Every fourth grader who has ever watched the Olympics has tried, and utterly failed, to hurl a discus-like object. There is not a fourth grader alive who can throw a discus in the direction they intend. Wally was living in some sort of fantasy world. We were self-actualized.

Our cry of 'WALLY' echoed off the building, drawing attention from every quarter of the playground. Students and teachers alike turned just in time to see Wally release the stone. We all ducked. The stone flew toward the parking lot. Wally's momentum kept him spinning. He lost his balance and somersaulted across the ground.

We watched the rock soar out over the teachers' parking lot, higher and higher. It reached the apex of its flight, hung suspended for a split second, and then started to descend. It was whistling like a falling bomb. It gained velocity as it fell. It gained mass as it gained velocity.

The rock bounced off the hood of the principal's car, ricocheted off the headlight of another car, and smashed through the windshield of a school bus.

There was a great rending of metal and a cacophony of crashing glass.

Wally *heard* the rending of the metal and the smashing of glass but didn't *see* anything because he was still somersaulting across the ground. He naturally assumed that he had smashed Wonder Woman's jet. When Wally quit rolling he leapt into the air and shouted, "I did it! I did it!" as the teachers arrived.

"Wally!" one teacher demanded, "What on earth do think you are doing?"

He quit jumping and surveyed the path of destruction his rock had wrought. He turned green. His eyes large and wet, Wally looked up at the ring of teachers surrounding him. Wally swallowed and said, "Um. I was…We were…I was trying to…I was…I was trying to, um, hit Wonder Woman's jet with a rock?" Fortunately, school psychiatrists had not yet been invented.

We went back to class, and Mrs. Baird went to the back chalkboard, picked up the purple chalk, and made a mark beside Wally's name. She stopped in front of Wally's desk and said, "Wally. I'm so disappointed in you. Don't you think that Wonder Woman would be smart enough to park her jet on the roof?"

Wonder Woman was too clever to be tricked into revealing her identity by a bunch of fourth graders. We were stumped. We could not force Mrs. Baird to show her true colors. Finally, Alicia Snitch, hoping to end our senseless struggles and shut the rest of us up for good, tried a direct, frontal assault. She raised her hand in class. When Mrs. Baird called on her, Alicia asked, "Mrs. Baird, are you Wonder Woman?"

Mrs. Baird laughed, and then said seriously, "I'm not at liberty to divulge that."

We didn't need *Encyclopedia Brown* or the *Hardy Boys* to decipher that answer. We rapidly became the best-behaved class Halfdollar Elementary had ever known.

Time passed. October was drawing to a close. The colder weather meant having recess inside. It was much harder to put ourselves in peril inside- short of burning the school down- and none of us were that eager to find out if Mrs. Baird was Wonder Woman. Our interest flagged. Our thoughts turned to other things.

One of our classmates had a birthday. His parents hired a clown to come to our classroom. The clown goofed about and then filled up helium balloons for the students. When the clown left, he forgot his helium tank.

There were two big lockers, doorless cabinets, in the back corner of the classroom. They were eight feet tall and sat at right angles to each other and the walls, making sort of a cube with a doorway. We stowed our jackets, boots, and lunch boxes there in the mornings. Mrs. Baird also used the area to store things we weren't using in the classroom presently. The Pinto, the Nina, and the Santa Maria were back there.

Our class was studying the human respiratory system at that point in the curriculum. We learned all about the lungs, trachea, epiglottis, bronchioles, inhaling oxygen, exhaling carbon dioxide, alveoli, the works. We learned that when you inhale, the oxygen goes down your trachea, into your bronchi, then to your alveoli. The blood comes by and the carbon dioxide jumps out of your red blood cells into your alveoli, and the oxygen jumps out of your alveoli into your red blood cells. We learned that the surface area of all the alveoli in two adult lungs is almost equal to the singles area of a tennis court, and eighty times the area of our skin! It was fascinating to us.

And then it was almost Halloween. A big school party was planned for the Friday before Halloween. We were allowed to wear our Halloween costumes to school, and we were going to trick-or-treat from classroom to classroom. We were going to have a contest. Who had the Funniest Costume. Who had the Scariest Costume. Who had the Best Over-All Costume. But remember, this was the 1970s so we weren't all going to win.

At the end of the day, all the students were going to go into the auditorium, and the teachers were going to stand on-stage with costumes on. We students were going to get to judge which teacher had the best costume. The whole school was looking forward to the event. It had never happened before. We were intrigued by the idea because we were kids, and kids know that teachers are adults, and that adults are not creative. What would the teachers wear? Would the gym teacher come dressed as the librarian?

Mrs. Baird told us that our class was going to get to watch a scary movie in our classroom because we had been doing so well that year.

The day arrived. We were in our desks, in our costumes. Doctors, nurses, football players, cheerleaders, astronauts, scuba divers…other non-gender specific costumes. The bell rang. 8:30. No Mrs. Baird. 8:35. No Mrs. Baird. 8:40. We were distraught. This was the greatest day of our lives. We did not want a substitute teacher.

Finally, at 8:45, the door opened, and Mrs. Baird came in pushing a cart. She was wearing a dress. On the cart was a lump covered in brown butcher paper. She said, "You guys have done such a good job studying the human respiratory system that I have a surprise for you."

We gathered around the cart. We were thinking, 'Cupcakes!'

She grabbed the piece of butcher paper and pulled it off.

Underneath the paper was a complete set of raw cow lungs. Still steaming from the butcher shop.

Your average fourth grader is ill-prepared to see cow lungs at any time of the day, but first thing in the morning is the worst possible time. We cringed at the sight and smell. Mrs. Baird pressed on with the show. She reached under the cart and pulled out a spool of about fifty yards of surgical tubing.

Mrs. Baird said, "I want you to see how lungs inflate and deflate." She cut a twelve-inch straw from the tubing and inserted it into the windpipe of the cowless lungs. She said, "Remember, only blow. Don't suck." Then she took a deep breath and blew into the straw. The lungs expanded, and then she quit blowing and the lungs deflated.

We each got to try and inflate the lungs. I didn't want to make the lungs expand. I wanted to make the lungs explode. I stuck my straw into those lungs, took as deep a breath as I could, and blew until I was red in the face. I blew until I could barely stand up, but the lungs did not explode. They barely moved. I learned that I had the lung capacity of a Dixie-cup.

All the boys gathered around the lungs, and we all stuck our tubes in and blew as hard as we could. Even teamwork couldn't get the lungs to explode so eventually that got boring. Mrs. Baird wheeled the lunged cart behind the lockers with the rest of the detritus from the school year, and we got ready to watch our scary movie.

The movie was *The Blob*. *The Blob* was an old movie when I was in the fourth grade. If you ask your adults about it don't call it a movie. That will confuse them. Call it a picture show.

In the movie, a meteor crashed into a Pennsylvania field near Phoenixville. The meteor cracked open and inside was a blob about the size of a volleyball. It looked like it was made out of red Jell-o. It would latch onto people and consume them. It could only roll a half a mile an hour, and yet it was able to chase down healthy, adult, human beings running full speed. The more people the Blob ate, the bigger it got. It was awesome. And terrifying.

I know what you're thinking. You're smart. If you weren't smart you wouldn't be reading this book. You're thinking, "Well, duh. The Blob is a ball. Just run up hill. Or close the door."

It wasn't that easy. There's a scene where there is a lady in a bathtub- but it is 1958, so there are a lot of bubbles. She's just relaxing. Having a drink after a hard week. The Blob rolls up to the bathroom door. You're thinking, "She's safe; the door is shut." Think again. The Blob flattens itself out and oozes under the door. The lady has fallen asleep, and then the Blob creeps up the side of the tub and *BAM! BOOM!* The lady is gone.

Pretty soon the Blob was as big as a beach ball. Then a VW Bug. Then it was the size of this room.

Most of us sat wide-eyed in front of the movie screen. But Mrs. Baird had told us that if we got too scared we could excuse ourselves from the film to go and sit behind the lockers. This was a tough choice for some. Which was scarier? The movie, or going to sit behind the lockers, in the dark, with raw cow lungs? Who knew when the cow's ghost might show up, looking for her lost lungs.

Alicia Snitch was the only person too scared to watch the movie but brave enough to sit behind the lockers.

The Blob was now a huge, hissing, pulsing red mass of destruction. The Army was called in. People shot pistols, rifles, rocket launchers, flamethrowers, but nothing stopped the Blob.

It's an actor named Steve McQueen versus a gelatinous alien sphere. Who knows which one is smarter?

And then the Blob heads to the other side of town but the people on the first side of town don't have the decency to pick up the phone and call the people on the other side of town to warn them.

The people on that side of town are in a movie theater, watching a movie. The Blob squeezes itself out of the projection room and into the balcony. It sucks up a few people. The Blob slides over the railing into the main part of the theater and pandemonium erupts. People are running out all the exits at once, but by now the Blob is so big it can go out all the exits at once, like a giant octopus. Sucking people in left and right.

I caught something odd in my peripheral vision, and I began to hear a hissing in our classroom. But I was too focused on the movie to look. The students in my class were wound up by the movie, all of us trying to stay cool, not scream. Wally was sitting next to me. Wally was wound pretty tight. The littlest things could set him off, so when he shrieked, I hardly paid attention. He pointed. But not at the screen. He was pointing toward the lockers. I looked to see what he was screaming at and, as I did, I began to scream too. The rest of the class joined in. The Blob was in our classroom! It was emerging from behind the lockers!

A wet, hissing, pulsating, expanding mass of gore rose above the lockers. It had a long, bloody tentacle trailing from behind it.

"THE BLOB, THE BLOB!" we screamed. We ran for the door of our classroom. I was picking up smaller kids and throwing them at the Blob. "Eat him! Eat her! Leave me alone!" I'm not proud of that.

The Blob beat us to the door. We couldn't get around it.

Mrs. Baird was saying, "Calm down. We'll take care of this."

And then we heard a scream. A long, loud, shrill scream. It came from behind the lockers. We'd forgotten about Alicia Snitch. She was back there, where the Blob had come from. As we turned to look, we saw Alicia rise up from behind the lockers- the long, bloody tentacle from the Blob wrapped around her. Her very life force was being sucked from her as the Blob grew larger and larger.

Mrs. Baird said, "Don't panic. I'll take care of this." Mrs. Baird grabbed the front of her dress and ripped it off. We all gasped and stared dumbfounded. Underneath her dress was Wonder Woman's patriotic bathing suit! Complete with the golden WW, the calf-high boots, and the golden rope. Wonder Woman stood in our very midst. She produced a golden tiara, from somewhere, and threw it at the Blob like a boomerang.

The Blob exploded. We were coated in a fine, red, bovine mist. Hunks of lung fell about the classroom. Alicia Snitch fell with a thump back behind the lockers.

We followed Mrs. Baird, nay, we followed Wonder Woman, behind the lockers. She picked up Alicia Snitch and unwound her from the bloody tentacle. The tentacle still hissed softly.

We saw how Alicia, in her deep and secret need to know if Mrs. Baird was Wonder Woman, had taken the remaining surgical tubing, stuck one end deep into the cow lungs, fastened the other end of the tube to the helium tank the clown had left, and then turned the helium tank all the way up, thus inflating the lungs and making a very realistic blob-like creature rise into our room.

Wonder Woman said nothing. She carried Alicia Snitch and put her in her desk. Then Wonder Woman walked to the back of the classroom, picked up the piece of purple chalk, and made a mark beside Alicia's name.

Corn Maze

We were ten years old and had achieved the rank of Bear in Cub Scouts. Well, Uncle Deebo was nine. But Skeet and I were ten.

In the Boy Scouts, the ranks go Scout, Tenderfoot, Second Class, First Class, Star, Life, and Eagle. If you equate this to the military, Scout, Tenderfoot and Second Class are the enlisted men, First Class is a junior grade officer, Star and Life are your company grade officers, and an Eagle is a general. In Cub Scouts, when I was a Cub, we had Bobcat, Wolf, Bear, and Webelos. So, in the great scheme of things, a Bear Cub Scout is a helpless kid in a funny blue shirt with no skills and lots of adult supervision.

We were at the corn maze. The corn maze was seven miles out of town and thus it was a massive undertaking to get us children there. There was twenty-one Cub Scouts at the maze that day.

The adults gathered us in a circle, and we paired off using the buddy system. Because there were twenty-one of us, that meant either ten groups of two and one kid left out on his own, or nine groups of two and one group of three. Me, Skeeter and Uncle Deebo teamed up to keep track of each other.

The buddy system is set up so kids can keep an eye on each other. In the water, it makes sense.

"Bil, where's your buddy?"

"Um, at the bottom of the pond?"

On land, the buddy system just ensures that kids aren't alone when they stray from the group. On land, the buddy system is like a two for one deal. If you lose one kid, then you can assume you lost two. In our case, it was three. The buddy system is just another way for adults to slack off under the guise of teaching children responsibility.

If you have gotten this far into your life and don't know what a corn maze is then you should be ashamed. A corn maze is a maze cut through a corn field. They generally operate around

Halloween and often entail chainsaw murderers, blood-thirsty ghouls, and brain-thirsty zombies jumping from hiding spots and trying to scare the life out of teenagers. Teenagers go into corn mazes at night when the monsters can hide and attack properly. Ten-year-olds don't get to go into the maze at night with the zombies and murderers because ten-year-olds are "too young" for that, or so we had been told. We went to the maze during the day, when the monsters were napping, or grocery shopping, or picking up their laundry, or whatever monsters do during the day.

Farmer Daedalus's corn maze was 8000 square feet of twisting pathways through nine-foot-tall corn stalks. There was a big sign as you entered that read, "No Smoking, No Lighters, No Matches, No Snacks, No Walkie-Talkies." The rules were written in different colors; some more faded than others because rules had been added as it was discovered they were needed.

It was a hazy day. It had rained earlier in the day, and mist was rising off the ground.

As we entered the maze we were led, flanked, and followed by inattentive adults relying too heavily on our senses of responsibility. People have called me many things, but never Responsa-Bil.

I like to read books about prisoners of war. One of my favorites is about Colditz, a castle to which the Germans sent the most notorious Allied escapers. These guys built an airplane in the attic, dug tunnels, melted gum wrappers to make counterfeit badges so they could dress up like German guards and walk out the front gates, and had people at home send them women's clothing so they could slip out of formation on the way to the exercise field and walk off toward Switzerland. These escapes took weeks and months to plan, coordinate, rehearse, and orchestrate. The escapers required split second timing and precise diversions. Skeeter, Deebo, and I escaped wholly by accident. The group turned left, we turned right, and we were free. We didn't even notice that the group was missing for some time.

When we did realize that the group was lost, it didn't matter much to us. We made our way through the rustling corn stalks laughing, joking, and lying to each other.

Deebo said, "You know, each year Farmer Daedalus makes the corn maze in a different shape."

"What do you mean? It's a corn field. It's corn field shaped, like a huge rectangle," I said.

"No, dummy," Uncle Deebo corrected. "Not the outside of the corn maze, the inside. If you look at it like from an airplane or a helicopter, you can see that the paths through the field make a shape."

"Like what kind of shape?" Skeet asked.

"Like a jack-o-lantern or a pumpkin."

"How do you know?"

"Farmer Daedalus has pictures of them taken. They're in the barn. Plus, my brother told me. He said he climbed up on the hill over there and looked down on the maze, but you can't do that anymore because Farmer Daedalus put up camouflage netting because kids would go into the maze with walkie-talkies, and then kids on the hill would guide them through."

"Plus," Skeeter added, "Farmer Daedalus jams the radio signals in the area."

I don't think any of this was true. A simple look up would have proven there was no camouflage netting. The radio jamming signals may have been harder to not see. The point is: Boys lie.

Farmer Daedalus's corn mazes were legendary. People came from hundreds of miles away to get lost in them. Other farmers bought kits and plans and planted their mazes so that the corn grew in a certain design. Farmer Daedalus was old school. He grew a field of corn, then he went in with nothing but an idea and a machete. He didn't come out until his maze was complete.

Of course, as Farmer Daedalus grew older his mazes became less coherent. One year the maze was a huge circle, the next year there was no way out, and the final maze Farmer Daedalus ever made went straight for half a mile and ended at a cliff above the river. That was quite a kick for the teenagers in the pitch black of night.

"Anyway," Deebo said, "he makes the mazes in shapes."

"Yeah," I said, "it's true." In all honesty, I had no idea about the shape of the mazes, but Deebo and Skeeter were having such a good time discussing it that I figured I ought to know something about it as well. So I said, "One year, like ten years ago, he made the maze in the shape of the Devil. And then, at midnight, the Devil, the real Devil, showed up in the maze."

"Wow," said Deebo in awe.

"What time is it?" asked Skeeter.

"About two o'clock," I said.

"What shape is it in this year?" Deebo asked with some trepidation.

"A hippo," I blurted.

"Why a hippo?"

"They're the deadliest animal on the planet. I saw it on *Wild Kingdom*. Plus, there's a pond right in the middle of the field, and that's where the hippo lives."

"What are you talking about?"

I said, "My brother told me that at midnight the creature that the maze is shaped like rises up out of the middle of the maze and wanders through the corn. Eating people, or whatever." I regretted that as soon as I said it. Now we all had a vision of a giant hippo stalking us through the maze.

The mist seemed more present, more ominous.

"Getting dark early today, don't you think?" asked Skeeter.

"You guys got flashlights?" asked Deebo.

"Yep," Skeet and I answered.

"Do you think we need them yet?"

"It is getting awful dark."

It was getting darker but not so dark that a flashlight was going to do us any good.

We pulled out our flashlights and switched them on.

"Maybe we should ration them," I suggested. "Just use one at a time."

Deebo and Skeeter agreed.

All three flashlights were dead fifteen minutes later.

Something crossed the trail in front of us. It came out of the corn on the left and moved into the corn on the right. We heard the thump of its feet, saw its dark mass, but couldn't identify it.

"Was that the hippo? Why would the hippo be out already? It's not midnight?"

"Maybe today is the solstice."

"What's the solstice?"

"They have one every season, and the fall solstice is one of the shortest days of the year."

"Are you sure?"

"Yep."

"But all days are twenty-four hours."

"Nope, summer solstice is the longest day of the year. It's like forty-eight hours."

"How can a day be longer? Or shorter?"

"The hours are shorter. There's still twenty-four, but they're faster on the fall solstice so midnight comes about eight hours early."

We were moving slow, staying together.

"You know," Skeeter said, "when Farmer Daedalus closes the maze, at night I mean, a twelve-foot electrified fence rises out of the ground to surround the maze so no one can get in."

"What if you're not out?"

"The fence only goes up when everyone is out. You see, there's motion sensors throughout the maze. At just before midnight, Farmer Daedalus sounds a foghorn, and you have to leave the maze. The fence comes up when everybody is out. He can tell everyone is out because none of the motion sensors are being set off. See?"

I didn't know where this newfound information was coming from but just the act of speaking it seemed to make it true. Or a least possible.

"But what if like, just when the horn went off, you were standing perfectly still for some reason? Like you were paralyzed with fright? So you didn't trip the motion sensors?"

"Then you have to spend the night in the maze. With the hippo."

Skeeter, Deebo and I walked even closer together.

"Where do you suppose the group got off to?"

"And," Deebo added to the general fund of made-up facts, "once the fence is up, Farmer Daedalus releases wild animals into the maze. You know, to eat intruders." And then Deebo added, "My older brother told me. He told me that after the fence goes up, but before he releases the animals, Farmer Daedalus flies over the maze in a helicopter that has a tranquilizer gun on the front. But not an ordinary tranquilizer gun. It's like a Gatlin gun and can shoot 500 tranquilizers a minute. He knocks out anyone still in the maze."

"And the animals can find you," Skeet said enthusiastically, "because they are wired into the motion sensors, and they track you down as you flee."

Gulp.

Whatever was in the maze with us crossed the trail ahead of us again.

"Regular wild animals or ex-o-tic animals?"

"What's an ex-o-tic animal?"

"You know, non-indigenous. Foreign. Animals from other places. Like lions and kangaroos are ex-o-tic. But only if they are where they shouldn't be. I mean, a lion isn't ex-o-tic in Africa, and a kangaroo isn't ex-o-tic in Australia. And an opossum isn't ex-o-tic here, but it would be if you took it to Africa."

"How would you get it there?"

"Do kangaroos eat people?"

"Does that mean ex-o-tic dancers are from foreign countries?"

"Why would you ask that?" I asked.

"Cause I saw a sign that said 'Ex-o-tic Dancers,' and my mother told me not to ask about it. But I'm thinking about it now. She told me never to go to a place with ex-o-tic dancers. I guess my mom doesn't like foreigners."

We pondered that and kept a sharp eye out for lions and kangaroos. And dancers.

"You guys have any idea where we are? Or how to get out of here?"

"I don't know. This is like a twenty-thousand-square-foot maze. The group could be lost in here for days, and we'd never find them."

"They can't be lost in here for days 'cause of the ex-o-tic animals and the fence. They'll be eaten up."

"I feel bad for some of those younger scouts, like the Bobcats. I bet they are getting pretty scared about now."

"Sure is dark."

"How come only teenagers can come into the maze after dark?" I asked.

"My mom said, 'Don't ask about it,'" Deebo said. "She seems to say that more and more."

"My older brother," I said, "said it was because boys and girls go on dates in the maze. And it's dark, so the girls are scared. And then the zombies and chainsaw murderers come out, and the girls hold the boys' hands and cling to the boys for protection."

"My older sister," said Deebo, "says that is a sexist attitude and demeaning to the female gender. And that girls are just as capable of fending off chainsaw murderers as boys."

Quoting and/or citing your older sister was not the same as quoting/citing a male relative. If a boy says, "My aunt, sister, mother, grandma…says X," then it is probably true. If a boy says, "My older brother, dad, uncle, grandpa…says X," then it probably isn't true.

We weren't panicking just yet. Oncoming darkness, wild animals, chainsaw murderers, killer hippos, and necking teenagers were one thing, but the real problems were about to be revealed.

Skeet said, "I gotta go to the bathroom."

Deebo said, "I'm hungry."

I said, "Just pee over there. Pee anywhere. It's why we joined the Boy Scouts. So we can pee outside."

"I'm hungry," Uncle Deebo said again.

"How long have we been in here?" I asked.

"Long enough to be hungry," Uncle Deebo said.

Once that kid got hungry he lost all interest in other subjects. If chainsaw murderers came charging out of the corn, Uncle Deebo would ask if they had anything to eat. Brain eating ghoul? Uncle Deebo would remind him he should share.

"What's that noise?" Skeeter asked. "It sounds like a helicopter!"

"Dive for cover! Dive for cover!"

We dove off the trail and into the corn stalks to avoid the tranquilizer spraying machine gun mounted on the approaching attack helicopter. How had our lives gotten this complicated?

"We can't let them see us. They'll open up on us with the tranquilizer Gatlin!" Uncle Deebo screamed.

Sure enough, a helicopter came in low over the maze. It stayed in the area for some time, as if it were searching for something, as if it were flying a grid pattern in the hopes of tranquilizing kids who had stayed in the maze too long. Or perhaps it was trying to locate lost maze participants because their parents and Scout leaders were worried because they had become separated from the group.

Skeet, Uncle Deebo, and I emerged from cover when we were sure the helicopter was gone to search some other section of the maze.

"I'm starving!" Uncle Deebo announced. "Anybody got anything to eat?"

"The sign out front said, 'No Snacks,'" Skeet said.

"Well," Uncle Deebo thought aloud, "we're in a cornfield. We could eat popcorn."

"I think we need a fire to make popcorn," I said. "You gotta heat the corn up so it'll pop."

"Can't make a fire," Skeeter said, "the sign said, 'No Matches, No Lighters.'"

Uncle Deebo reached under his shirt tail and pulled out what looked very much like a gun. He held it above his head and announced, "The sign didn't say 'No Flare Guns.'"

"Whoa, where'd you get that?" I asked.

"What's it for?" asked Skeeter.

"I think," Uncle Deebo said, "that when people are lost at sea they fire a flare into the sky so the Coast Guard can rescue them."

"Cool," I said, "I wish we were lost. Then we could use it."

"Wouldn't do us any good," Uncle Deebo explained. "The coast is like four-hundred miles away. There's nobody in the Coast Guard close enough to see the flare."

"Good point."

"Where'd you get it?"

"My brother Tommy. He's in the Coast Guard. He accidently brought it home from his ship. And I accidently saw it in his room, and accidently picked it up, and accidently brought it with me today."

This was not stealing or deliberate rule breaking. This was an accident.

"So," continued Uncle Deebo, "I figure we can start a fire by piling up a bunch of cornstalks and then firing this bad boy into it. Then we can make popcorn."

And so, we did.

And the next year, the sign outside the maze read, "No Smoking, No Lighters, No Matches, No Snacks, No Walkie-Talkies, No Flare Guns, and NO @#$! CUB SCOUTS."

Wally! Come Down Right Now!

Afghanistan, Albania, Algeria, American Samoa, Andorra, Angola, Anguilla, Antigua and Barbuda, Argentina, Armenia, Aruba, Australia, Austria, Azerbaijan.

Hanging around the perimeter of our school gymnasium were flags from countries from all over the world. The flags were hung in alphabetical order. Our fifth-grade teacher, Mr. Woodcraft, decided that each student needed to learn an alphabetical list of the countries. We didn't each have to learn all of the countries; we each got a chunk of countries. We had to pick one of those countries and do a report on the culture and history of that country.

This was going to culminate in a shindig in the gymnasium on a Friday night. Our adults would be there, we would eat food, and then each child would stand up and recite their list of countries while pointing to the corresponding flag and then present their report.

"...Australia, Austria, Azerbaijan... I did my report on the country of Australia. Australia is a country. It is also a continent. It is an island. It is in the ocean. People live there." Basic fifth grade public speaking.

And each child's adult would think to themselves, "My child is the smartest, brightest, most creative child in the whole school system."

And all those adults would be wrong, except mine.

Every day in class, we had to stand up and recite our list of countries. One day, a girl got up to recite her list, which was composed of the last several letters of the alphabet. She said, "Venezuela, Vietnam, Virgin Islands, Wake Island, West Germany, Yemen, Yugoslavia, Zambia, Zimbabwe."

When she sat down, my buddy Wally raised his hand and asked, "What about Wallis and Futuna?"

Mr. Woodcraft said, "What about Wallis and Futuna?"

Wally said, "Wallis and Futuna is a country."

Mr. Woodcraft said, "I don't think Wallis and Futuna is a country."

Wally said, "I know it's a country. It's in the South Pacific located between Fiji and Samoa. I know it's a country because my mom was in the Peace Corps. She met my dad on Wallis and Futuna, and they fell in love, got married, and had me. In that order." Wally said, "I am named for the country of Wallis and Futuna. My name is Wallis Futuna Fenstermacher."

"That be as it may," said Mr. Woodcraft, "I don't think it's a country."

Wally said, "It is a country, and I demand you formally recognize Wallis and Futuna as a country."

Mr. Woodcraft said, "We don't have a flag in our gymnasium for Wallis and Futuna, and therefore I refuse to formally recognize Wallis and Futuna as a country!"

This pretty much sums up American diplomatic policy. If your flag does not hang in the gym of a rural American school, you don't exist, and that's all there is to it.

This was in the days of the superpowers- the USA and the USSR. Teachers are essentially superpowers. Wally knew that a tiny little country like Wallis and Futuna didn't stand much of a chance in a full-frontal assault against a superpower. But he also knew he wasn't beaten. He just had to step back and wait for the winds of political change to shift so he could press his point at a later date.

We went to gym.

Our gym teacher was a woman named Ms. Grunkle. We knew she was a woman because we had to call her '*Ms.*' Beyond that, we had no indication whatsoever. Nothing about her said physical or education. Except her wardrobe. She wore standard 1980s gym teacher clothes: a white polo buttoned all the way up to the bottom of her lowest chin, white polyester coach's shorts with the three metal snaps, white tube socks pulled up to her knees, and white tennis shoes. She always wore a whistle and carried a megaphone. She only communicated through the bullhorn. In the gym she shouted, "Run! Run!" In the hallway she shouted, "Don't Run! Don't Run!" It was very conflicting information.

I believe she was ambulatory. I think she could walk. She just chose not to. Ms. Grunkle was a pioneer of the three-wheeled, electric gym teacher scooter. She rode it back and forth along the floor of the gym while shouting at us through the bullhorn.

Ms. Grunkle would blow her whistle at the beginning of gym class and then shout, "Okay, boys and girls, let's shape up!" She would motor her scooter over to the reinforced gym record player and put on a record such as *Rejoicing in Jumping Jacks*. The voice would come through the speaker: "Now, let's get those hearts pumping! Jumping Jacks are fun. Ready? One, two, three." All the while, Ms. Grunkle would roll back and forth on her scooter shouting, "Get those arms up, Lepp! Let's see your feet come off the ground, Barth."

And then it would be time for the rope. It used to be that in every school gym in America there was a rope hanging from the rafters. Four stories above the ground. The rope was eight inches in diameter. It came all the way down from the ceiling to about a foot off the ground. There was a huge knot tied in the end. We children were supposed to climb to the top of the rope, touch the ceiling, and then climb back down as part of our physical education. Very few children were strong enough to climb all the way to the top of the rope; fewer still were strong enough to climb all the way back down.

When a child reached the top, one of two things would happen. Either they would sort of let go of the rope, at which point they would come down the rope at about 711 miles an hour, and by the time they reached the bottom of the rope all that would be left of them would be some ashes, some callouses, and some blisters. Or they would entirely let go of the rope. In which case they would be like, "Ahhhhhhh! Ahhhhhhhhhh!" as they plummeted. You'd think they would go *Splat* when they hit the ground. But no. No. Our teachers were concerned for our physical well-being. They put a mat at the bottom of the rope. That mat was at least as thick as my t-shirt. That way, you only broke most of your bones when you hit. Not all of your bones.

We children sat in a big circle around the bottom of the rope, most of us hoping we would not be called on to climb the rope. It was like a strange game of Duck, Duck Goose. Ms. Grunkle would drive around us shouting, “Lepp, climb the rope!”

I have never been particularly athletic, nor coordinated. I could grab hold of the rope and get my feet on the knot, but that’s as high as I could get.

“Barth! Climb the rope!” Skeet could grab hold, get his feet on the knot, and then climb until his feet were maybe two feet above the knot. Then he slid down.

“Fern Dale,” Ms. Grunkle shouted, “climb the rope!”

Fern Dale was a snooty, snotty girl whom I’m pretty sure could be found in the middle of the night, in the middle of the woods, in the middle of a clearing, with a cauldron and a fire saying, “Rats’ tails, frog eyes, all boys must die.” Sweet little thing. Incidentally, she grew up to be much more than that. But back then, she was just snooty.

Fern Dale grabbed the rope and started to climb. She got to where her feet were maybe eight feet off the ground, and then she froze. I don’t know if she ran out of strength, or got scared, or both. But she froze. Eight feet off the ground.

Ms. Grunkle, in her kind and compassionate way, drove around shouting, “Fern Dale, climb up or climb down! Fern Dale, climb up or climb down!” The more she yelled, the more upset poor Fern Dale got. Fern Dale started to cry. Her nose began to run. She needed to wipe her face. She couldn’t get her face to her hands because her arms were extended above her head, and she couldn’t get her hands to her face because she wouldn’t loosen her grasp. But she needed to wipe her face, so she wiped her face on the rope. Those ropes were abrasive, made of raw jute, steel wool, and barbed wire. The rope cut poor Fern Dale’s face. She started crying harder as the tears rolled into the scratches.

Ms. Grunkle decided she was going to have to be more pro-active in rescuing Fern Dale. But she wouldn’t get off her scooter. She rolled to the edge of the mat, but the trike was rear-wheel drive and didn’t have enough power to get on the mat at such a slow speed. She backed up ten feet and came in hot. She hit the edge of the mat, flew all the way over it, and took out three kids on the other side. They were gone. The janitor came in, sprinkled that red stuff on them, and pushed them away with the big mop. We never spoke of them again. Then, Ms. Grunkle figured out she could back onto the mat, but she still wouldn't get off the scooter, so she still wasn't tall enough to get Fern Dale.

Ms. Grunkle gave up trying to reach her. She rolled off the mat and over to the intercom mounted on the wall. Ms. Grunkle buzzed Mr. Woodcraft. Mr. Woodcraft, a tall man, came running into the gym and helped Fern Dale down.

Fern Dale got to do what every child got to do in the 1980s when they were upset at school. She got to go to the bathroom, wash her face with cold water, get a Kleenex, come back in, sit down, and deal with it.

Then Ms. Grunkle shouted, "Fenstermacher! Climb the rope!"

Fenstermacher was, of course, Wallis Futuna Fenstermacher. Wally was one of those kids who never stopped moving. Some part of his body was always moving 100mph. There was no Potential energy about Wally. He was pure Kinetic energy. Nowadays, they give you something for that; back then we just let kids go.

We never even saw him get up. Wally launched from the circle and was a third of the way up the rope before he ever grabbed it. Wally touched the ceiling, then he climbed back down the rope. As soon as his feet touched the knot, he shot back up the rope. He was going up and down, and up and down.

"Fenstermacher!" Ms. Grunkle bellowed, "What are you doing?"

"Climbing the rope!"

"Quit climbing the rope!"

Wally was an obedient child. Just because you can't stop moving doesn't mean you aren't obedient. When Ms. Grunkle said, "Quit climbing the rope," Wally quit climbing the rope. But when she said, "Quit climbing the rope," Wally was at the top of the rope. So, there he was, four stories above the ground.

"Fenstermacher! Fenstermacher!" Ms. Grunkle didn't know what to say. Then she said one of those stupid things adults say to children. "Wally! Come down right now! Come down here and get your punishment!"

Wally was up. The punishment was down.

Wally didn't say anything, but I know what he was thinking.

"Nope. I'm not comin' down. And you sure aren't coming up."

"If you don't come down I'm calling Mr. Woodcraft," warned Ms. Grunkle.

Again, Wally was quiet, but I know what he was thinking. "Go ahead. He's not coming up here either."

Mr. Woodcraft came in the gym saying, "Fenstermacher, you're getting on my last nerve. Come down right now."

Wally stayed silent.

The roof of our gym was held up by metal trusses. The trusses were twelve inches apart. The rope was tied to one of the trusses at the far end of the gym. Wally reached up with one hand and grabbed the truss. He reached up with the other hand and grabbed the truss. Wally did a pull up, and he was in the ceiling.

Mr. Woodcraft said, "Wally! You better think about what you are doing!"

Wally thought about it. He reached down, grabbed the rope, and hauled it up into the ceiling with him. Now nobody was going to get him down.

The teachers called the principal. Figuring Wally needed rescued, the principal called the fire department since they were the folks in our small community responsible for rescuing people.

Pretty soon the fire department came running in with extension ladders. One of the firefighters set up his ladder under Wally and started climbing. When he was about halfway up, Wally swung down so that he was hanging from the metal truss. He reached out and grabbed the next truss, then the next. Wally monkey-barred clear down to the other end of the gym. The firefighter climbed down his ladder, took it to the other end of the gym, set it up, got about halfway up, and Wally monkey-barred back to where he had started. The fireman climbed down his ladder and followed Wally while Ms. Grunkle drove back and forth shouting, "Wally! You come down right now!"

Pretty soon the fire department figured out they weren't going to get Wally. They figured out Wally didn't need rescued. People who need rescued need rescued because they don't have any other avenue of escape. Wally had plenty of avenues of escape. Wally didn't need rescued. Wally needed trapped. That is not the fire department's purview.

The adults discussed who in our community was responsible for trapping things.

The humane officer showed up with his big net on a long pole, like you see in the cartoons, but it wasn't nearly long enough to catch Wally. He went out to his truck and came back a couple minutes later carrying a long, thin, rectangular box. He set it on the ground, flipped some latches, opened the box, and there was a tranquilizer rifle.

The humane officer began explaining what a tranquilizer gun was. But we didn't need anyone to tell us what a tranquilizer gun was. We'd grown up watching a TV show called *Mutual of Omaha's Wild Kingdom*. Every week on that show there was Jim, standing on a helicopter skid with a tranquilizer gun chasing a dingo across the Australian Outback, or in the back of a pick-up bouncing across the African savannah chasing a white rhinoceros while Marlin Perkins, safe in a studio in New York City, was saying, "Now Jim is going to shoot the white rhinoceros with a tranquilizer dart, but he has put just enough tranquilizer in the dart to subdue the white rhinoceros, not kill the white rhinoceros. Be careful, Jim. And should the white rhinoceros veer into the truck, that's okay because we are covered by Mutual of Omaha's insurance."

The humane officer was saying to us, "I'm putting just enough tranquilizer into this dart to subdue Wally, but not kill Wally."

Wally was hanging four stories above the ground. It didn't matter how much tranquilizer you hit him with, it was going to knock him out, and he was going to fall, then splat!

The firefighters went and got their big net.

Wally was monkey barring back and forth, the firefighters were following under him with their life net, and Ms. Grunkle was driving back and forth yelling, "Wally! Come down right now!"

The humane officer was tracking Wally through his scope. Tracking. Tracking. He fired. And missed. Not by a little. We were a small West Virginia hunting community. He missed so bad he had to quit his job, change his name, and move to Ohio.

We watched the dart soar toward the ceiling, hit one of the metal trusses, ricochet, come back down, and hit Ms. Grunkle in the shoulder. She went over like a white rhino. She took her scooter with her when she fell. She still had her hand locked on the throttle, and so she was spinning in circles. We were trying to get out of the way.

Finally, the adults did what they should have done in the first place.

They called Wally's parents.

Mrs. Fenstermacher, Wally's mom, ran into the gym doing what any adult would do thinking their child was hurt in the gym. She was scanning the floor. Then she looked up, and there was Wally hanging four stories above the ground.

"Wally!" she said, "What are you doing up there?"

"Hanging from the ceiling, Ma."

"Why don't you come down?"

"I'm not comin' down, Ma. I'm not comin' down until Mr. Woodcraft formally recognizes Wallis and Futuna as a country."

Mr. Woodcraft grunted and mumbled. "I'm not gonna recognize Wallis and Futuna as a country."

Mrs. Fenstermacher did not react in a way the other adults anticipated or appreciated. Mrs. Fenstermacher had been in the Peace Corps. She was sort of a hippie. She liked protests. She raised her fist and yelled, "You go, son! Fight for what you believe in!"

Wally did a pull up, and he was back in the ceiling. He stayed in the ceiling. For a long time. He lived up there like a bird in a box store.

Sometimes during lunch- our gym and cafeteria were the same room- Wally would swoop down and steal your fried chicken. He'd drop us a note if he needed anything. We'd sneak in after school, and he would lower the rope, onto which we had tied a basket. We'd drop in whatever supplies he needed, and he'd haul it back up.

Finally, it was the night of the big gala. We were in the gym with our adults. We'd eaten. Kids were standing up, pointing to their assigned flags, reciting the country names, and reading their reports. The girl got up to do the last several letters of the alphabet. "Venezuela," she pointed to the flag for Venezuela. "Vietnam, Virgin Islands, Wake Island…" After she said "Wake Island" and pointed to the flag for Wake Island, but before she could say "West Germany" and point to that flag, Wally, Wallis Futuna Fenstermacher, unfurled himself from the ceiling. He was hanging by his knees between the flags of Wake Island and West Germany. And he wasn't wearing anything. Well, he had on his underwear. He'd used the paints he'd ask me to send up in the supply basket to paint himself so he looked just like the flag of Wallis and Futuna. It has a red background, a white cross pattée , and the French tricolors in the corner. He was just hanging there, painted like the flag for Wallis and Futuna, hanging between the flags for Wake Island and West Germany, his hair dangling like fringes.

The whole place went silent. Wally's parents stood up. I knew what they were thinking. "Our child is the brightest, smartest, most creative child in the whole school system." And you know what? They were right.

Then Mr. Woodcraft stood up. He stared at Wally for a long time. Wally, painted like the flag for Wallis and Futuna, hanging between the flags for Wake Island and West Germany. Mr. Woodcraft stared for a long time. He cleared his throat. He rapped his knuckle on the table like he was hitting a gavel on a podium and said, "Well, I guess I formally recognize Wallis and Futuna as a country."

I think what we can learn from all of this is that even a seemingly insignificant person, perpetrating a seemingly mindless act, while clinging to nothing more than the moral high ground, can, in fact, change the hearts of the stubborn and the minds of the ignorant.

Ice Sledding

Skeeter and I were nine years old when we decided to discover the origins of Skitter creek. We packed a couple of peanut butter sandwiches and headed up stream.

It was a bitter, cold day, and the creek was frozen solid. We were walking right down the middle of the frozen creek when we heard the ice crack.

We slipped and slid to the bank and laughed about how close we had come to falling in. If you think we were smart enough to stay off the ice after that then you must have started reading this book right here.

Generally speaking, you don't want to fall through the ice because you don't want to drop into frigid water, or maybe get stuck under the ice. But that's when you are on a pond or a lake or a river. Skitter creek was only ankle deep in most places. Maybe knee deep. Not deep enough to get wet enough to endanger yourself.

There are no vital organs in your legs, reasoned Skeeter, and thus getting wet up to your knees can't be that bad.

We found a long stretch of ice, got a running start, and slid as fast as we could, like you do in your socks on a wooden floor.

The ice started to crack. I went for the edge, but Skeeter skidded to a stop on the middle of the frozen creek. We stood in the otherwise silent winter wood listening to the ice creaking and cracking as we watched the fissures spread. The speed of sound and the speed of sight raced to the creek bank as Skeet stood still, his arms out to balance himself, as the ice broke into chunks. He was balancing on a good-sized piece of ice, maybe as big around as a trashcan lid.

"Now what are you going to do?" I asked.

"Shhhh…." He whispered, as if my voice would be enough to upset the equilibrium.

He jumped toward the shore. He didn't make it. He had very little traction on the ice so instead of jumping he lurched, a little, with one foot. That one foot landed on the edge of a second ice chunk, which caused that chunk to flip up and over. Meanwhile, Skeet's other foot, the one that hadn't really gone anywhere, fell off the far side of the chunk he was standing on. And then he was standing in shin-deep, icy water.

"I guess I didn't move quick enough," he said.

There was no choice but to head home, and since he was already wet, Skeeter walked right down the center of the ice. I would dash for the shore every time the ice started to crack, but Skeet would try to ride it out. I'm not sure what success in this endeavor would have looked like, but I feel Skeeter never achieved it.

His pant legs were frozen solid from about mid-thigh down by the time we got home. He said his feet were cold. I believed him. He got the hair dryer to thaw his pants enough to get to the laces on his boots, which he also had to thaw.

"It's obvious what the problem was," he said when he finally got the boots off and had begun hacking away at his socks. "I was *standing* on the ice. All my weight was in one place."

"You're just figuring that out now?" I asked.

"What we need to do is lie on the ice."

"That's what you learned from this?"

"Yep. Tomorrow I'm taking my sled."

And he did.

"Think about it," he said the next morning while placing his sled on the ice. "The chief problem with sledding is the hill is almost never long enough, so eventually you stop sledding, and then you gotta walk back up the hill. But creeks flow downhill, even if it's gradual. If we can get going on this ice we'll never stop. We can sled forever," he explained.

"Or until we go so far south that the creek thaws. Then you run into the same problem. You gotta drag the sled back," I said.

"If we go so far that we get to where it's warm, it won't matter because we won't want to go sledding anymore. Nobody sleds when it's warm."

"So you plan to sled all the way to a region with a different climate?"

"Yep."

"I shoulda brought a sandwich."

Creeks flow downhill, descending from a higher elevation to a lower elevation. Often the decline is so gradual it's imperceptible. Other times it's very dramatic, like at a waterfall.

Skeet and I had to push ourselves along with our hands for large sections. Sledding down a frozen creek is a cross between swimming and cross-country skiing, but slower. You hear the word 'skiing,' and you think, 'Fast and fun. Gravity does most of the work,' but that's downhill skiing. Nordic skiing takes a lot more effort. It's like the difference between fast-water kayaking and canoeing on still water. Canoeing down a river seems fun, romantic, but then you find out that paddling is tedious. And nobody goes row-boating for fun… not for long anyway. Sledding on a flat stream is like dog sledding, but from the dog's perspective. In kayaking, white-water rafting, and downhill skiing you have the forces of nature working for you. In canoeing upstream, cross-country skiing, and ice-creek sledding you are working against the current, gravity and/or friction. However, as far as we knew, we were the first people to ever cross-country sled down Skitter creek, so it was a fun, if slow, adventure.

Then we hit the part of Skitter creek where there are several quick, but small, steps down as the elevation drops maybe twenty feet over about a hundred yards. We picked up speed, which allowed us to coast all the way to Dead Deer Canyon. The creek gets very narrow very fast at that point, drops about 100 feet over two hundred yards, and the walls rise like a tunnel as the creek descends. We hit Dead Deer Canyon going fast, and then picked up more speed. We went from cross-country sledding to bobsledding in less than a quarter mile. There was no learning curve. Fortunately, Skeeter and I were used to limited learning curves.

People going downstream, in the movies, realize they are approaching a waterfall when they hear it.

It's difficult to hear a frozen waterfall. We didn't realize we were approaching one until there was no more creek in front of us.

Transportation pioneers face many challenges. Somebody had to be the first person on a horse. I'm sure the creator of the first horse-drawn wagon faced challenges. Early steam engines exploded. Internal combustion engine? No way that worked the first time. We've all seen news reels of the first flying machines, and then rockets crashing, collapsing, and exploding. An important key to being a successful transportation pioneer is to survive the test run.

A runner sled has two thin, steel runners, or blades, attached to a frame on which smooth birch boards are bolted. The rider sits or lays on the boards. At the front of the sled is a wooden bar set perpendicularly across the runners. This bar is about a foot long. You can, in theory, put your feet or hands on this bar and, by pushing or pulling one way or the other, steer the sled. You can move the steering bar maybe an inch to the left or right, so steering is limited. Like the learning curve. There are no brakes apart from your feet and hands.

Your best chance for avoiding a collision on a runner sled is bailing out since you can't really steer or stop it. Bailing out usually means landing in the snow, but we were blasting down an iced slope populated by large rocks and log jams. A lot of fallen trees and branches, and other dangerous detritus, like dead deer, had washed into Dead Deer Canyon over the past millennium. Much of it had become wedged in the narrow walls.

I bailed off the sled rather than going headfirst over the waterfall. I dug my heels into the ice and grabbed at vines and rocks to slow myself down. My sled flipped over, bounced off a log, crashed into the wall, and wedged between two rocks.

Skeeter chose to ride it out. We were familiar with the falls. It wasn't a huge drop. Maybe six feet, with a wide, deep pool beneath it.

I halted my slide just on the edge of the falls but Skeeter never even tried to slow down.

The brand name of the sleds Skeet and I owned was *The Flexible Flyer*.

The Flexible Flyer is neither of those things.

Skeeter's sled tipped off the edge of the icy falls, and he and it went straight down. Headfirst.

Some tenacious water was still flowing in the creek, deep beneath the ice. Enough of that moving water fell out beneath the lip of the frozen falls to roil the pool of water at the fall's base and thus keep it from freezing. A large circle of water was opened like a mouth in the ice below the falls.

Skeet went straight into that open mouth, sled and all. Never even hit the rim.

He popped up after a couple of seconds. He pulled his sled out of the water and put it on the ice. I scrambled down the cliff and grabbed the front of his sled. He grabbed the back, and I managed to haul him out of the water.

We burned the remains of his sled in the fire I built to thaw Skeeter.

Over-Solving

My buddy Mike had an older brother and older sister, both of whom learned to drive about the time *Smokey and the Bandit* came out.

I highly recommend the film. If you haven't seen it, all you need to know for now is that Burt Reynolds, as the Bandit, helps bootleg a whole bunch of beer across the South while driving a 1976 V8, 455, Pontiac T-Top Trans Am. The car was very cool, and very fast.

One day my buddy Mike's mom told her husband that she thought the kids needed to learn to drive a stick shift. Mr. Brown agreed and said he'd go see if he could find a deal on a stick shift for the kids to learn on. A few hours later he came tearing down the street and screeched into the driveway in a 1976 V8, 455, Pontiac T-Top Trans Am. "What?" he said to his wife. "You said the kids needed to learn to drive a stick shift, so I bought a stick shift."

This kind of action may be described as 'over-solving' a problem.

When Frank Barth, Skeeter's dad, heard this story, he went out and bought a 1976 V8, 455 T-Top Pontiac Trans Am. When he pulled in the driveway his wife asked, "Why?" And he said, "Skeeter will need to learn to drive a stick shift."

Mrs. Barth said, "Frank, Skeeter won't be sixteen for four more years."

Frank said, "The clutch ought to be good and broken in by then."

Frank was a world class over-solver.

Skeet and I were twelve when Frank got that car. It was August, and very hot. We were moping around and starting to get on Frank's nerves. One day he snapped at us, "Get out of here! Why don't you boys go check the mail or something?"

That was something we hadn't done in a while, so why not?

When I was a kid there was no email. There was just regular mail. Getting a letter addressed to me was an exciting thing that generally only happened around my birthday or Christmas. I often received cards from family members on those occasions, and those cards often contained a few dollars. Thus, mail was treasured and looked forward to.

Mail changes a bit when you are a teen. Maybe you meet someone special at a summer camp and fall in love. You know this person is your true life-partner, your soul mate. You are destined by the gods to spend forever with that person, but alas, at the end of a week-long camp, you are torn away from that person, and they go home to some far off and exciting, exotic foreign city like Toledo, or Harrisburg. What are these lovers to do?

Back then, there were long distance fees if you wanted to call a person outside your area code, so you couldn't call your beloved without your parents getting mad when they got the phone bill. Instead of calling your beloved, you wrote impassioned epistles and missives and dispatches.

The *ding* of an incoming text will never have the same effect as opening your mailbox to find a scented envelope from your darling on which they have taken the time to draw hearts and XOXOXOXOXO.

But that's not what I'm talking about. I'm talking about when we were twelve. When Skeet and I were twelve years old, we'd never met anyone from Harrisburg or Toledo, and we certainly weren't interested in scented envelops.

Another kind of mail we got was the chain letter. These were the grandparents of chain emails but back then they came in an envelope, with your name on them. You could open them without releasing a virus. Often, they were purported to have been written in blood. Chain letters came in two varieties, one positive, one negative. Basically, they said: "This chain letter has been going around the world. You must copy this letter, in your own blood, and mail it out to ten other people…" That's a lot of blood. After that introduction, the letters went positive or negative. The either read, "If you send it out to ten other people, all your dreams and fantasies will come true, and you will live long and prosper," or, "If you don't send it out to ten other people, all your worst fears and nightmares will come true, and you will suffer a grievous injury and possibly death." Both themes generally ended with, "Don't tell your parents."

Quite the conundrum. You had to handwrite the letters. In blood. You had to address the envelopes, not in blood. You had to get stamps. You had to mail the letters. That wasn't easy to do without your parents getting wise. My mom immediately became suspicious if she saw me writing outside of homework. She got unreasonable if she saw me writing in blood. Where was I supposed to get envelopes? Or stamps? Stamps cost money. How were my parents not going to know?

"Uh, mom, can I have ten envelops, ten stamps, a quill, and something that will hold a cup of blood?"

"Why? Did you get a silly chain letter? You don't need to waste your time on those. I've told you that."

The letters had a deadline. "Mail out the ten letters in ten days, or else!"

You would lie awake in bed the night of the deadline awaiting doom, unable to sleep, waiting for your worst nightmare to come true, as well as trying to decide exactly what your worst nightmare was. And then you'd wake up in the morning and everything would be fine, and a small part of your brain would acknowledge that *maybe* the letter was a hoax. But why take chances?

Anyway, Mr. Barth told us to go check the mail. Low and behold, Skeet had gotten a letter. It was a chain letter. It was a little different than most chain letters because instead of insisting you mail out ten other letters written in blood it required a single task.

Skeeter's letter read, "Dear Skeeter, you have been selected for great fortune and luck if you can complete the following task. You need to build a slip-and-slide. But no ordinary slip-and-slide. You need to build the greatest slip-and-slide ever seen. If you do this within three days of receiving this letter all your dreams will come true. If you do not build the slip-and-slide expect doom and regrettable terrors."

He showed the letter to me. "Are there unregrettable terrors? And what's a slip-and-slide?" I asked.

He explained: "We need a long strip of plastic, water, and dish soap. Most slip-and-slides are like ten feet long, and wide enough for one person. But I've been instructed to build the world's greatest slip-and-slide, soooo, I'm thinking a little bigger…"

We headed out the next morning, eager and smiling, knowing we had something to do. Skeet's dad yelled, "Son, you're not supposed to go anywhere 'til you wash the car." We pretended not to hear.

Skeet's mom said, out of our hearing, "Frank, I don't think writing those boys that letter was a good idea."

"Nonsense," said Frank, "It gives them something to do, and it gets them out from under foot."

"Seems like begging trouble," Mrs. Barth said.

Frank pretended not to hear.

Halfdollar City Pool sat on a hilltop. The front, or shallow end, of the pool was in-ground, but the back of the pool sat about fifteen feet off the ground and was supported by a huge, cinder block structure. The pool was half in-ground and half above-ground, thus catering to both the redneck element of the county and the more refined citizens.

Behind the exposed walls of the deep end was a field that belonged to Angus Fester. The field descended down, down, down and ended at Skitter creek. Skitter creek also flowed beside Skeeter's house and yard. The hill behind the pool was the greatest sledding hill in town, and thus was a perfect hill for a slip-and-slide. The hill was a hay field when it wasn't covered in snow, and Angus Fester had left several large rolls of white plastic in the field. It was the plastic that would eventually encase his haybales, making those giant marshmallows you see lined up on farms.

A couple of well-placed kicks got the plastic rolls unrolling down the hill and, before long, we had a six-lane slip-and-slide. Earlier we had picked up a couple of five-gallon buckets of industrial dish soap and commercial grade floor wax from the supply closet at the school. We liberally applied these lubricants to all six lanes of the slip-and-slide.

Dozens of kids were showing up in their bathing suits to take part in the festivities.

Skeeter turned the water on and the slipping and sliding began. A kid can build up a pretty good head of steam going down three hundred yards of haybale plastic coated in liquid wax, and we were having a great time.

The folks in the pool soon realized that the water level was dropping. A lifeguard leaned over the fence and yelled at us, "Hey! What are you doing? Turn off that drain valve! You're emptying the pool!"

Skeeter yelled back to her: "Turn around! You're a lifeguard at the pool. The pool is behind you. You have no authority in this direction."

The lifeguard yelled back, "I'm a lifeguard where the water is! And right now most of the water is going down that hill! I'm calling Sheriff Hasbro!"

Lifeguards may only be lifeguards in one direction but Sheriff Hasbro was the Law of the entire county. Kids cleared out quick.

Skeeter and I had another surprise waiting when we got home. Mr. Barth's new 1976 Pontiac T-Top Trans Am Firebird was now beside the creek. In a tree. A swimming pool worth of water had flowed from the pool, down the slip-and-slide, into Skitter creek, and had caused a bit of a flash flood. The flood waters had swept through the Barth's yard and lifted the Trans Am into the tree. Mr. Barth was standing in the backyard looking up at the car.

Mrs. Barth was leaning on the railing of the back-porch, sipping iced tea, and smiling.

Mr. Barth's lips moved, but no sound came out. He knew this was his fault. He knew his wife had been correct. He knew she was watching him, and that he couldn't yell at us because he had written the letter. His face went through several varied expressions, from rage to anger to frustration.

Finally, he sighed and said, "Thanks for washing the car."

Skeet said, "I waxed it, too."

Mr. Barth said, "Well, you may have over-solved that situation."

The Inflated Easter Bunnies of Halfdollar

February is the point in the year when Winter loses all its allure. You no longer want to have a snowball fight or go sledding. You just want it to be Spring. And Spring is right there, just over the horizon.

Skeeter and I were in eighth grade and had utterly run out of things to do. We decided to take a drastic step. We decided to go to the Halfdollar Public Library.

When I was in the eighth grade I was not much of a reader. I did not start to read recreationally until I was a sophomore in college. One of the reasons I didn't read much is because I've always been a slow reader. Another was because teachers saying things like, "Reading can take your mind on a journey," didn't really resonate with me. My response was, "I like my mind right where it is."

I did not just say, "Don't read." You should read, and if you've made it this far into this book, you likely already agree with me. However, if you run into a reluctant reader, don't say, "Reading can take your mind on a journey." Say, "Hey, kid. Read this book. There's stuff in here your adults don't want you to know."

One of the best things about books is that, unlike movies, TV shows, and video games, no one, thank the Lord, has gotten around to rating books yet. We're close, but not there yet.

If you are watching *Attack of the Zombie Chainsaw Piranha Bloodthirsty Sorority* on TV and your mother walks by, she is going to say, "Stars and gardenias! What are you watching? You'll ruin your mind!" On the other hand, you can be sitting on the couch, in the living room, in broad daylight, reading a book and thinking, "Mm, mm, mm, my mother does not want me to know this." When she walks by and sees you reading, she will say, "Oh look, they're broadening their mind!"

If you want your kids to read, tell them there is seditious stuff in books, that books are free at the library, and that the innocent looking librarians know where the best stuff is. (But hurry!

Because the good books are getting pulled from the shelves and the good librarians are getting overwhelmed!)

We kicked the doors open when we arrived at the library because that is how we liked to enter places. The little librarian gasped and said, "What are you two doing here?" We were accustomed to this greeting, especially when we entered buildings that housed antiquities and things of great value. The librarian continued, "I hope you didn't bring those tiny fishing poles." This was in reference to an embarrassing, if understandable, mistake we had made when Skeeter and I had learned that they had microfiche at the library.

We applied for our library cards and since this was before the computer era, there was no way to do a quick background check and thus deny us our cards. We took our cards and headed for the stacks.

One of the first series of books that Skeet and I discovered was James Fennimore Cooper's *The Leatherstocking Series*.

I know what you are thinking. You are thinking, "Really? You didn't like to read? And you started with James Fennimore Cooper?"

The answer is, yes. The first two books in that series are *The Deerslayer* and *Last of the Mohicans*, and they are fantastic. Then you get *The Pioneers*, *The Prairie*, and I don't even remember the last one because they get progressively less interesting after the first two.

The books are about Natty Bumppo, or Hawkeye, and his Native friend Chingachgook. They're running around upstate New York during the French and Indian War. Everyone has a flintlock, a big knife, and a tomahawk. People are getting shot, stabbed, eviscerated, and brained. We were eighth grade boys. There was little more interesting to us than a good evisceration.

About the only other regular reading I did back then was the *Scouts in Action* page in *Boy's Life* magazine. It wasn't as gory as an evisceration, but there was always trauma. Skeeter and I were Boy Scouts, and each month we received a copy of *Boy's Life*. I flipped to the illustrated "Scouts in Action" page as soon as I got my magazine. That page depicted an actual Boy Scout risking his life to save someone else's life, thereby earning the Medal of Merit or the Medal of Honor.

A Scout is walking home and sees a little old lady drive her car into a frozen pond. Disregarding his own personal safety, and after exhausting all efforts to reach, throw, or row, the Scout jumps into the pond and saves the old woman, thus earning his Medal of Merit. Or a Scout is walking home and sees a house burning down. Disregarding his own personal safety--it is imperative to disregard your own personal safety-- he runs into the house and saves the little old lady who had lit the fire because she was cold- because she had just driven her car into a frozen pond.

Skeet and I wanted our Medals of Merit almost as badly as we wanted our Eagle Scout badges, but, as far as we were concerned, you just don't happen across tragic accidents with enough frequency. We did discuss the possibility of one of us getting grievously wounded and having the other guy save him and earn his medal. Then, when the first guy recovered, the other guy could get hurt. But we could never decide who should get hurt first, and thus we never earned our Medals of Merit.

There is a beautiful scene in *Last of the Mohicans* in which Hawkeye's pal, Major Duncan Heyward, a British officer, is captured by the Mingo. The Mingo are going to kill him, but not in some quick and easy way. They are going to burn him to death, but they are going to slow cook him. Like, you put the roast in the oven, go to church, and when you get home, it's done. The fire is going to progress up his body, singeing his skin, melting his guts, boiling his eyes. It was going to be an all-day affair, and Hawkeye just didn't want his friend to suffer that way. However, Hawkeye knows he can't run into the camp to save Major Heyward because there are too many Mingo, and Hawkeye would be killed himself. Instead, he does the only other thing he can think of. He goes off into the woods, takes aim with his flintlock, and shoots Major Heyward right between the eyes. Kills him dead, but at least he didn't have to suffer.

We thought it was probably the greatest thing ever written. Skeeter and I swore that if we ever had the opportunity, we would do that for each other. Nowadays, young people have their mobile devices, and they send each other texts like 'U R MY BFF.' Skeet and I said, "I will shoot you in the head." Strangely, it is the exact same sentiment, just a different way of expressing it.

Many of the major battles of the French and Indian War had been over for some time by the time Skeeter and I were born, and people no longer used flintlock rifles except to give themselves an excuse for a few more days of deer hunting. Nobody in their right mind would sell Skeeter and me black powder. About the only thing we had in common with Hawkeye and his pals was that there were still some trees left in North America, and we celebrated some of the same holidays. One of those holidays was Easter.

In Halfdollar, West Virginia, in the 1980s, there were two main outdoor Easter decorations. The first was colored plastic eggs hung from leafless trees by fishing line. I never understood the plastic egg thing. It looked to me as if some mythical bird had flown by and laid magic, floating eggs. I never once looked at that decoration and thought to myself "Jesus." Well, maybe I thought that, but I thought it with the wrong inflection.

The other decoration was the inflatable Easter bunny. These were not the same sort of inflatable yard decoration you see now. Now you can go to the local hardware store and buy a jack-o-lantern with Scooby and the Gang coming out it for Halloween, and a twelve-foot Santa at Christmas. The inflatable yard ornament of today has its own fan to inflate it. There are colored lights flashing on and off inside the thing, and it is all connected, by computer chip, to a light sensor. When the sun goes down the fan and lights kick on, and up goes your Santa. Sun comes up, the fan turns off and soon there is a twelve-foot Santa laying across your yard like he's been run over by a steam roller.

These decorations don't say 'Redneck' anywhere on them, but if your twelve-foot Santa is deflated into your aboveground pool, beside your trampoline, well, that says something about you.

The bunnies of the 1980s had no solar-powered fans, no light sensors that told the motor when to inflate the bunny, and no colored lights to illuminate the inflatable yard decorations. The inflatable decorations of the 1980s were not made of nylon, they were not mold resistant, they were not weatherproof, and they did not have weights to keep them in place should a strong wind blow through your yard.

The inflatable Easter bunny of the 1980s was plastic, or maybe vinyl, with sharp seams, and a little valve you pinched and blew into to inflate the son-of-a-gun. They came in several pastel colors and could be used as a flotation device in the event of a water landing. The bunnies did not come with an anchoring system, so if you didn't stake them down, and there was a breezy night, whichever neighbor had the first fence would have two dozen bunnies blown up against it. A pastel bunny dune halfway down the street.

Most people used binders twine or clothesline to tie their bunnies to trees and fence posts to keep them from blowing away.

Some people would have as many as a dozen bunnies lashed to trees around their yard. It may sound lovely, but you need to keep the science of the whole situation in mind. The bunnies, once inflated, became mere pawns in the great game of physics.

If you take a bunny into your house and blow it up- and let's just be clear that I am talking about inflating a plastic bunny. If you are going to explode an actual rabbit, you should do that outside. (Don't blow up a rabbit.)

If you take a bunny into your house and blow air into it, what causes that bunny to be inflated is that the air molecules you have forced into it are bouncing around the interior surface of the bunny, pushing out the sides, and causing it to be inflated. Those air molecules are moving at a speed related to the ambient temperature. Because it was the mid-1980s, that ambient room temperature was about 70 degrees because we did not listen to Jimmy Carter and put on a sweater and turn the thermostat down.

Honestly though, Carter blew it. If he had come on the TV and said, "Turn down the temperature and put on a sweater, or we are going to have screwy little light bulbs that aren't as bright and take a long time to light up," he'd of gotten reelected.

The Easter season falls at the end of Winter and the beginning of Spring. That means that Easter bunnies bound to trees and fence posts were subject to rapidly changing, often extreme climatic conditions. The temperature could drop well below freezing at night, then soar up into the 80s during the day. Thus, the molecules of air trapped inside the pastel bunnies were in a constant state of flux. The molecules were either cold and slow, or hot and fast. While hot and fast is a condition we often ascribe to rabbits, it is not a characteristic you want in your Easter Bunny.

If you blow up a bunny at room temperature and bind it to a tree with a piece of string, the molecules of air in the bunny react to the outside temperature. As the temperature drops, the bunnies droop until they are hanging limply over the string, and they look like starving prisoners. Conversely, if the temperature soars, the air molecules inside the bunny speed up, causing the plastic bunny to expand until it looks like it is being cut in half by the rope around its waist.

The Easter Bunnies were suffering. I expressed my concern for the bunnies to Skeeter, and he and I developed a plan.

We couldn't set the bunnies free, so we did what Natty Bumppo would have done.

Late Friday night, we loaded up our pellet guns and set out to spare the inflatable Easter bunnies of Halfdollar from their misery, just like Hawkeye had done for Major Heyward. One shot between the eyes, and the bunnies were spared. Sometimes Skeet and I could hear the bunnies sighing in relief. Sometimes they'd whistle.

Our task completed but our hearts heavy, we returned home, knowing we had acted honorably.

Skeet and I had failed to anticipate the uproar our actions might cause. All over town, a hue and cry went up. We did not tell anyone that it was we who had done it. Another thing we learned from the Natty Bumppo books is that you are supposed to be humble and not brag about your heroic deeds. Though nobody knew we'd done it, still Skeet and I were stung when folks called the perpetrators 'vandals' instead of 'heroes.' Nobody saw it for the act of mercy that it was. Skeet and I met in secret to discuss our options.

We decided to rectify the situation. On Saturday night, armed only with a roll of duct tape and our lungs, Skeet and I once again took to the yards of Halfdollar. We patched the hole in each of the slain bunnies and re-inflated them.

So that, on the third day, all the bunnies had risen.

The adults took our pellet guns, even though they could not prove it was we who had done it. But they did not revoke our library cards. Skeeter and I have continued to read, and act out, great moments from American literature.

Strike Anywhere Matches & Anything Can Stretch

Uncle Deebo was not our uncle. In fact, he was a year younger than we were, and not related to me or Skeet. Uncle Deebo was the seventeenth, and quite unexpected, child in the Stalnaker family.

Uncle Deebo's older siblings had regular names like Noggin and Holster, but by the time Deebo was born, his parents were tired. They couldn't think of a name, so they called him 'The Boy,' figuring something better would come along. Through the wonders of time and syllabic manipulation, 'The Boy' became 'Da Boy,' which became 'Deebo.'

Uncle Deebo had, as best we could tell, twenty-three nieces and nephews, many of whom were much older than Uncle Deebo. It was not uncommon to be walking down Main Street and hear some matronly niece holler, "Uncle Deebo, pull your pants up right now! Or I'll tell Granma!" Everyone in town called him Uncle Deebo.

Uncle Deebo was a good guy to have around. As the youngest of seventeen kids, he had heard and seen things we had never even thought of. His oldest brothers and sisters were much older than Deebo, but they held fast to their fraternal and sororitorial responsibilities rather than adopting paternal relationships. They shared things with their little brother that adults don't always share with children. These episodes and anecdotes Deebo generously shared with us. But his siblings weren't always kind or truthful in the information they shared with Deebo. By the time the poor kid was eight, he fully believed that not only did aliens exist, but that they existed solely to come from the stars to kidnap Deebo. He lived in fear of aliens.

One thing Uncle Deebo introduced Skeeter and me to was strike anywhere matches. We had already discovered matches and their potential, but Uncle Deebo had a vast and never-ending store of both matches and exotic ways to ignite them.

Uncle Deebo walked around with his pockets full of strike

anywhere matches and sang a little song he'd composed:

Strike anywhere matches.
Stike 'em fast as you can.
You can strike 'em
on your front teeth, on your thumb,
on a wall, on your bum.

Strike anywhere matches.
Strike 'em on your hat band.
Strike 'em on your calluses if you're an old farm hand.

You can strike 'em on your zipper.
You can strike 'em on your shoe, Mister.
You can strike 'em on your sister
if she's a hairy upper lipper.

Strike anywhere matches.
You can strike 'em anywhere.
Strike 'em in the kitchen
or on the road when hitchin'.

Strike anywhere matches.
You can strike 'em anywhere.
You can strike 'em on the run.
You can strike 'em on the fly.
You can strike 'em in the sun.
or even in the rain- if it's dry.

"Okay," Uncle Deebo would say, "here's today's way to strike a match." He'd reach into his front pant pocket and pull out a handful of Ohio Blue Tips. "You take the match and stick it, head up, in an old log. Then you take out your hatchet like this… You center the blade over the match head and then…" *WHACK*! He'd raise and lower the hatchet in a flash and strike the match. With practice, a fella could split the match and leave both sides of the head burning.

The next week he showed up with a BB gun. Without a word he grabbed a fistful of matches from his back pocket and set them up in a log the same way he had with the hatchet. He paced off twenty feet, aimed his BB gun, and shot the BB across the tip of the match. *WHOOSH*!

A month later he showed us the greatest technique of all. He dropped a match down the barrel of the BB gun and pulled the trigger. The match flew down the barrel of the gun, scraping along the interior of the gun, and emerged from the rifle as a soaring and glorious burning projectile.

Many a night we would sit in the yard and shoot matches, like comets and shooting stars, into the darkness. Skeet and I made paper airplanes and did our darndest to shoot them down with our little surface-to-air missiles.

As Boy Scouts we were supposed to be able to light a fire under any conditions with no more than two matches. We practiced the art of the two-match fire, but Skeet and I adopted Uncle Deebo's habit of carrying dozens of matches on our persons because we also practiced the art of the twenty-match fire.

Strike anywhere matches are harder to come by these days. If you look them up on that giant store on the Internet, you will see them for sale. There are two price options: New or… Used. One reason you rarely see strike anywhere matches anymore is because we live in a litigious society. People sue each other whenever they can. I read that strike anywhere matches are a safety threat because a mouse could chew through the box, then chew on the tip of a match, causing the match to ignite. When the match ignites, it can set the box on fire, and then your house could burn down. I also read that if you shake a box of strike anywhere matches, the match heads will rub together, a match will ignite, the box will explode, and your house will burn down. I think that if you are shaking a box of matches, you just have to live with the consequences. You shouldn't be allowed to sue.

When I was a Scout we would go on hiking trips. In our backpacks, there would be a loaf of bread, a pound of bologna, a pair of clean socks we had no intention of changing into, and two hundred thousand strike anywhere matches. Uphill, downhill, plenty of jostling. Never once did a Scout combust. I watched kids tumble down steep ravines, head over heels (nobody pushed them, I swear), their strike anywhere match-laden packs jouncing and bouncing in every direction, and never once did one of those Scouts explode. Not once did a Scout erupt from the scores of matches rubbing together in his pack.

Skeeter and I decided to test the theory that you could, in fact, strike a strike anywhere match anywhere. We were kids and thus we were scientists. All kids are, or at least should be, scientists, ever testing and exploring the world around them. We learned that you cannot, no matter how hard you try, strike a match on pudding or underwater, but that you can strike them on stale bread and Grape Nuts.

It was during the summer of our great match-testing experiments that we struck on another idea. We were trying to strike matches on a bowl full of Jell-O when Skeeter said, "It's not gonna work; the Jell-O is just too smooth."

"What we need to do," I said, "is stretch the Jell-O."

"What would that do for us?" Skeet asked.

"It's simple physics," I explained. "Jell-O is composed of two naturally occurring elements: Jell-O powder and water. The powder is crystalline, dry, and grainy, so you oughta be able to strike a match on it. The problem with Jell-O is that the water molecules have bonded with the Jell-O molecules." I continued: "It's common knowledge that Jell-O crystals are mined from a huge strip mine in Utah."

"Is that so?" Skeeter asked skeptically.

"Sure. It is deposited in striated layers beneath the desert. The deeper you go, the darker the crystals get. The lighter colored flavors, like lime and lemon, are near the top. You have to dig way down deep to get to grape," I explained.

"Ok," Skeet said, "but what's that have to do with striking matches on Jell-O?"

I said, "See, you mix the Jell-O crystals with water, and the water atoms surround the crystal atoms. If we could stretch the Jell-O far enough, the crystal atoms would stick out of the water atoms like stones in a creek. Then, when we drag the match along the stretched Jell-O, the match head will rub on the grainy Jell-O atoms, but miss the water atoms, and ignite."

Skeeter stared at me and said, "Why stretch the Jell-O at all?

Why not just strike a match on the Jell-O powder before the Jell-O ever gets made? Before anyone adds water?"

"Anybody could strike a match on unmade Jell-O," I acknowledged, "but I'm talking about a survival situation here. Let's say you were on a picnic and suddenly a blizzard hit, and you needed to light a fire but all you had to strike the match on was some already-made Jell-O. You'd need to know how to strike a match on the Jell-O."

Again, Skeet stared. "Let me get this straight. We're on a picnic, a blizzard hits, and the only thing we have to strike a match on is a bowl of Jell-O?"

"Precisely," I said.

"Why can't we strike the match on the wood we're going to burn in our fire? Or on the picnic basket? Or on our zipper, thumb, hatband, jeans, flatware…or something like that?"

"It's all wet, or frozen," I patiently explained. "The Jell-O is our only hope."

"So," Skeet summed up, "we're in a situation where the easiest means to light a fire is to stretch Jell-O taut enough to strike a match on?"

I nodded.

"Then," he said, "I'd say we'd be doomed. You can't stretch Jell-O."

"Sure you can. Anything can stretch. At least a little."

"I agree with you there," Skeet conceded, "but not everything can be stretched far enough that you can strike a match on it."

"Now," I said, "you are putting words in my mouth. I said Jell-O can be stretched far enough to strike a match on. And I said anything can stretch. I never said anything can be stretched far enough to strike a match on."

"But how would you stretch Jell-O?" he asked.

"You could suck it through a straw," I replied.

"But then it would be in the plastic straw, and you couldn't strike the match on the plastic straw," he countered. "And anyway, not everything can stretch. You can't stretch a cinder block."

"But you can strike a match on a cinder block," I said. "So you don't need to stretch it. Besides, I think you can stretch a cinder block."

"Nope," Skeet said, "all you can do is break a cinder block. If you pull hard enough it'll just break."

"But just before it breaks, it's gotta give a little. If you pull just a little bit shy of 'hard enough,' it'll stretch, at least a little."

"Prove it."

And thus, Skeet had laid down the challenge for me to prove that anything can stretch.

"Skeeter," I said, "anything can stretch. We'll work up to a cinder block."

He nodded slowly. He thought it over and then said in agreement. "Of course, some things can stretch farther than other things."

"Naturally," I agreed.

"For example," Skeet mused, "I bet you couldn't stretch a Coke bottle nearly as far as you could stretch a frog."

"Welp, that's probably true," I said. "No use standing around all day. We got work to do."

"Yep," Skeet agreed. And then he said, "We're gonna need to build a stretching machine."

When you're a kid and you get an idea like that you want to make sure that you get it early in the morning. You want to have the whole day ahead of you when you hit upon a really good theory. You don't want to get a grand notion like 'anything can stretch' a half an hour before bedtime. You won't be able to sleep because you'll just worry all night long about your theory. You'll worry what to do about it. You'll worry that someone else will hit upon the very same notion and do something about it before you get out of bed. If you're going to hit upon a theory as hot and potential as 'anything can stretch' you want to hit upon that baby in the early morning of a hot, bright summer day.

A great notion is a doorway into a whole new world of possibility, and a kid needs a whole day, at least, to swing that big door open. The best thing about a notion, a theory, a hypothesis, is that you have to prove it. You can't just have a great notion and let it go at that. Not if you're a kid. The whole point of getting a notion is so you can run tests and experiments.

And experiments are the bread and butter of a healthy childhood.

As it turns out, Skeet and I each owned half a stretching machine. If you're a kid with proper perspective you have everything you need to test any notion you can conjure. As a kid you always have enough to get to work experimenting on any proper notion. Or at least you have half of what you need, which is why you have friends. They supply the other half of anything you might need. My half of the stretching machine was a Huffy. Skeet's was a Schwinn.

We tied a rope under the seat post of each bike, and then we would select objects to perform stretching tests on. We'd choose an item, like a sock, measure it with a yard stick, record the pre-stretched length of the object in our notebook- twelve inches and five little lines- and then tie the ropes from our stretching machine around each end of the object. Then, we'd mount our machines and peddle in different directions. The ropes would stretch the object, and then we'd measure it again and record the post-stretching machine length. Eighteen inches and eleven little lines. Simple.

Examples of our notes read something like:

Garden hose- stretched three feet

Old tire- stretched, but wouldn't stay stretched long enough to measure

Plastic spatula- stretched some but mostly broke

Sister's hairdryer- stretched the cord right out of the thing

Sister's hair curler- same result.

Cat- didn't stretch far but stretched loud. Ran off before we could measure it. Skeet still bleeding. (Don't stretch a cat, or any other living creature including your siblings, big or small)

The problem, of course, was a matter of power. Our stretching machine was limited by the amount of power Skeeter and I could exert on the pedals of our bikes.

There are certain things you say as a child that you know are just trouble. As soon as you utter them you know a spanking or a grounding is in your future. These things start as an idea, and if you could keep those ideas quiet you'd be better off in the long run, but there are some ideas, no matter the consequences, that you just have to speak. And once spoken, they must be carried out.

I said, "My dad owns half a stretching machine."

Skeet nodded. "Mine too."

"No use asking them; they'd just say 'No.'"

"Yep."

My dad may not have known that he owned half a stretching machine, but he did. He owned a V-8 Ford station wagon. Skeeter's dad owned an International Harvester Scout.

The first thing we stretched with our new machine was a cinderblock. We stretched it right in half. Then we stretched an old tire a good long ways. We were stretching that tire right toward a stretching world record when we inadvertently stretched the back bumpers off both our dads' cars. That little catastrophe not only ended our stretching experiments for the day, but probably cost us a Nobel prize.

Unable to continue our physical experiments in stretching, Skeet and I came upon another idea, a more metaphysical bent on our original theory. That theory, of course, was that anything can stretch. Anything included all things. Physical or abstract. A guy could stretch a tire till the bumpers came off; we had hard evidence of that. But how far could one stretch time? Or pleasure? Or even truth?

We didn't forget about Jell-O though. We concluded that we lacked the means to stretch Jell-O far enough to strike a match on. We did not conclude that it was impossible, just that we needed better, more sophisticated equipment. But we did manage to find an old bicycle inner tube which could stretch a long, long way.

"Maybe we can't stretch Jell-O," I said to Skeet, "but I bet if we strung this inner tube between two fence posts, like a giant slingshot, we could launch Jell-O a hundred miles."

"Shoot Jell-O and save the matches?" he smiled.

"Question is," I said, "how do we get the Jell-O to hold still long enough to get slung."

Skeet thought about it for a second and then smiled and said, "Jell-O balloons."

Genius. Funnel Jell-O crystals into a balloon, fill the balloon on the faucet, tie the balloon shut, shake vigorously, and put it in the refrigerator to set over night.

We were down at the reservoir. Our inner tube was stretched between two posts. We had a cooler of Jell-O balloons. We were launching them over the dam and into the water. Flavoring the town's water supply.

There was a parking lot at the reservoir where older kids parked and, um, discussed philosophy. Skeet and I didn't have philosophy partners at that point, so we shot Jell-O balloons instead.

There we stood, in the cool of the evening, fireflies flickering, stars twinkling, jets passing way overhead, launching handcrafted, brightly colored Jell-O balloons into the night. The balloons were an artwork in and of themselves. Beautifully colored, as heavy as a regular water balloon, but considerably firmer.

The biggest difference between a standard water balloon and a Jell-O balloon is that if you hit somebody with a water balloon they will get wet but will likely come away from the event a little bit cleaner. If you hit somebody with a Jell-O balloon, the contents are more viscous, and your victim will get all sticky and attract bugs the rest of the day.

Sheriff Hasbro flew over us as we were launching our balloons. He had just bought the county a helicopter, and he was testing it out. It was one of those huge, double-rotor, cargo numbers. Dusk was ebbing into darkness when he went over. He flew across the water, then turned the big ship around and headed back.

We were not trying to hit the Sheriff's helicopter with Jell-O balloons. He had the cargo doors open on both sides of the copter. We were merely attempting to shoot Jell-O balloons *through* the helicopter as he slowly turned. He completed his turn and then illuminated a blinding spotlight on the front end of the enormous craft as he headed back in our direction.

Uncle Deebo, who you may have forgotten was in this story, crested the dam, coming from the reservoir. He was running full out.

"What's he doing?" Skeet mused as he selected another Jell-O balloon.

"Who knows," I said, "but he sure is in a hurry."

Uncle Deebo barreled toward us, bathed in the spotlight from the helicopter. He headed straight toward our slingshot. He was screaming, "The aliens are here. They're here to abduct me."

We had him directly in our sights and were blasting him with Jell-O balloons.

Uncle Deebo noticed us in his path. A Jell-O balloon glanced off his shoulder; another hit his chest. He looked left toward Skeet, then right toward me. Uncle Deebo screamed in terror and warning: "They're here! The aliens are here for me! Aliens are following me! They're dropping their eggs on me! They're trying to impregnate me! I knew they'd come someday!" He was blinded by fear, running as fast as he could from the pursuing perceived UFO.

He was headed straight for our slingshot. It was waist high. I didn't want him to run into it and get hurt. I yelled the only thing that came to my mind.

"Duck!"

Skeet, having the same thought, yelled, "Jump!"

Uncle Deebo did both. He jumped with his feet and ducked with his torso. His body left the ground, but awkwardly. He was bent forward at his hips. He flew through the air looking very much like a person trying to both hurdle and duck under an object, and yet he managed to get every part of his body over the slingshot. Everything but his left foot. The slingshot wrapped around Uncle Deebo's ankle.

"Oh Lordy!" he shrieked. "The aliens got me! They have me!" He flew a little bit farther forward, stretching the old inner tube behind him, but, as you well know, anything can stretch but nothing can stretch forever. When the slingshot ran out of give, it took. Uncle Deebo slammed onto the asphalt parking lot, and the slingshot began dragging him back toward us. Uncle Deebo was screaming incomprehensibly.

Hand to God, I wanted to help, but I couldn't stop laughing. Uncle Deebo had seen Skeet and I standing there, but I don't think it ever registered in his panic-stricken mind just who we were. Now he thought we were aliens, dragging him to his death.

Skeet managed to say, "Poor fool must have been fishing down by the pond when the Jell-O balloons started dropping out of the sky, and Hasbro turned on that giant spotlight." Skeet launched into another fit of laughter.

Uncle Deebo, out of breath, paused in his screaming. For a brief moment all that could be heard was the soft scraping of Uncle Deebo being dragged slowly across the parking lot as the slingshot pulled him closer to us.

And then Uncle Deebo's pants burst into flames.

A matronly niece yelled out from one of the parked cars, "Uncle Deebo! You put your pants out right now, or I'll tell Grandma!"

Church Organ

There is no standard pipe organ. Pipe organs can have a dozen pipes, or thousands of pipes. The pipes are organized in ranks, and the ranks contain pipes ranging from a few inches to eight feet tall. The shortest pipes produce the highest notes, the biggest pipes, the lowest. A pipe organ can have sixty-one pipes per rank and one rank per note. There are two types of pipes in an organ: flue pipes and reed pipes. Flue pipes work like whistles. Air is forced into the base of the pipe or through the toe hole into the foot. This air is then squeezed around the languid, causing the sound which then resonates through the pipe. The other type of pipe is the reed pipe. In a reed pipe, air is forced into a pipe, the air vibrates a reed, and the sound passes up through the resonator.

I often sat in church staring just past the preacher, who was also my father. Had the preacher looked at me he may have thought I was looking at him. I wasn't. I was looking at the pipes in the pipe organ. Every week I tried to count the pipes, or at least devise a method by which to count the pipes. There were just so many of them and some of them were so tiny. I also wondered how they made their sounds. I couldn't figure out if the air came up through the pipes or was sucked down the pipes. Many of the pipes looked sort of like whistles, with a slot near the base. Did the air go in there, or come out of there?

There were four groups of pipes. There was a group on either side of the altar. The other two groups were on a twenty-foot stand situated behind the alter. The pipes on either side of the altar were arranged so that the shortest pipes were closest to the altar, and then they rose away like an arch, or wave, until the tallest were farthest from the altar. The pipes on the top of the stand behind the altar were arranged in a similar fashion, with the smallest pipes in the middle and the tallest on the ends. Centered in the swoop of the pipes at the top was a stained-glass window depicting Jesus in flowing red robes opening his arms and welcoming us to Him. The whole configuration of pipes looked like an outline of Batman's cowl and open cape, with Jesus rising like the Moon behind him. That image was very comforting. No matter what I encountered in life I knew that either Jesus or Batman would be there for me.

One Sunday as I sat staring at the pipes I had an idea for a way to figure out if air came out of the pipes.

It was not difficult for me to gain entry into the church when no one else was around because my father was the pastor. I let myself into the sanctuary and, with the help of a step ladder, had a closer look at the pipes. Some seemed to be made of steel, others copper, and some were wood. The wooden pipes were square, which was useless to me. I needed a round pipe, preferably about the diameter of my big toe. Said pipe needed to be located in the second or third row back. The first row would be too obvious; any farther back than four, and I wasn't sure I would be able to observe the results of my experiment. It sounds better when you say, "Observe the results of my experiment," doesn't it?

The next Sunday I sat in church and stood during the hymns, paying special attention to a certain area of the pipes. Not being a musician, and there being upwards of a thousand pipes in the organ, I had no way of predicting which pipes would be employed during any given song. That first Sunday, I was left to conclude that either my experiment had failed, or the correct note hadn't been hit. I checked on my preparations during the week. Everything seemed in order. But it was very much like trying to pick the Powerball number. I added some elements to my experiment so that instead of just selecting one pipe for my trials I had six components. I figured at least one would hit.

Halfway through the choral anthem the next Sunday, about three pipe rows back, a red balloon stood up in the midst of the pipes and came to attention. It didn't inflate very much, just enough to stand it up, and then, just as quickly, it deflated and fell back down. I had proven that air came out of the top of the pipes. Score one for me. I felt eyes on me and turned to look at Skeeter. We weren't allowed to sit together. He'd seen it. He winked.

The next week, another balloon inflated. This time, several

people saw it. There were chuckles, murmurs of approval, and grunts of disdain. In the church prank-scoring system, that counts as a perfect ten. I didn't want to push my luck so I snuck into the sanctuary later that week and removed the rest of the balloons.

In the Methodist church, bishops are appointed by a national council to the various conferences around the country. The bishop is the head of your conference. A new bishop will try to come to each church in his or her conference during the first few months of their appointment to present the sermon and do a meet-and-greet. The quality of this sermon reveals if the person has been elevated to a high position because they are a good theologian or simply to get them out of the way. And, because the Methodist church is a covered dish denomination, they also come for a meal.

It came to pass that our conference was assigned a new bishop, and the Sunday dawned when that bishop would preach in our church.

I was sitting in my pew reading the printed bio of the new bishop in the bulletin when I came across a paragraph stating that our new bishop had, early in his ministerial career, been a liturgical clown. I would say, "Don't laugh," but that's the whole point, isn't it?

Liturgical clowns bring the message of Christ through clowning. And they are serious about it. However, when you are sixteen years old and you read that the most important person in your local religious hierarchy is a clown, it is hard to suppress a giggle. I looked back to see if Skeet had gotten that far in his reading. I saw his eyes open wide. He smiled and looked up at me.

The bishop was striding toward the pulpit to start his sermon, and the organist was wrapping up whatever he had been playing with a sustained note. Then a low, horrified murmur filled the church. The bishop naturally assumed that this murmur was directed at him. But then he saw that the whole congregation was looking up toward the pipes of the organ, where a very long, thin, green balloon was filling with air. As the bishop turned to look where the congregation was looking, the balloon popped free of the pipes and went *bthththththth.*

I thought, "I'm dead. I thought I got all the balloons!"

The bishop followed the movements of the balloon and deftly snatched it out of the air. He tied a knot in the balloon, twisted it a few times, and then handed a T-Rex to one of the acolytes. He said, "I see I'm not the only clown in this church."

I liked the new bishop immediately and immensely.

Methodists don't gamble. It is a rule. But our congregation did operate a Bingo game. But it wasn't gambling. Sure, you had to pay twenty-five cents per card to play, and if you got a bingo you received a certain number of quarters based on how many cards had been sold, but, as everyone explained, that wasn't gambling. That was just a way to keep score. And a ten percent tithe was automatically deducted from your score before it was handed over to you. An average score for a game was about eighty quarters, less ten percent. Because we weren't gambling, just keeping score, and because we were tithing, the weekly Bingo games had been more or less tolerated by those in the church and community who would have otherwise spoken out against them.

The new bishop, however, couldn't ignore the games. It was his job to have a say in that sort of thing. One Friday night he came to our church to witness Bingo night. He bought four cards and, during the course of the evening, scored 144 quarters. He won it, er, scored it honest. Nobody at Halfdollar United Methodist church would rig a Bingo game just to make the new bishop happy. Scoring that many quarters made the bishop feel like there was nothing wrong with our weekly Bingo games.

Lillian Crimm didn't like it though. Lillian Crimm was a member of the church, a long-time member of the church. She'd been a member of the church so long that she believed certain rites were vested in her, whether anyone else believed that or not. One rite she believed was hers was to win at Bingo. The second time the bishop announced "Bingo!" Lillian jumped to her feet and held a boney finger in the bishop's face. "I think he's cheating!"

Another old lady, Beatrice Humphrey, said in a stage whisper, "If anybody knows enough about cheating at Bingo to spot it, it would be Lillian."

People did not suspect Lillian cheated. People knew Lillian cheated. She kept her cards from week to week sealed in individual Ziploc bags and would just pick up where she left off. She could get a bingo in one ball. But communities choose to tolerate and ignore certain things, and we tolerated Lillian Crimm's Bingo cheating. She, however, could not tolerate the bishop winning twice, especially when she had been so close to winning, twice!

She accused the bishop of horrible things.

Beatrice Humphrey said, "You should consider the log in your own eye before you go pointing out the speck in another's eye."

The bishop had been in the church business for a long time, long enough to know that each church is blessed with at least one Lillian Crimm. He kept his cool, detached himself from the argument, put his score in his pockets, was presented with myriad apologies, and made his exit with polite handshakes.

Lillian swept up her cards and left the church.

The Bingo had always been controversial, and Lillian's cheating was gnawing at some of the other players. Her outburst toward the bishop was a downright embarrassment to some of the folks in the church. It was enough to start a movement to end the Bingo games.

Letters were sent to the local paper and various church offices. Because Methodists aren't supposed to gamble it wasn't hard for those in favor of shutting down the games to gain a following. A decree came down from the bishop himself. The games had to end.

Lillian was furious. At the end of the last session Lillian was so overcome that she snatched up the cage with the balls and ran off. Well, she was old and used a walker, so she shuffled off. Other folks gave chase.

Beatrice Humphrey caught up to Lillian in the sanctuary and a struggle ensued over the cage of Bingo balls. Both women grabbed opposite ends of the cage, then fell backwards. Bingo balls exploded from the cage in all directions showering the pews, the altar, the choir loft, and even the balcony. Bingo was dead.

After the scrum my dad said to Beatrice, "I thought you were going to kill her."

Beatrice responded, "Kill Lillian Crimm? I've known that lady for a long time. She won't die 'til she gets her way. She won't be truly dead 'til she gets her last bingo."

But she was wrong. Lillian Crimm died later that year. My dad made me promise that no balloons would come out of the pipe organ during the service. I was pretty sure they were all gone by then.

Lillian's was a well-attended funeral. Despite her cantankerousness she was an important member of the church and community. She was a veteran of the OSS during WWII. Lots of folks showed up. It was an open casket affair, and Lillian was laid in the coffin with her war medals on her chest, a red plastic rose in her hands, and a nearly completed Bingo card beneath the rose. It was in her will.

The bishop, having formed a strange bond with Lillian, was scheduled to say a few words at the funeral. He stood when it was his turn and approached the coffin as the organist was finishing up a hymn. The organist hit a long note. There was a wheeze amongst the pipes, and then a *POP*!

We all watched as, not a balloon, but a Bingo ball shot out of one of the pipes, hit the ceiling, fell, bounced off the offering plates, and headed straight toward the bishop. He raised his hand to catch it but before he could, Lillian Crimm sat up in her coffin, snatched the ball out of the air, said, "B-8," looked at the card she had in her coffin, and yelled, "Bingo!" and then dropped dead…again.

Beatrice Humphrey stood up in the back of the church, pulled her purse up her arm, and said, "Well, I saw what I came to see," and left.

Geomorphology & the Rope Swing

Geomorphology is the study of the changes of the earth's surface over time. The natural geomorphic outcome for continents without beaver dams will include more ravines and steeper valleys, due to the cutting erosive forces of flowing water.

Skeeter and I were the undisputed Rope Swing Kings of Halfdollar. We had a string of rope swings up and down Skitter creek that rivaled what anthropologists call *The Great Euphrates Rope Swing Culture*.

The rope swing, for those of you who grew up in the Gobi, or Antarctica, or are otherwise aquatically challenged, is a simple device by which one enters the local swimming hole. The local swimming hole is any hole wherein water exists and into which a person can fit themselves. The difference between a swimming hole and a swimming pool is that chemicals cannot be intentionally introduced into a swimming hole. Chemicals can be present in the swimming hole, but only those chemicals which occur naturally through mine run-off, factory pollution, and fertilizer.

In its simplest form, the rope swing is a rope tied high in a stout tree. The user grasps the rope, swings out over the swimming hole, lets go of the rope, and drops into the water. The rope swing adds endless fun to swimming sessions. You can dive from the rope, flip, perform a cannonball, a can opener, a belly flop, or a back smacker. Not only is the rope swing fun, it is also dangerous. Nowadays you could probably lose your insurance if you even mentioned the words 'rope swing' in public.

The Seventies was the last decade a kid could go out and Kid properly. When my mother said, "Go out and play," she meant, "Go put yourself in harm's way." If I didn't come home from play bleeding, or at least limping, I'd have some serious explaining to do. "Just what have you been up to, young man? Coming home clean and unscathed!? Wait 'til your father gets home!"

The rope swing remains, to this day, the great holdout of unsafe play. Putting safety devices on a rope swing would make it more dangerous. There can be no safety belt or harness because the object of the rope swing is to fall off it. Wearing a helmet is out of the question because you'd drown. The rope swing is so thoroughly unsafe, so streamline in its danger, so utterly hazardous, that trying to make it safer only serves to increase the ways you can be hurt. You can skin your knees being drug across the ground, you can let go too soon, you can let go too late, you can slam into a tree, you can land wrong, the rope can break, the branch can break, the tree can break and fall on you as you crash into the jagged rocks below! OH! Blessed be the rope swing! And, as if it were not dangerous enough in its raw form, Skeet and I endeavored to make the rope swing more fun, and thus potentially more lethal.

One of our best and most complicated maneuvers was called *The Tarzan*. *The Tarzan* involved two rope swings, one on each side of the creek. The object was to fly out on the first rope, let go mid-stream, and then try and catch the rope hanging on the opposite side of the creek. Momentum carried you into the trees on the other side of the stream before swinging you back out over the creek. The trick was to disguise your screams of terror and pain as a Tarzan call as you crashed through the blackberry bramble.

And then there was the rope we had that was way too short. We called it *The Rope Too Short*. You had to get a running start and leap for the rope. There were various perils involved in this style. First, you really had to dedicate yourself to the jump so if you missed the rope, you were still going into the creek but not necessarily into the most desirably deep section.

A variable on *The Rope Too Short* was to get the short rope swinging before you made a jump for it. We called that *The Rope Too Short, Already Swinging*. You had to run and jump to catch the already swinging rope above your head while you flew through the air. You had to commit to the jump, so you were going into the water, just maybe not the most optimally deep part of the water. This was not a technique we recommended for most rope swingers, but it was useful for inducing long periods of convalescence in younger siblings.

The real challenger was what we called *The Roulette Wheel*. For *The Roulette Wheel* we tied the rope near the far end of the branch, rather than nearer the tree. This resulted in the branch bending toward the river as you swung out. Just before you hit the water, the branch would spring back skyward. This spring would launch the rope swinger into the sky, often above the branch. The trick was to hold onto the rope as you ascended. If you did this just right, you would spin like a roulette wheel through the sky. The problem was that the branch would sometimes snap. This was okay if you were above the branch because you had time to miss the branch as you descended, but if the branch broke above you you had to dodge it as it came crashing down. This was the other reason we called this style *The Roulette Wheel*: You often ended up black, blue, and red.

Skeet and I had perfected these various forms, and our rope swings were the envy of swimming holes for miles around. Kids came upstream and downstream with clipboards and slide rules and protractors to study and diagram our rope swings.

Then the drought hit. Skitter creek all but dried up. Our swimming hole became a puddle, then a trickle, then a mud hole, then a sand pit. We built a dam to try and capture the flow and refill our hole, but there was so little water in the creek that the sticks and rocks we used for the dam got bored and left.

Desperate, we went to the city pool one day, but they had a sign that said you had to take a shower *before* you got in the pool! We had a hard and fast rule about doing anything that required we shower first. To top it off, there were no rope swings allowed in the pool.

That night, when the pool was closed, we slipped over the fence. We slipped into the pool. We did not shower first. It wasn't hard to get into the pool after closing, just jump the fence and there you were. The problem was that the pool area was well lit, and thus it wasn't hard for Sheriff Hasbro to spot intruders as he made his nightly rounds. If you took the precaution of sliding a picnic table up against the inside of the fence and wore your shoes while swimming, you could exit the pool premises in the classic Leap-Vault-Dash move perfected by generations of trespassers.

Skeet climbed the high-dive and tied a stout rope round the board, about a foot back from the end of the diving board. The diving board was the nearest thing to a tree branch that the pool offered. Skeet jumped off the board holding the rope. Skeet splashed into the pool, still holding the rope. He sank into the water, still holding the rope. The diving board bent like a fishing pole hooked to a whale. Skeet bent the diving board as absolutely far down as it could go and then the board rebounded. Skeet had just unleashed the world's most untamed Roulette Wheel. Still holding the rope, Skeeter rose from the water like a missile. Still holding the rope, Skeet was flung fifteen feet above the diving board, which was now bending up toward the sky because Skeet was still holding the rope. The diving board bent as far upward as it had downward and then it rebounded yet again, jerking Skeet out of the sky like a fly on a frog's tongue, because Skeet was still holding the rope.

It was hard to see the expression on his face as he came down because by now Skeet was locked into a horizontal spin as he tumbled out of the sky, pulling about three Gs every rotation, and nearing Mach speed. He did not look happy. He hit the water, still holding the rope. There was a terrific sound when Skeet hit the water.

Imagine the sound of a two-ton block of Jell-O, dropped from 30,000 feet, landing on an ice rink. *SLAP*. To this day, I am unsure if that sound was made by Skeet hitting the water, or if he achieved Mach One just before hitting the surface and thus caused a sonic boom. Either way, Skeet hit the water hard and fast, so fast that the water was caught off guard. There was no splash, just that *SLAP*. Hybrid sonic/hydro waves danced across the shatter surface of the pool. The water wasn't displaced by the impact; it simply crumbled.

When I had Skeet properly reassembled, and after the water had gotten its wits back, I took my turn on the rope swing. I did not climb the diving board. I stayed on the deck and walked as far back as I could, pulling the diving board down, and toward me. My back to the fence, my arms outstretched, the diving board bent toward the water, I said to Skeet, "Let me show you how it is done."

I lifted my feet, and the diving board, all tension now released, sprang upward. I was whisked above the pool deck like an air hockey puck. I shot out over the water like a bird of prey. I was really moving. And then I noticed that I was no longer over the deep end of the pool. And then I was no longer over the shallow end. This was going to be a hard landing. I decided to let go of the rope. Be it madness or ignorance, I thought it was better to be free than to be tethered. I let go of the rope while I was still far out over the shallow end deck of the pool. I cleared the fence, flew over the picnic shelter, and skidded to a stop in the mulch on the playground.

Maybe the pool was not the best place to rope swing.

Sheriff Hasbro pulled up in his cruiser as we were limping away. He'd undoubtedly heard Skeet's sonic boom and had come to investigate. We were too beaten and broken to run. Skeet, thirty feet of stout rope coiled around his arm, looked up at Sheriff Hasbro and said, "Does this have something to do with the fact that we failed to shower before getting in the pool?"

The Sheriff shook his huge head and said, "Boys, this drought has gotten to all of us. My guess is that you just learned a valuable lesson about tying ropes to high dives."

He had a higher expectation of our ability to learn from our mistakes than we did.

"I tried it myself once," he continued, "back during the drought of '51. Back when I was the rope Swing King of Halfdollar. 'Course, when I was your age, I weighed at least a hundred pounds heavier than either of you. I displaced enough water with my splash that it rained pool water for three days afterwards. Farmers from bordering counties wrote me thank-you notes. I hit the bottom of the pool so hard that there is still a two-foot deep, double crescent pothole in the bottom of the pool."

"Oh," I said, amazed, "so that's why they call the deep end Hasbro's Bottom."

We all laughed, and he let us go.

Later, when we were mended, Skeet and I were cutting across Angus Fester's cow pasture on our way to Skitter creek when we came across an old claw-footed bathtub Fester used as a water trough for his cows. We looked at the tub and smiled. Each of us taking one end, we hauled the tub down to the stream. We placed the tub in the creek and used buckets to fill it as best we could.

One thing about trying to rope swing into a bathtub is that there is not a lot of room for error. Another thing about trying to rope swing into a bathtub is that a fella ought to study up on his Newtonian physics and parabolic arcs. Newton's Law states that a body in motion stays in motion. Skeeter and I were unaware of this law. We didn't realize, until after the fact, that as we executed our inverted parabolic arcs over the tub, we could not simply let go right above the tub and drop into it. We sailed over the tub and landed on the rocks of the creek bed. This led to a game we called: *Who Can Get the Most of Their Body in the Tub at Once*.

Next, we went to the dump and collected all the mattresses we could find. We placed these all around the tub and tried to bounce into the tub. This was slightly less effective than trying to drop into the tub from above.

Skeet and I went back to Skitter creek to ponder the problem the next day, and that's when we remembered the beaver dam. Well, we didn't remember so much as we were reminded of the beaver dam. We heard a great *boom* from upstream, and then a sustained, "Yee-haw."

"Oh man," I said to Skeet, "I bet that that was Angus Fester blowing up that old beaver dam."

Angus Fester's property bordered Skitter creek. The beaver pond was way above Angus's farm, but Angus used the water from the creek to irrigate his fields. We reckoned the drought had hindered his irrigation efforts, and now he was blowing up the dam to free the water in the beaver pond.

There were no beavers in the pond anymore. They cleared out under mysterious circumstances. One day they were there; the next day Angus Fester complained to the Department of Natural Resources that the beaver dam had to go. The DNR guy told Fester that you can't remove a beaver dam supporting an active beaver population. Soon thereafter, the beaver population was gone. There was no significant investigation, and no charges were brought against Fester, but many in town suspected he had assassinated the beavers.

And now, he was blowing up the dam.

Skeet and I raced through the woods. We needed to get to the dam and plug it before all the water leaked out because there wasn't going to be any new water to re-fill the dam in the foreseeable future. This was no time for platitudes like, 'Don't worry about it; it's just water over the dam.' There was a drought on. Any water over the dam was water gone. We'd have nowhere to go for a swimming hole if we couldn't patch the hole and stop the flow. That would make the summer abysmal. And one had to be careful with dams lest they break the ocean.

Fester was long gone by the time we reached the dam, so we set to work.

It is said that beavers can repair a ten-foot hole overnight but since Fester had dispatched the beavers through some sort of beaver-icide, we were fresh out of beaver aides to help us in our plight. Skeet and I heaved logs and rocks and mud into the breach. Fortunately, Fester's hole was wide, but not very deep. Not unlike the slob himself.

Within thirty minutes we had the dam fairly well rebuilt. We'd stopped most of the drainage Fester had created. We stopped to survey our new swimming hole. It was impressive. The beavers had built several dams, one dam nearly thirty-five feet across and at least seven feet tall. They'd managed to back water up over at least four acres of land and had thus created a nice patch of wetlands which was flourishing, despite the drought.

"Beavers," Skeet said in an uncharacteristic and educated tone, "are keystone creatures. Keystone creatures," he continued before I could ask, "or keystone species, are creatures that modify the natural environment in such a way that the overall ecosystem builds upon the change. Keystone Species are species who enrich an ecosystem in a unique and significant manner through their activities, and the effect is disproportionate to their numerical abundance. Like here, where a couple of beavers built a few dams which, in turn, created this wetland, which has become the habitat for many other creatures."

"Duh." I said, "Like I didn't know that."

"And," he went on, "this wetland is about to become the natural habitat of the two undisputed Rope Swing Masters of the Universe."

"Amen," I said.

It occurred to us that Angus Fester wasn't going to be happy about the dam not being blown up, and thus he was likely to try and blow it up again. What we needed to do was re-introduce a beaver to the beaver pond. If there were a beaver present in the pond Fester could not legally blow up the dam.

"It would be unfair," I said to Skeet, "to put a real beaver in the pond. Fester would just kill him. If we put a beaver up there we'd have to explain the situation to the beaver first. We couldn't just let him go into the circumstances blind. And I'm not sure either of us speaks beaver well enough to adequately explain the situation."

"That would have to be one brave beaver," Skeet said.

"Right now, let's just focus on getting our rope swings up to the pond," I said.

We spent the day establishing several swings in the area and were just testing the last one when Angus Fester came tramping out of the woods.

Angus said, "What the…? I wondered why there was no water coming 'outa this dam. I should have figured it was you two messin' around up here. Y'all are on private property, now clear off."

"Fester," I said, "this ain't private property, or if it is, it ain't your property. And you ain't got no right messin' with this dam. Don't you know you are disturbing an ecosystem here?"

"I'm tryin' to water my fields! Now, clear out!" With that, he lit a stick of dynamite and tossed it at the dam. Skeet and I dove for cover. This was getting serious. We ran off into the woods after the explosion but returned as soon as we saw Fester leave. Once again, we heaved logs and debris back into the breach.

Fester couldn't do much to keep us out of the beaver pond. Well, he could throw dynamite at us but he couldn't go to the law because, in the first place, he didn't own the land the beaver dam was on, and, in the second place, Sheriff Hasbro couldn't stand Fester. Fester spent more time in the County drunk tank than he did at home, so Hasbro knew him well. Hasbro wasn't about to go out of his way to help Fester.

Skeet and I made a bold move. We went to Hasbro ourselves. Hasbro had told us at the pool that he was a rope swing aficionado so we thought he might help us out in our current situation. Hasbro was not happy about Fester throwing dynamite around. He said he'd look into it. And then Hasbro said, "Boys, geomorphology is the study of the changes of the earth's surface over time. The natural geomorphic outcome for continents without beaver dams will include more ravines and steeper valleys, due to the cutting erosive forces of flowing water."

I looked at Skeet. We both smiled and said, in unison, "Duh."

Who knew rope swinging could be so educational?

Hasbro said, "I want you two to take care of that beaver dam. I'm deputizing both of you to be official beaver dam deputies."

We smiled.

The next day, when we got to the beaver dam, there were three pallets of sack-crete, bagged concrete, lying beside the old logging road that went past the dam. Sack-crete is handy because you don't need to mix it with sand; you just add water, and it sets up all by itself. The concrete inside the bags will form a nice, solid, eighty-pound block if the bag gets wet. That's where those pillow shaped concrete blocks in the corner of your garage come from. Osmosis.

There was a note taped to one of the pallets that read, 'Dear Beavers, thought this might help you dynamite-proof your dam.'

Three pallets of sack-crete is 162 eighty-pound bags. Lord knows how a beaver would move something like that. Besides, there were no beavers around. Skeet and I took it upon ourselves to help the absent beavers with the task. It took us all day, but by dusk Halfdollar was home to the most heavily fortified beaver dam this side of the Chicago Zoo.

When we arrived at the dam the next day, Fester was already there inspecting the new structural attributes of the dam. He was cursing loudly. He tried a couple of sticks of dynamite, and, because the sack-crete hadn't set up all the way, he did manage to move parts of the dam, but he could not blow it apart. We swang in peace and quiet after he gave up.

It was the next day, Thursday, that things came to a head. We heard a tractor making its way toward the dam from Fester's property as we were swinging. Pretty soon we could see Angus driving his new tractor up below the dam, pulling a wagon loaded with cases of TNT.

"Uh-oh," I said to Skeet.

We heard another vehicle approaching down the old logging road as Fester was getting off his tractor. Sheriff Hasbro's pick-up truck pulled to a stop just beside the dam. Sheriff Hasbro was rarely seen driving anything except his official car, but it was a small town and we knew everybody's personal car. Whereas we rarely saw Sheriff Hasbro without his Sheriff's vehicle, we had never seen him out of uniform. Sheriff Hasbro stepped out of his truck wearing nothing but a bathing suit. Granted it was a bathing suit made with enough material to drape over the whole of Kansas, but it was a bathing suit nonetheless.

Hasbro was a big man-- six-foot eight at least and nearly four hundred pounds. His body was pale and covered in thin wisps of red hair. He stood there before us looking like a mangy, red-headed polar bear hide stuffed with coconuts. He said, loud enough for Fester to hear, "Boys, I understand you got some nice rope swings up here. Thought I might come up and try them." And then he said, looking down stream toward Angus Fester, "Why, hello Angus. What on earth are you doing with all that TNT?"

"Uh, nothin'," Fester said.

Sheriff Hasbro selected one of the many rope swings we had hanging around the beaver pond. He hung his weight on it to test the strength. "Seems sturdy enough to me," he said. "Watch this, boys." Hasbro backed up the bank of the pond, rope held tight, and then he lumbered toward the edge of the pond and leapt into the air. He swung out over the beaver pond with eloquence. He ran like a hobbled warthog but he flew out over the surface like an osprey. We could see the rope give a little as Hasbro arched out over the water. The branch the rope was tied to gave a little and then, with the branch bent way over, it rebounded and slung the Sheriff up, up, up into the sky. He looped out over the water and started to rise above the branch. He looked like a lesser moon of Jupiter sailing through space. The tree shuddered a little as Hasbro's circular swing reached the top of its circle. The branch was now being pulled upward. The ground around the tree gave a bit. The huge oak was lifted out of the ground an inch or two like a small child being lifted by one arm. Hasbro was performing the most beautiful *Roulette Wheel* maneuver anyone had ever witnessed.

Fester, not generally one to appreciate art and beauty, said aloud: "My good Lord! Look at that!"

Hasbro was way up there. The ground around our feet began to crack as the roots of the tree dislodged. There was a partial eclipse. The branch the rope was tethered to let go of the tree. It didn't snap off, or sheer off, or break off; it just gave up. There was no crack, just a sigh. A resigned whisper as the branch simply retired. The tree thumped back into the ground. Hasbro continued upwards. Five limbs, his four and the one from the tree, were spread across the sky like a giant star. And then he was headed down.

Sheriff Hasbro might be the Sheriff in Halfdollar, but gravity is still the law.

"Watch out below, boys! I'm coming down!" came a cry from an altitude Sir Edmund Hilary wouldn't have dared without oxygen.

And down he came. Like an asteroid. Like a spaceship reentering the atmosphere. Like a cliff-diving manatee, he careened toward the water.

"Oh, man," I said in a church whisper, "this is amazing."

"Amen," said Skeeter.

Fester, who had walked over to stand beside us, said, "He was always the Rope Swing King, ever since we were kids. My only wonder," continued Fester, "is how he's gonna dodge that branch."

I nodded. The branch Hasbro had pulled from the tree was below him. "How is he going to avoid landing on it?" I muttered.

"Looks to me," Skeet said, "that that branch has had the same thought. It looks like that branch is deliberately trying to get out of Hasbro's way."

Sure enough, the branch seemed to be slipping sideways of its own accord, out of Hasbro's path. The branch may have been broken, but it did not pine to be kindling.

Hasbro pulled his knees up to his chest, wrapped his arms around his shins, and yelled, "Cannonball!" just before entering the water. Hasbro didn't merely cause a splash; he created a waterspout of oceanic proportions. Half of the water, mud, cattails, leaves, and loose beaver sticks in the pond soared skyward in a spout. There was a slurping sound as water resting in the mud three feet below the pond floor was sucked out of the ground and displaced. Wells went dry. The water table, already as fragile as an old card table due to the drought, folded its legs inward. It was as if God had suddenly switched a huge wet/dry shop-vac on above the beaver pond.

The other half of the water in the beaver pond rolled away from Hasbro in the meanest liquid concentric circle since Atlantis sank. An eight-foot-high wave with an ever-expanding diameter raced out of the pond, knocking over trees, boys, farmers, and boulders alike. The massive, concrete-reinforced beaver dam was no match for Hasbro's rolling wall of water. The dam crashed open, flew apart, and was scattered on the waters of the now fast-flowing Skitter creek. Fester shouted with rage as his new tractor, wagon, and tons of TNT were washed into the next county. Hasbro, with a huge smile on his face, sat stuck in the mud in the center of the dry beaver pond. He was looking up at the sky.

The water Hasbro had forced into the sky met the hot summer air and, before our very eyes, formed deep gray nimbostratus clouds. "Well," said Hasbro, "the pond is gone but the creek is flowing. Sorry 'bout yer tractor Angus."

And then the heavens opened. Hasbro's clouds spread out over Halfdollar, and sweet rain fell. Yes, the pond and the dam were gone but Hasbro had ended the drought. And in an election year, to boot.

Hasbro arrested Fester for Intent to Blow up a Beaver Dam and for throwing dynamite at us. Hasbro said in his closing remarks at the trial: "Angus Fester, you deliberately tried to blow up a beaver dam, and you tried to keep these boys from creating a swimming hole for rope swinging. These are crimes against both the natural world and the fabric of humanity. I've said it before, and I'll say it again. Geomorphology," Hasbro said, staring hard at Angus Fester, "is the study of the changes of the earth's surface over time. The natural geomorphic outcome for continents without beaver dams will include more ravines and steeper valleys due to the cutting erosive forces of flowing water.

"The social-geomorphic outcome for continents without beaver dams would be a world with fewer beaver ponds and thus fewer rope swings. This is even more devastating than erosion alone. A world without rope swings is a world without kids banding together to step into harm's way in the name of fun. Our society already has enough cultural, religious, and racial ravines. Fun bridges those gaps. It is in play that we can forget all our differences and just enjoy each other. In play we are all the same. Beaver dams equal world peace.

"Furthermore" continued the good Sheriff, "life is like a turn on a rope swing. Life is essentially a short, wild, uncontrolled, inverted parabolic arc out over unknown waters cluttered with submerged perils, on a rope too thin, tied with a granny knot to a branch too weak. If you can survive a belly flop under those conditions, you can survive anything."

Egg Babies

Ms. Gurdak was smoking a cigarette when we walked into Health class.

I went to high school a long time ago. You could smoke in school. Well, not the kids. Just the teachers. The kids had to go out back.

Ms. Gurdak was a frugal woman. She lit her first cigarette of the day with a strike anywhere match and then, not wanting to waste matches, she lit each new cigarette from the butt of the last one. She would take the old butt and stand it up on the edge of her desk when she was in the classroom. Which was handy because we didn't have a clock in the classroom; we knew class was about over at eight cigarette butts in. Did I mention she was our health teacher?

We walked into class, and she was smoking a cigarette and holding a carton of eggs.

As we took our seats she said, "I'm going to give each of you an egg. And you're going to have to keep this egg safe for three weeks. That way, you can learn what a pain in the, uh, what a responsibility it is to be a parent."

Skeeter raised his hand and said, "Ms. Gurdak, I don't think I need to carry an egg around for three weeks to prove that I'm not responsible enough to be a parent."

"'Course you're not," she said. "Y'all are just babies yourselves. You don't need to be raising babies. That's the whole point of the assignment. None of you are ready to have a kid. You have your whole lives ahead of you. You have a kid now, and that complicates things. Babies are fragile, both physically and psychologically. I'm not saying someone your age couldn't raise up a decent baby; plenty of young folks have. I'm just saying, you numbskulls need to see how much time and care it takes to have a baby. I want you to think of this assignment before you go plucking apples from the trees or stealing honey from the hive."

The real reason our teacher was having us do this assignment is because the school board had decided that the teachers could not teach us certain biological facts about the birds and bees. It was the same reason they weren't teaching us how to make gunpowder. If we knew how, we might.

Ms. Gurdak started passing out the eggs. The experiment turned immediately from an exercise in responsibility to an exercise in sociology. When she gave a girl an egg, the girl would be overcome with emotion.

"Oh, it's the most beautiful egg I've ever seen. I'm going to name it Emily. I'm going to make it a skirt."

Charolais wasn't as verbal about it, but she was tender in her actions toward the egg. She accepted the egg Ms. Gurdak gently placed in her palm, looked at it, then put the palm of her other hand over the egg. Safe and warm.

When Ms. Gurdak handed a boy an egg, he would grunt and try to steady it in the pencil holder on his desk. The egg would roll down the desktop and he would catch it and put it back. Over and over, like a punishment in Hades.

Except Fred Ware. Fred was a big guy. He stared at his egg, and you could hear him thinking, "Scrambled…Fried..."

When she got to me, Ms. Gurdak looked at the egg carton, took a drag on her cigarette, and said, "Lepp, I'm out of eggs," as though it were my fault.

There were thirteen students in the class but only twelve eggs in the carton. This salient point illustrates why she was teaching health, not math.

"That's okay," I said. "I'm like Skeet. I don't need a three week assignment to prove that I'm not responsible."

She nodded in agreement and said, "Your, and Mr. Barth's, irresponsibility are exactly why you need to do this assignment. You're going to have a baby, too. Y'all stay right here." She left the classroom.

Ms. Gurdak walked back into the classroom a few minutes later carrying a five-pound bag of flour. She plopped the bag down on my desk and said, through a cloud of smoke and flour, "Here, Lepp. This'll be your baby."

"But," I protested, "everybody else has an egg. How come I gotta lug around a five-pound bag of flour."

"Mostly," she sneered, "cause yer a smart-aleck."

Skeeter raised his hand and said, "Ms. Gurdak? I've been sitting here contemplating how unready I am for this situation. I understand the awesome responsibility. I have decided to give my baby up for adoption."

Charolais sneered at him.

Ms. Gurdak didn't respond.

I learned my very first parenting lesson later that day. I came around a corner on the way to the cafeteria and Wally Fenstermacher, totally unprovoked, whipped a pencil at me. I saw the pencil coming, and I learned that you shouldn't use your baby as a human shield. It's effective but frowned on. (People do it all the time now. They carry their babies in those backpacks you wear on your front. BabyBjorn, I believe they are called, from Norway or Sweden. They tell you it's healthy for the baby. The baby is near the parent, feels the warmth, the heartbeat, feels safe, whatever. I don't buy it. 'BabyBjorn' is probably Norwegian for 'human shield.')

The pencil Wally threw *thunked* into my baby bag of flour. A stream of flour leaked from the bag.

I grew up watching Westerns. I knew that when you get shot with an arrow, you should push the arrow through, rather than pull it out, then you pour whiskey on the wound and cauterize it with a red-hot brand. I got ready to push the pencil through but realized I didn't have a red-hot brand. I was about to pull the pencil out when I heard Ms. Gurdak's voice. She said, "Don't do that, Lepp. You gotta take this serious. You need to take that baby to the doctor."

I laughed, but she was serious. She said, "Doctor Mortimer knows all about our little experiment. If anything happens to your baby serious enough to merit a doctor you need to get a note from him saying you brought the baby in. Whole town knows. Everybody'll be watching to make sure you and your classmates are taking proper care of your babies."

"Everybody?" I asked.

She sucked on her cigarette and nodded. "Everybody."

Doctor Mortimer was old. He had what people called then 'the palsy.' He was a great doctor, except his hands shook continuously. It didn't affect his job unless you needed stitches. If you needed stitches Dr. Mortimer would call Marty, the mechanic from down the street. Marty had the steadiest hands in town. He would come into the doctor's office, wiping his hands on a greasy rag, and sew you up. Then you paid the doctor bill and went to get your car from Marty. Only one of those was covered by Medicaid.

Flour was leaking from around the pencil wound in my baby bag of flour. I thought about going to Dr. Mortimer's. I thought about Ms. Gurdak giving me the flour because I was a smart-aleck. I made a decision, shrugged, and said, "My baby's hemorrhaging too bad. I can't wait for a doctor. I gotta call an ambulance." I turned and ran down the steps to the payphone mounted by the office. I pulled a dime from my pocket, dropped it in the slot, and dialed the direct line to the local paramedic. With a pal like Skeeter, it was useful to know the paramedic's number.

We only had one paramedic in town. Our little town of Halfdollar was located within half an hour of two hospitals but that meant it took an ambulance half an hour to get to you and half an hour to get back to the hospital. A lot of people died in that transition period.

West Virginia is one of the oldest, sickest states in the Union, which gives a whole new meaning to 'Almost Heaven.' The good people of Halfdollar had hired Handy to be the local paramedic. The town rented him a little apartment and bought him an ambulance. It was worth it to cut a half hour off emergency trips.

Handy was a paradoxical paramedic. Like Ms. Gurdak, he smoked all the time. He only ate red meat and potato chips. "I became a paramedic," Handy had told me, "'cause someday, I'm gonna catch a full-on heart attack. This way, I'll be there for me when I need me."

He answered the phone after five rings saying, "Handy speaking."

I was thinking, "Five rings? What was he doing? What if this had been a real emergency?"

"Handy, this is Bil Lepp. I need you down at the high school. My baby got stabbed."

"Lepp? You ain't gotta baby," he said, not the least bit hurried.

"I do now."

"What? Who's the mother?" Handy asked.

"Ms. Gurdak?" I said.

"That's disgusting," Handy said.

"It was an assignment," I explained.

"That doesn't make it any better!" Then he chuckled and said, "Oh yeah. That crazy ol' bat Gurdak made us carry eggs around when I was in school, too. Is it an egg? 'Cause if your baby's an egg, I can't do nothing about it. That's like Humpty's Dumpty."

"Humpty Dumpty," I corrected.

"What?"

"You said, 'Humpty's Dumpty.' Humpty didn't have a Dumpty. Humpty was the Dumpty."

"What are you talking about?" Handy asked.

"You said it like it was possessive. Like the Dumpty belonged to Humpty. The Dumpty didn't belong to the Humpty. Humpty WAS the Dumpty."

"Are you sure? I thought Humpty had a Dumpty. You know, 'Humpty's Dumpty fell off the wall."

"I'm pretty sure it was a whole Humpty Dumpty, not Humpty's Dumpty, that fell off the wall."

"What is a Dumpty, anyway?" Handy asked.

"I don't know," I said. "I always thought it was his last name."

"Whose last name?" Handy asked.

"Humpty's."

Handy said, "I don't reckon I know anybody by the last name of Dumpty."

"I'm pretty sure they're from England."

"That would explain it," he said. "Leave it to the Brits to name somebody Humpty. But anyway, if you're in England, there ain't much I can do for you. I can't get my ambulance over there quick enough."

"It's not an egg," I explained. "I have a five-pound bag of flour. And I'm at the high school."

"She given out bags of flour now?"

"Just to me. 'Cause I'm a smart-aleck."

"Figures," Handy said. "I guess I ain't doin' nothing else. You at the high school, you said?"

"Yep. I'll be in the parking lot."

"Be there in a sec."

"Handy?" I asked, "Could you run the lights and sirens?"

Skeeter and Charolais walked up while I was on the phone. I explained what was happening. Skeet found it as funny as I did. Charolais did not. Charolais was still holding her baby cupped in her hands. Skeet had his in the pocket of his t-shirt, which is a perfectly sensible place to carry an egg. Unless you get hugged.

Charolais Fester was the smartest, funniest, prettiest girl in town, even if she was named for a breed of cows. She may have been the smartest, funniest, prettiest girl in the world; it's just that we hadn't been far enough out of town to make an objective claim such as that. Her father was a peckerweed, and her brothers were shallow louts. Her mother, Helen Fester, was one of the finest women I ever knew. Helen was small and had been born into a bad situation, only to marry into a worse one in hopes of escaping the first. Charolais was her only child that ever tried to be decent, and it hurt Helen that most of her kids had turned out poorly, despite her best efforts.

But not Charolais. She was good. Couldn't help it. She saw how bad her father and brothers were, and she stood in the world to prove that just because she was born a Fester, it didn't mean she was like them. Charolais was four foot nine by the second grade and never got an inch taller. Skeeter fell in love with Charolais in the second grade, and for whatever reason, she fell in love with him, too. Maybe just to prove she was human.

Charolais did not think calling the ambulance was funny.

Handy pulled into the parking lot ten minutes later. Which didn't make any sense because his apartment was three minutes away. He got out of the ambulance and stared at me as I rushed toward him. I thrust my baby at him. He took the bag of flour in his hands, yanked the pencil out, put a piece of gauze over the hole, and wrapped about three feet of surgical tape around the bag. Which is exactly what I would have done.

"Would 'of got here sooner," he said, handing me my baby

back. He reached into the front seat of the ambulance and withdrew a bag of flour. "But I stopped to get this. 'Case we needed to do a transfusion."

Skeet looked at the bag Handy was holding and said, "Good thing we didn't need it. You bought bleached. Bil's baby is whole-wheat. Transfusion could of killed him."

Handy chuckled. Charolais didn't.

Charolais turned and walked away.

Skeeter looked at me, then at Handy. He said, "Somehow what you two just did with a couple bags of flour got me into trouble with my girlfriend."

The next day, all the girls in our class showed up with their babies wearing tiny dresses and bows. They'd painted hair and faces on their eggs. Many of the girls had also brought cribs made from baskets or liberated from doll houses. Most of the boys had shoeboxes stuffed with toilet paper or cotton balls. I had my bag of flour wrapped in a towel in my backpack.

Charolais was giving me the cold shoulder.

At lunch I went over to her and asked her what the trouble was. She said, "You're not taking this baby thing serious."

I said, "What do mean?" I patted my backpack. "Baby is safe in here, wrapped in a towel."

"That's what I mean," Charolais said. "You are doing the least amount of work possible to get through this assignment. Maybe some of the girls have gone too far building strollers and pretending to change their egg's diapers, but you are acting like you are trying to get a five-pound bag of flour through a couple weeks of transport. You're not taking it seriously."

"Of course, I'm not taking it seriously. It's a stupid assignment."

"Well," she said, "you should take it serious. Babies are serious."

"I know that," I said, "but this isn't a baby. It's just a five-pound bag of flour."

She was upset. She stamped her foot and said, "It's not just about a bag of flour. It's about responsibility. To get through this assignment you need to care. Part of it is to teach us to think, 'There's this other thing I need to keep safe.'"

I patted my backpack again. "It's safe. Wrapped in a towel. Most of the guys don't even have their eggs anymore. I've done more than most."

"Great," she said. "You're not the worst dad. When you have a wife and kids I'm sure they'll be satisfied to know that even though you don't try hard, there are dads who do less."

"It's a bag of flour," I said.

"Why do you refuse to see it as anything more?"

"What are you talking about?" I had been being obtuse, but now I really was confused.

"I'm talking about that flour has potential," Charolais tapped the table with her fist. "It could be lots of things. Bread or cookies or gravy."

I laughed at her and said, "Or it could be a parachutist. I could drop it off the building and there would be a tremendous explosion."

Charolais's face reddened. "Don't you dare! Don't you dare drop that baby off the roof."

"It's a bag of flour," I said, leaning back toward obtuse. And I was thinking about gravy.

We stared at each other for a long moment. Charolais and I had been friends since the second grade. We didn't fight often. She broke the silence and said softly, "Why are you so determined to make a joke of this whole thing?"

I said, "Because it is a joke. Carrying around a bag of flour doesn't teach me anything."

"It's not that hard to do," she said. "You just *decided* it was stupid, and now you are determined to screw it up someway or another, as though by screwing up the assignment you can prove the stupidity of it."

"What?" I asked.

"You've got this feeling deep down in you, Bil, that you can't be allowed to be perceived as successful. For some reason, you don't dare excel."

"Why should I excel, Charolais? What's the point of doing well at carrying around a bag of flour?"

"It's not about the flour," she said. "It's about doing well for the sake of doing well." She walked off.

Later that week, we started studying Greek myths in our humanities class. Fred Ware looked uncomfortable throughout the lecture on Kronos. After our teacher explained that the Titan leader Kronos had eaten his own children to prevent them from overthrowing him, Fred Ware was truly troubled. His stomach growled.

The next day he walked into health class without his egg.

"Ware?" snarled Ms. Gurdak, "Where's your egg?"

"We were studying Kronos in our humanities class. Let's just say, the coup was averted."

"Ware, if this was Humanities, you'd get an A. But this is Health. So, you get an F."

Skeeter was excited on the way to school Monday and said he had a surprise for the health class. He wouldn't tell me what it was, but he did tell me to go into the classroom before him and get everyone looking at the door. I ran ahead.

Ms. Gurdak demanded, "Barth? Where's your egg?" when he walked into class.

Skeet lifted a brown paper sack and pulled out a Mason jar filled with clear liquid. An egg floated in it. Skeet took the lid off and fished the egg from the liquid. He held the egg above his head so we could all see it and announced, "I'm now the proud parent…"

We gasped when he dropped the egg toward the ground. It didn't break. It bounced twice and then rolled to a stop at Ms. Gurdak's feet, "…of a bouncing baby boy." He bowed, then continued, "I soaked it in vinegar all weekend. The acid in the vinegar eats away the calcium carbide that composes the shell and turns the egg all rubbery. If you soak a chicken bone long enough you can make it soft and tie it in a knot. See?" He pulled a chicken bone with a half-hitch tied in it from his back pocket. "I made it into a necklace."

Ms. Gurdak said, "Barth if this was science class, you'd get an A. But this is health class, so you get a F."

Charolais glared at Skeeter. She hugged her arms around herself and stormed from the classroom. She bumped him hard on the way out and said, "Idiot."

Genevieve Mortenson and Toad Gilky had been getting together and breaking up with each other since seventh grade. They were together when Ms. Gurdak handed out the eggs. They'd broken up since. Genevieve got custody of both eggs. Toad took care of them on the weekends. Skeet and I slipped into the school cafeteria Sunday night and pasted pictures of Toad on all the milk cartons, proclaiming him a Dead Beat Dad.

I didn't bring my flour baby with me on that excursion because I didn't want to be implicated on charges of corrupting a minor.

That night I lay in bed looking at the bag of flour on my desk. The little guy was growing on me. He was talented. He didn't need an alarm clock. He was self-rising.

I did research on him. Mostly because he was adopted, and I might need to know about his medical history sometime in the future.

Flour, I read earlier that day, is a staple ingredient in the diets of many cultures. Because of this, shortages of flour can cause great political unrest. I learned that the word 'flour' derives from a French term meaning 'the finest part of the meal' with 'meal' in this case meaning 'food derived from grains.' So, the finest part of the meal is flour because all the course elements of the grain have been stripped away.

My little baby bag of flour was the finest part of the meal and full of potential to cause political unrest. I was proud.

One by one all the boys failed the assignment. All but me. I was the only boy left with a baby, and this caused trouble. The girls liked me more because I was the only boy left with a baby. The boys disliked me because the girls liked me more than them. The boys would pass me in the hall and say mean things like, "How's your little hippy baby? How's your flour child?"

I had conflicting feelings about my bag of flour.

Charolais found me on the roof of the gym Friday. "What are you doing?" she asked.

"Putting the final touches on my flour baby's parachute. I'm going to drop him off the roof."

"Why?" she demanded. "It's over in three days. You turn that bag of flour into Ms. Gurdak Monday morning, and you'll get at least a C. You've gotten that five-pound bag of flour through the last few weeks because deep down you do feel responsible for it, or at least you must want to prove you can. I hear what the other guys say about you, what they call you, just because you kept a five-pound bag of flour alive. You've stood up to them this long. Why not a few more days?"

"I got the flour through these weeks because of you, Charolais. That discussion we had in the lunchroom. I did it. I got the baby this far to prove to you I could do it. But now I'm going to drop him off the roof. I earned it. I all but completed the assignment; now I get to wreck it."

"What? Why?"

"I gotta."

She was furious, but she was trying. "Look at me, Bil," she said. "Who am I?"

I was confused but I played along. "Charolais Fester."

"That's right," she said. "I'm Charolais Fester. I'm that girl named for a cow. I'm nothing but 'that Fester girl.'"

"Wait," I said, but she kept on going.

"People in this town don't expect anything from me, or from my family, except failure. If a Fester screws up, big or small, folks'll say, "Well, what do you expect from a Fester." It don't matter how hard I work, how much good I do, or who I become. The first time I screw up folks'll write me off. It doesn't matter I've gotten further in school than any of my brothers. That I'll be the first Fester to graduate from any institution that doesn't include the word 'Correctional.' No one expects me to succeed.

"You, though? You and Skeeter? Both of you come from good families, with two, sober, nice parents. It would shock the world if you failed but even if you do, they'll say, 'Well, he's a good boy just sowing some wild oats. He'll straighten out.'"

I was silent. It was one of those moments where someone has spoken the truth but you can't decide if you are ready to admit it. I nodded and said, "We're in the same boat, Charolais."

"What?" she asked.

"To get noticed. To be different than what folks expect of us, we have to present ourselves as the opposite of expectations. You have to work hard to be seen as good. I have to find ways to skirt the system and monkey with the works if I want to get noticed for anything but what folks expect. Fact is," I continued, "you're stronger than me."

"How so?" she asked.

"'Cause you work hard to be the best in the world. That takes faith and courage. But I'm too chicken to really screw up. I'm not going to rob a bank or get in fights. I'm too cowardly to be as bad as I would need to be to really shock folks. I go home at night and maybe I get yelled at, or grounded. You go home and no matter how good you did during the day, no matter how noble, you gotta see your father, unless he's in jail. And then you get…" I didn't finish.

She cocked her head, smiled. "You're an idiot, but not as dumb as you put on." She paused, touched my shoulder. "You don't got the guts to rob a bank, so you're going to drop a flour baby off the roof of the gym?"

"That about sums it up," I said, choking up a bit.

"Don't," she stated. "Don't do it. Turn that ugly, five-pound flour baby in on Monday morning. Don't do it for anybody but me. Make me proud of you."

What could I do? Charolais was one of my best friends and possibly the smartest person I knew, but I'd never done much for her. I could do this. I held my flour baby away from the edge of the roof and asked, "You going to the football game tonight?"

"Yea," she said. "Me and Skeet, even if that pewckerweed soaked his egg in vinegar to make it bounce. Genevieve Mortenson doesn't have a date 'cause she and Toad broke up, again, so she's gonna sit at the travel choir bake sale table the whole game. She's gonna babysit a bunch of egg babies for us. She'd probably watch your flour for you."

"Next to you and Fern Dale," I told Charolais, "Genevieve is about the most responsible person in the school. But why on earth does she date Toad Gilky? I mean, I know they're broken up right now but they'll get back together soon."

Charolais winked at me. "There's just not that many available boys in the school. She's gotta date somebody," Charolais said. "Even good girls date morons sometimes."

I dropped the flour in my backpack and said, "I'll think about letting her babysit."

I kept my flour baby in my backpack during the football game but several people, Charolais included, gave their eggs to Genevieve at the traveling choir bake sale table. Genevieve had a small basket with a towel folded at the bottom of it. She carefully laid, well, placed, all the eggs into that one basket. With a bored sigh, she said, "I'll be here. All night. You guys go have fun."

I saw Genevieve pushing her way through the crowd midway through the third quarter. She looked frantic. I saw her grab Charolais by the shoulder. I started moving toward them. I heard Genevieve saying, "They're gone. Somebody took the egg babies."

The other egg parents were gathering around. "I'm so sorry, guys. I got up for just a second. Toad came by. He asked me to talk with him. We went behind the bleachers to make out… I mean make up. When I came back the babies were gone. Someone took the whole basket."

"Did they leave a note?" Skeeter asked.

"No," Genevieve whispered. "I'm so sorry, guys."

"A note?" Charolais asked Skeeter. "Are you serious? Nobody kidnapped the eggs. Somebody just took them."

Charolais got good grades. Charolais worked hard at school. I could see she was upset with herself for losing her egg at this point. She felt she'd made a bad choice leaving the baby with Genevieve. She hadn't made a bad choice. Genevieve was a responsible person. You could trust her to watch your baby. Usually. I smirked.

Charolais punched me. "It's not funny. Somebody stole my egg baby! I know why you're smirking. You didn't leave your flour baby with Genevieve. You've got your stupid five-pound baby in your backpack. You were going to throw it off the roof and I stopped you, and now my egg baby is gone, and you think it's funny." She punched me again. Hard.

Toad Gilky was coming toward us. Genevieve was crying. Charolais was punching me. Toad was saying, "There's a note, there's a note. Some kid brought me a note."

"What?" Charolais asked. She stopped punching my arm and snatched the note from Toad's hand. "Who gave you this?"

"Some kid. One of the Wilkins twins. She said she found it taped to a stall in the women's bathroom. It had an envelope." Toad pulled a crumpled envelope from his pocket. He held it up for us to see. On the outside it read, "Please give this letter to Genevieve Mortenson or Toad Gilky."

"Holy crap," Charolais said. "Somebody did kidnap our egg babies! This note says, 'You should be more careful with your eggs. I'll call the Gilky house at midnight with more information. Don't go to the authorities.'

Skeeter giggled.

Charolais punched him in the stomach. "This isn't funny, idiot."

Now most of us were laughing. "Charolais," Skeet tried to explain, "we're laughing at you."

She hit him in the arm.

"Because you're overreacting. You're not upset because your egg baby got kidnapped. You're upset because you gave your egg baby to Genevieve. Ms. Gurdak gave us the egg babies to illustrate exactly why we shouldn't run off behind the bleachers, and then you gave your egg baby to Genevieve because she's about the least likely person in our class to go behind the bleachers, and then she did, and your egg baby got kidnapped, and now you're gonna fail the project. And that's why you're so upset."

"Shut up. What time is it right now?" Charolais asked.

"It's almost ten," Skeet said. And then he said, "Oh, wait, there's Sheriff Hasbro. We better go tell him."

"No, don't!" Charolais tried to stop him. "What are you doing?"

"There's been a crime. Ms. Gurdak told us that we had to take this seriously, and the town was in on it," Skeet explained.

"Skeeter, no!" Charolais called. "It's not even your baby. You turned your baby into a rubber ball! The note says don't go to the police."

But he was gone, and soon headed back our way, Sheriff Hasbro right behind him. The Sheriff said, "So y'all got yer egg babies kidnapped? You ever heard the saying about all your eggs in one basket? Skeeter here says y'all got a note."

Charolais handed him the note. "It says don't go to the authorities."

"Course it does," Hasbro said. "They all say that."

"Have you read a lot of kidnap notes?" Charolais asked.

"Nope. But I've seen a lot of movies. Y'all did the right thing coming to me. I reckon we better head over to the Gilky house."

"Uh," Toad said, "maybe I could run home first? Let my dad know you're on the way?"

"Sure, Gilky, that's a good idea," said the good Sheriff, smiling.

By 11:30 we were all gathered at the Gilky household. The phone rang at exactly midnight. Charolais answered. "Hello? Yes. Okay."

"We have to bring a loaf of fresh baked bread, a jar of mayonnaise, a can of paprika, a chopped onion, one of those funny egg plates, and an egg timer to the back of the school at two in the morning."

Skeet grimaced. "That's sick."

Genevieve sniffled. "I'm so sorry."

"This used to be a nice town," Sheriff Hasbro said. "I'll have to stake the place out."

"Why a loaf of fresh baked bread?" Toad asked.

Everybody looked at me.

"The kidnapper wants Bil's flour."

I gasped.

Charolais stepped up and gripped my shoulder. She said, "Bil, you've debated over and over what to do with the flour baby. Now it's time to decide. Are you going to sacrifice your baby for the lives of the other babies?"

I didn't hesitate. "Yes."

We were on the roof of the school gym. The gym stuck out at a right angle from the rest of the school. It had been recently added to the school. It was a prosthetic wing. I was holding my bag of flour two stories above the location where we were supposed to leave the ransom. It was a good place for the kidnapper because he could escape into the old part of the building, or the new gym, or off into the woods.

Skeet had put the mayonnaise and other ingredients in the proper location just outside the back door to the gym, and then, as directed, he had left. Sheriff Hasbro was sitting in a borrowed car in the parking lot.

Toad, Genevieve, Charolais, Skeet, myself, and several others were hanging over the edge of the roof. We were using the flour like a paint bomb in a bank bag. "When the door opens, drop the flour on the kidnapper."

"Who do you figure it is?"

"It's gotta be someone with access to the school after hours."

"Why?"

"They're going to come out that door."

"We don't know that."

"We have access to the school after hours," I said. "Skeet and I were in there recently."

"You guys put my picture on the milk cartons?" Toad asked.

"Yeah."

"Shhh, the door's opening."

"Drop the flour."

"Not yet. I gotta wait 'til he puts down the egg babies."

The kidnapper put the basket of egg babies on the ground then went to pick up the mayonnaise and other items.

I dropped the flour. A five-pound bag of flour falling twenty feet has an incredible terminal velocity. A raindrop falls at twenty miles per hour. A five-pound flour bag packs enough punch to knock out a polar bear. It hit with a 'whump' and a huge cloud of flour billowed out in all directions.

We heard a profanity. Sheriff Hasbro stepped around the corner of the gym below us and said to the kidnapper, "No, don't strike that match with all that flour in the air. You'll blow us all sky high."

"I don't care if I do. I never should of given Lepp that bag of flour."

We ran downstairs and surrounded Ms. Gurdak. Sheriff Hasbro asked her, "So, why did you do it?"

Ms. Gurdak struck the match anyway, lit the cigarette, and took a drag. She said, "Teach you all a lesson." Then she shrugged and said, "Gaylord." That was Hasbro's first name. "I've known you since you were a boy. You carried an egg around in my class, got an A. You've done yourself proud. Your daddy was a no good…; well, he was no good. Gave your whole family a bad name. But you didn't let that get in your way. You worked hard. Overcame that. You're a good lawman. People respect you."

She sucked on the cigarette and said to Charolais, "Fester, you come from a crappy family, too. Worse than Gaylord's. But I see your grace and goodness. I see the light in you. I see how hard you work. You do Good, girl. You keep these numskulls," she waved her cigarette at me and Skeet, "in line. People see you in this town. They know you're different than your dad and brothers. You keep doin' what you do, and you'll do us all proud. You're a good girl. A good, good girl."

Then she said, "Lepp?" and took the final drag on her cigarette. She brushed flour off her shoulders, and then flicked the cigarette butt at me. She said, "You're a smart-aleck."

Fortune Cookies

When the Chinese restaurant opened in Halfdollar, it was a cause for celebration. We had never had a foreign restaurant. There was a Chinese restaurant in the next town over, but that wasn't even in the same county.

Sheriff Hasbro was a big man. He was six-eight or six-nine and weighed about 380 pounds. He never sowed his wild oats; he ate them. So it came to pass that his doctor told him he had to lose weight.

Truth was, you didn't need to be all that fit to solve crime in Dry County, West Virginia. If someone committed a crime and fled the scene before Sheriff Hasbro arrived, that was no big deal. He'd just show up at their house, or Mom's house, or girlfriend's, or wherever else everybody knew they'd go. But one day Sheriff Hasbro decided it was time to lose weight. He was in a pickle, though. He couldn't jog. "Hell, I'd have to lose 200 pounds before I could jog. And walking just isn't quick enough." So, he got a bicycle. Well, he had a bicycle built. You're average Schwinn wasn't built for Hasbro's bulk.

Sheriff Hasbro had an old army buddy who went on to be an engineer at Harley Davidson. The two exchanged a few letters and before long the world's sturdiest bicycle arrived in Halfdollar. It was a monster. It was actually a tricycle, with ape-hanger, chopper handlebars. It went downhill with no problem. Uphill was a different situation, so the trike had a motor to get Hasbro uphill. He would coast downhill, motor uphill, and pedal on the flat. But there's not much flat in Halfdollar. Hasbro didn't get much exercise, but he sure looked funny.

Once the Chinese restaurant opened, with its buffet, Sheriff Hasbro dedicated himself to ensuring the peace and safety of the establishment by parking his trike out front for several hours every day.

The owner of the restaurant was named Hank, and most folks in town assumed he was Chinese. I suppose he was ethnically, but he was about as Chinese as I am Dutch. Some long time ago his ancestors left mainland China, came to America, intermingled with folks from other cultures and ethnicities, and shazam, Hank could trace a lot of DNA back to the Ming dynasty but that guy was about American as apple pie and good ol' xenophobia.

But because Hank 'looked' foreign lots of folks assumed he was. Lots of folks thought he couldn't speak English. This assumption was based on several things. First, he looked foreign. Second, he was hard to understand. You'd hear people say, "Y'all, 'at fella talks funny. He's got an accent."

And Hank did talk funny...'cause he was from Boston.

I try to promote West Virginia in my stories, stick up for the state, accentuate the good and debunk the stereotypes, but to pretend that there are no morons in West Virginia would be dishonest. We have a state legislature, just like you.

Because lots of folks thought Hank couldn't understand English, they said things around him that were none of his- or their- business. Pretty soon Hank had the dirt on most of the folks in town.

Skeet and I worked for Hank. It was easy work, and we liked him. Hank would ask, "Who is so and so," and we would point them out the next time they came in. Hank was putting faces to the gossip.

We had one branch of folks in the county who had formed their own little social group, and there was plenty of gossip about them.

They called themselves a church. The outside of their building looked like a church, but what those folks believed differed greatly from most mainstream American Christian churches in those days. Nowadays they would fit right in, sadly. They weren't really hurting anybody with their crazy Jesus, so for the most part we just let them be. Whatever was wrong with them, most folks thought it wasn't contagious. Again, time proved us wrong.

Their preacher liked to yell and scream and warn his congregants about the dangers in this world. He was fond of talking about how everyone was out to get them.

When your primary religious dogma is based on the idea that everyone is out to get you, you are not practicing religion. You are living an exceptionally self-centered existence. Sure, the world may dislike you, but they aren't going to come all the way to Halfdollar to do something about it. They'll launch a strike on LA or New York City and hope the effects trickle down to you.

That preacher was named Lester Gwinn, and Lester only had one eye.

Pastor Lester Gwinn lost his eye when he was in the Army. Not in a heroic way though. He'd been stationed out in California and was driving down the road, admiring the women in their bikinis, looking at the ocean, watching the sunset, and eating a corndog. He was watching the women so intently that he forgot he was driving until sideview mirrors started bouncing off the side of his car. His car had drifted to the right, and he side-swiped eleven parked cars. He swerved and hit a dump truck, which stopped him. He remembered he had been eating when the corndog stick went into his eye.

He was medically discharged from the Army. He was disgruntled that they had not given him a Purple Heart. They fitted him out with a glass eye. Lester was depressed and had no way to get home or make money. He was in a bar one night, and the fella next to him told Lester a joke. "You hear about the guy who bet the bartender $10 he could lick his own eye?"

"No," said Lester, trying to figure out if he was being made fun of.

"Well," continued the joke teller, "this fella bets the bartender, and the bartender takes the bet, and then this guy pulls out his glass eye, and licks it!"

The guy didn't tell jokes well.

Lester could have gotten sore but instead he saw a job opportunity. He made his way from California to West Virginia, stopping in at every bar, betting people he could lick his own eye. When he got back to Halfdollar it took about six minutes to run out of people to make that bet with because we only had one bar, and Lester was out of work again. So, he became a preacher, like people do. They figure if the disciples could do it, so can they. A lot of people think Jesus or the Holy Spirit call them to preach. Some of those people need to keep in mind that they might be wrong. Thinking that just because you fish and sin you are qualified to be the next great disciple is like equating Kim Kardashian to Helen Keller because they both learned to talk.

Skeet and I would sneak over to Lester's church sometimes when those folks were holding services, and we'd watch through the windows or sneak up into the balcony. Lester Gwinn would get rolling into a sermon, then pop out his glass eye and hold it up screaming, "This is the eye of the Lord, and it sees all!" Sometimes he'd roll it down the aisle. It was terrifying and way better than the sermons we were accustomed to at the Methodist church. I doubt he had read the Bible, certainly not any commentaries, and so he made interesting mistakes. I'll never forget when he told the congregation that Jesus, "…suffered under Pontius's Pilates."

Lester ranted and raved about Hank and his restaurant because Hank was an easy target and not related to anybody in town. Lester told his congregation that foreigners were dangerous. Of course, Lester had eaten at the restaurant. Everyone in town had. Lester liked the food, but not Hank, or China.

His congregation would go there after church on Sundays, circle the buffet, and lock hands. Then, Lester would pray reverently over the food, exorcising all the demons Hank may have slipped into the grub. Then everybody in Lester's group would eat, just to see if the exorcism had worked. Sometimes they had to have seconds or thirds, just to make sure.

Hate the sin, love the dinner.

Hank didn't care, so long as they paid. They were lousy tippers, but Hank could live with that since Skeeter and I were the waiters. But Lester was a complainer. Nothing was ever right for him, so naturally, he got on Hank's nerves. And because Lester was stupid he believed Hank couldn't understand him, so he talked bad about Hank within earshot.

Hank was a funny guy. He had a trick where he would take a fortune cookie, wrap it in a wet paper towel, and microwave it for a few seconds until it got soft. Then he would pull out the original fortune and replace it with a brand new one that Hank had made himself. When the cookie re-hardened Hank would present it to a specific person about whom he had heard gossip. It might say,

'Your husband knows,' or 'Your wife knows about the $500 you lost on the Superbowl,' or 'To get an A in math class, tell your teacher you know what he keeps in his cabin.'

Hank was a nice guy at heart and sincerely tried to help people through his cookies, more than hurt. If you were on a date and it wasn't going well, your fortune might say, 'Compliment her shoes.' Or a guy might get one that said, 'Her birthday is Friday.'

People went to the restaurant because the food was good, but also because there was almost always a dust up after somebody got their fortune cookies.

And Sheriff Hasbro was there to quell it.

One Sunday, when Hank had simply had enough of Lester, he went in the back and doctored a big batch of fortune cookies for the congregation. The fact that very few folks caught on to Hank's fortune cookie scheme boils down to humans' tendencies to believe in magic when we want to. Hank told people he paid extra for his fortune cookies to be custom-crafted and handwritten at a genuine Tibetan monastery in the Andean mountains. People believed it. Nobody asked what the Tibetan monks were doing in the Andes. Or how those monks knew everyone's business in Halfdollar. Or even how it was that cookies made a continent away, at the top of a snow-covered peak, arrived fresh and warm to a table, in a small town, in a different equatorial zone.

Hank made a point of delivering the fortune cookies himself. He simply did not trust Skeeter or me to get the fixed cookies to the proper people. It wasn't that we didn't know everybody in town; it was just that Skeeter and I occasionally delivered cookies to the wrong people simply to see the reaction.

This particular Sunday, Hank came out of the kitchen with a tray of cookies and hand-delivered one to every member of the congregation. A rapturous joy filled the restaurant as people read things such as 'You Will Go to Heaven,' 'Jesus Loves You,' 'God's Grace Will Embrace You.' Everyone was joyous until Lester Gwinn opened his cookie. He paled and then went red with fury. He stood and left the restaurant, his fortune fluttering to the ground. People scrambled for the fortune as soon as the door shut behind him. Someone read it aloud: 'Jesus thinks you're a hypocritical fraud with no Scriptural knowledge.' That's a lot of text for one fortune and a pretty Christospecific observation from a bunch of Tibetan monks in the Andes. But it worked.

Lester quit coming to the restaurant and told his congregation to stop going, but they didn't. It made Lester angry. He lost all variety in his preaching. He ranted about Hank and his evil restaurant from the pulpit. People quit the church. Lester grew distant and seldom left his home.

One day, we were at the restaurant. It was a slow period, so Skeet, Hank, Sheriff Hasbro, and I were chatting at the counter when a man came in wearing a paper bag over his head. He pulled a gun and pointed it at Sheriff Hasbro and Hank. He demanded the money from the register. Hank looked at Hasbro, who just nodded. Hank handed the money over and the thief ran out of the restaurant.

Sheriff Hasbro went back to the plate of food he had in front of him. Hank looked at us, then at Hasbro. "Excuse me, Sherriff," Hank said, "aren't you going after him?"

"Better to wait till he cools off," Hasbro said.

"But you don't even know who it was."

"Sure I do. It was Lester Gwinn."

"How could you possibly know that? He was wearing that paper bag and hardly said three words."

Sheriff Hasbro dabbed his mouth with his napkin. "Paper bag gave it away. He only cut one eyehole."

Mayhem Dressed as an Eight-Point Buck

It was two in the morning. Buck season opened a half an hour before sunrise. I was in my living room watching a movie, waiting for sunrise so I could go deer hunting, when there was a knock on the back door. I knew not to answer it. I knew that if anybody was knocking on my back door at two in the morning on the opening day of buck season, it had to be Skeeter. If Skeeter was knocking on my door at two in the morning on the opening day of buck season, he had come up with one of his plans. And I didn't want to go along with it.

But there was no free will involved. I was sucked up off the couch and drawn to the back door. There stood Skeeter, with a paper bag in his hand and a diabolical grin on his face. He didn't say anything. I got a sick feeling down in my guts. It's like the feeling you get, fellas, when you walk into a public restroom, and there are no urinals on the wall. "Something is very wrong here," you say to yourself.

I invited him in anyway. It was like letting a vampire into my house. I gave him all the power. He sat at the kitchen table, put the paper bag on the floor, and I went to brew up a pot of coffee.

I brought the coffee over and sat down. Skeet said, "I've been up all night, sewing." He reached down and picked up the paper bag. He reached inside and pulled out something long, brown, and furry. He flipped it open and pulled it onto his head. By God, that kid could sew. What he had made was a perfect replica of an eight-point buck's head.

"Don't worry," he said, "I made one for you, too."

So, there we were. Two young bucks drinking coffee at the kitchen table. (It is a terrible joke. I know. But if you had thought it up, you'da put it in your story.)

I knew the masks couldn't be the whole plan.

"That's not the whole plan," Skeet said. "I also took a mannequin, dressed him in hunter's orange, and tied him to the hood of my truck. What we are going to do (not 'Do you want to?') is drive around town. Like it's people season. And we got one. We'll drive up to the checking station and check our human. Everybody will think it is funny."

It was funny, but precisely the sort of funny that you don't want *your* dad to find out it was *you* who did it. We decided to hide out. We were sitting in Skeeter's truck on an old service road in the state park.

Skeeter had just gotten his truck, brand new, that summer. It only had about eighty thousand miles on the odometer, but the odometer was in the glovebox. It was mechanically disassociated from every other part of the vehicle. The first time I had gone to roll down the passenger side window, I turned the crank about a quarter turn and the window went *thunk* and disappeared into the door. We never saw it again. Which was fine in the summer because the truck didn't have air conditioning.

This night, however, it was twenty degrees. We had about four hours before sunrise. The cold wind blew right in the open window. We didn't have enough money to buy enough gasoline to run the truck, to run the heater, for four hours. We were freezing. I reached into the paper bag and pulled out my mask and put it on. Skeeter put his mask on, too.

It was warm and cozy inside that mask. Pretty soon, I fell asleep. My head slowly fell right out the open window. You know how, when you are sleeping, sometimes your subconscious will pick up on something and scream, "Wake up! Do something!"? But other times, your subconscious will say, "Now, open your eyes, but don't move."? That's what my subconscious was telling me.

I opened my eyes but didn't move my head. The sun was just turning the sky gray. I could see two lights, about six feet apart, about three feet above the ground, about twenty yards down the road. I could barely make out the silhouette of a large, American sedan. Two sun beams broke over the mountain top, came down the hill, up the road, and over the top of that car. One sunbeam went through a blue light on the top of that car; the other sunbeam went through a red light.

The door opened, and Sheriff Hasbro started to get out. He was a big man. It took him a long time to get out of a Ford Taurus. Our county didn't have much of a budget.

I was poking Skeeter, trying to wake him up.

Sheriff Hasbro was walking slowly down the road toward us, his big flashlight held on his shoulder. He had his other hand on his holstered pistol. Discretion is the better part of valor, they say, and Sheriff Hasbro was erring way on the side of discretion. He was no coward, but you don't want to just run up on a pick-up truck with a guy tied to the hood and two deer sitting in the cab.

The smartest thing for me to do was stay still. The smartest thing isn't really my strong suit. If you were ever a teenager in a small town, then you know that the cops are bored. So, they come looking for you, to see what you are doing. Being civic-minded young men, Skeeter and I endeavored to participate in activities which allowed local law enforcement an opportunity to practice the skills they had learned at the academy. I thought, "How often do you get the chance to scare the pants off a duly elected official of your county? I'm just going to make a little deer noise."

I snorted like a deer, sorta. It wasn't a good impersonation, but it was effective.

Sheriff Hasbro left the ground. He jumped so high that Skeeter had time to start the truck, defrost the windshield, and drive underneath Sheriff Hasbro, before he came back down. We made our way around the Sheriff's car and headed into town.

We were sixteen. We weren't lawyers. But we had watched a lot of *Starsky & Hutch*. He never said, "Freeze." He never said we were under arrest. He never read us our rights. How were we supposed to know we were in trouble? Who knew that it was illegal to impersonate a deer?

We headed into town. The road into Halfdollar is fairly straight, by West Virginia standards, but it is one of those up and down jobs. We could see the sheriff's car coming up over the hills behind us, but he wasn't gaining on us. I turned the CB to the Police channel to see what was going on.

"Tom," said Hasbro. Tom was the deputy. "There are two deer driving Skeeter Barth's pick-up down the highway. And I think they have Skeeter tied to the hood!"

Tom said, "Well? Good."

You can see where that might hurt our feelings. I turned off the CB, and we headed into town.

This was before the Internet, before most twenty-four-hour news channels; we didn't even get public radio back in our holler. What people did for their news in the morning was turn on their police scanners.

When we turned onto Main Street there were people lined up and down both sides, drinking coffee with their curlers in. I thought Orson Wells was landing spaceships on the courthouse lawn. I turned the CB back on in time to hear Deputy Tom say, "Sheriff Hasbro, I called the FBI, just like you said. They called Animal Control. Animal Control said you should consider them two deer armed and dangerous. You're allowed to use lethal force if necessary."

That was more than we had bargained for. Skeeter pulled to the side of the road, and Sheriff Hasbro pulled in behind us. He got out of his car, came over, made us take off our masks, yelled at us for a bit, then gave us each a ticket for Mayhem Dressed as an Eight-Point Buck.

We had to pay a little fine and do a little community service.

They say that true forgiveness only comes after you have honestly repented of your sins, promise to never do the same thing again, and swear to never take any glory from the original action. With that in mind, I can honestly say that Skeeter and I will never be forgiven for what we did that day.

Not Like a Sexy Centaur

Maine Coon cats, the largest house cats in the world, made their way into Halfdollar and mated with bobcats, or possibly racoons, thus producing a rare and gigantic family of invasive, feral cats which had no fear and no predators. These humongous cats soon eradicated every rodent, from moles to small livestock, in the region. They were the largest non-human carnivore in the county apart from a handful of black bears.

The bears left the cats alone except for one epic incident when one of the cats tried to eat a bear cub. The Mama bear and the tom cat engaged in a fight that rolled down the mountainside, out of the woods, and onto Main Street. The fight lasted three hours, tore the porch off Sullivan's store, knocked the steeple on Lester Gwinn's church askew, punctured the tires of three passing cars, and only ended when Sheriff Hasbro dispatched the cat with three well-placed, and necessary, shots from a .300 Weatherby. It took four full-grown men to load the carcass of the dead cat into the back of the county dump truck. The bear limped into the woods.

At least that's how some people tell it.

Our family had a cat at that time. Just a regular house cat. I'm not a cat person. I didn't want a cat. But I was a kid and not in charge. My sister got the cat.

My mom got a spray bottle and would shoot the cat with a jet of water to keep the cat from doing things like walking on the table or unrolling the toilet paper. The cat hated getting shot with water.

That cat could sense a can opener cutting into a tuna can from three rooms away. She would barrel into the kitchen and smash into your legs, often resulting in the tuna juice sloshing from the can and dropping onto the floor, or onto the cat. The cat would then spend a delicious few seconds licking the floor and savoring the tuna juice caught in her coat.

One day I bought a squirt gun. The next time the cat jumped on the table I shot it with a jet of tuna juice. The cat leapt from the table, incensed and enraged at being shot. She hissed and spun, but then smelled the tuna juice. She stopped spinning and eagerly licked herself clean.

She hopped up on the table and I shot her again. Unfortunately, that cat learned that if it did something bad around me, something both unpleasant and desirable happened. This led to an uncomfortable period with the cat following me around the house essentially purring, "I'm a bad kitty; spray me with tuna water."

At Christmas time, our church youth group would go out into the community and visit folks who didn't get out much. I drew Mr. Blevin. Mr. Blevin was more of a recluse than a shut-in, and he was an interesting old guy who told good stories.

I found him on his back porch, arms resting on the railings, a scoped, high-powered hunting rifle in his hands. He was scanning the woods and he said, without preamble, "Yep. I think it's back."

Mr. Blevin, like most of us, kept a conversation running in his head. But Mr. Blevin, unlike most of us, would start having his internal conversation with anybody who approached as if you'd been part of it all along.

"What's back?"

"You ain't never heard of the Maine Coon Wildcat?"

"Is that the cat that had the fight with the bear on Main Street?"

"One of 'um. I thought they was gone, but I got a feeling one of them critters is back. Been seeing huge cat prints out around my barn."

"Then they're real? I thought it was a myth."

"Boy, probably ten years before you were born, ol' Mrs. Clever was collecting cats. She was a cat connoisseur. Wanted to get the world's biggest house cat. She drove all around the country buyin' up big cats. One day she went up to Maine, got herself several Maine Coon cats, biggest house cats there is. Four feet long, sixty pounds, six toes on each foot. That's called polydactylism, havin' extra toes. Them cats is tough enough to survive Maine winters, outside. Hard critters. Anyway, she brought some here. Rumor has it she cross-bread them with a Eurasian Lynx. Maine Coon cats are known for their sunny dispositions but at least one of them big cats got a mean streak. Meanest cat you ever saw."

"Ok, well, Merry Christmas, Mr. Blevins," I said as I got up to leave.

"Merry Christmas to you, too," whispered Mr. Blevin while staring down his scope.

That night, I saw it. Heard it first. A slow purr. I was walking our dog, Deacon, and as he and I came around a corner we saw the huge cat standing in our path.

Deacon went nuts, like a dog is supposed to do. The giant cat arched its back, hair sticking straight up. Deacon strained at the end of the leash, growling and barking. The cat kept its distance. I wondered what would happen if I eased the tension on the leash, allowing the dog to move slightly closer to the cat. I took a half-step forward. The tension eased, and the leash sagged. The dog looked at me as if to say, "HEY! What are you doing? Keep me away from that cat!"

I pulled the dog away from the encounter so he could save face. I found the squirt gun of tuna juice in my pocket as we headed home. I shot one of the Wise Men in the nativity scene in front of the church with a full blast of tuna juice, more to test if the squirt gun still worked than out of malfeasance. The nativity scene was set up in front of the Methodist church where my dad was the preacher. The church was beside our house.

Skeet saw me as I entered my yard and headed over to join me in my living room, to watch TV. Sheriff Hasbro showed up soon after that to talk to my dad about food boxes for some folks in our community who were going to have a tough Christmas. Hasbro and Dad talked in the kitchen for maybe half an hour, and then Hasbro said goodbye to Dad, stuck his head in the living room to tell Skeet and me to stay out of trouble, and left.

He was back five minutes later. "Reverend Lepp," he said to my dad, "Y'all had three Wise Men in your manger scene, right?"

"That's the traditional number," my father agreed.

"Well, that's what I thought. There was three when I drove by on my way here forty minutes ago. But now, there's just two.

Looks like one wandered off on his own, or somebody stole a Wise Man."

Dad and Hasbro turned to look at me and Skeeter. We were listening in on their conversation from the doorway. It always intrigued us when petty crimes were committed in town for which we were not responsible. We put our hands up. "Not us," I said. "You both had eyes on us while this was being committed."

"Well, dang," chuckled Hasbro, "now I got no suspects."

Neither Skeet nor I had taken the Wise Man, but I had a theory as to what had happened.

I shot a second Wise Man with a healthy dose of tuna juice the next night while I was walking the dog.

There are certain lines which must not be crossed when playing a prank. Especially a prank that involves a church. It is okay to shoot a Wise Man with tuna juice to cause it to be dragged away by a giant Maine Coon cat. However, shooting tuna juice on Mary, or Baby Jesus, so they get dragged into the wilderness by a devil beast edges on sin. I hadn't decided on Joseph yet. He might think it was funny.

The first Wise Man to disappear was never seen again. The second Wise Man was discovered the next day. He had been thoroughly shredded.

Sheriff Hasbro came to my house and had me go get Skeeter, who lived next door. "I know you boys didn't abduct the first Wise Man because I was here with you when he went missing. I don't know you didn't steal the second Wise Man, but your parents seem pretty sure neither of you left the house last night during the time the crime must have happened."

"You mean we have an alibi?" Skeet asked eagerly. "Cool."

"So," Hasbro continued, "I don't think you guys are doing this, at least not directly, but I bet you know who is."

"Herod?" I suggested, helpfully.

Skeet didn't yet know I might be behind the vanishing Wise Men. He was less likely to inadvertently give me away if he didn't think I was involved. Skeet was my best pal and would never willingly sell me out to the law, but Sheriff Hasbro was a good lawman and could read faces. For now it was best Skeet didn't know, though he'd be ticked when he found out what I was up to and that I hadn't told him.

"Here's the thing," Hasbro continued, "you guys might not be doing this, but I bet you know who is. We all know if it ain't you, it's one of your friends. Fern Dale maybe? Toad Gilky? We also know I could make your lives miserable if I so chose. So, here's what's gonna happen. I'm going to stake out the manger scene and catch the culprits, and you are going to help me.

"Skeeter, we all know you can sew, thanks to the deer masks you made," continued the Sheriff. "I'm going to give you some money, and you are going to run over to Rainelle and go to the fabric store. You buy enough fabric to make a cow suit. Deputy Tom is going to put that cow suit on and stand in the manger scene, looking like the rest of the life-size critters in the background. He'll keep watch on the flocks, so to speak."

"Yes, sir," was all Skeet said. Hasbro passed over a handful of cash. The next morning, Skeet and I drove to Rainelle, bought fabric, and spent the day sewing, and assembling, a suit.

"This isn't a cow," Hasbro said when we showed him our finished product. "This looks more like a donkey."

"Yeah," Skeet agreed, "they didn't have enough cow material, so I went with, uh, a donkey. We thought it fit Deputy Tom's personality better."

The disguise was simple enough. Tom, the deputy, who wasn't very tall, wore a donkey head and torso on his upper half and the front legs of a donkey on his lower half. We had built the backend of a donkey that Tom could back up against and strap around his waist. He looked remarkably like the donkey statue that was already in the manger scene. Tom took his place in the manger scene just after dusk.

There are things you do in this life that you hope, with the passage of enough time, you can laugh about with the person to whom you did them, but until that day comes, you must stay mum. As we maneuvered Tom into position, I pulled out my little squirt gun and doused the back of Tom's donkey suit with tuna juice.

Skeet and I went back to my house. We made a show of going in the front door then snuck out the back door. We crawled across the yard and then crept through the back door of the church and into one of the Sunday school rooms from which we could watch what was going to happen.

I filled Skeeter in on the tuna juice gun, and what I'd been up to, while we waited to see what transpired in the stakeout.

It didn't take long. The big cat came out of the brush from behind Tom. Forty pounds of cat is a lot of cat, and Tom must have sensed movement behind him because he turned his donkey head and gave a little start at the enormous feline creeping toward him.

The cat crouched, and Tom knew he was in trouble but not why, which is the worst way to be in trouble. Tom had seen the shredded remains of the abducted Wise Man. He didn't want to suffer a similar fate.

The way to thwart an attack from a big cat is to stare the cat in the eyes and make yourself seem as large as possible. You never run from a predator. Only prey runs away.

Tom wasn't a wise man. He bolted.

Well, bolted isn't the right word for it because Tom was wearing a donkey suit and was strapped to a donkey rearend. Tom took a big step and started to drag the donkey end behind him, which made him look like a lame animal, exactly the sort of thing a big cat looks to cull from the herd.

Tom built up speed, but he knew he wasn't going fast enough. He had to shed weight, so he took off the donkey head and torso, tossing them behind him in the general direction of the Maine Coon cat. Tom was still wearing the donkey front legs and was still dragging the back legs, but because he'd taken off the head and wasn't wearing a shirt he looked like a centaur -half man, half horse- but not like a sexy centaur. Tom's physique was not that of a warrior. He was built for leisure, or as a result of leisure. He looked like a centaur that always got picked last for centaur games, like the centaur who stayed behind to correlate requisitions and proofread regulations.

Tom was running furiously with his front end but could do nothing but drag the back end, which slowed him considerably. He was reaching behind himself trying to unstrap the donkey rear end. The cat sprang and landed on the back half of the donkey just as Tom broke loose and took off down the street now looking less like a centaur and more like a satyr.

Skeet and I left the church to give chase. Many of the neighbors, having heard on their lawns such a clatter, came out to see what was the matter. Tom was running in circles with the cat chasing behind. As funny as it was, if that cat got hold of Tom, it was going to be ugly. I did what you do with a bad cat. I pulled out my squirt gun and blasted the cat with a jet of tuna juice.

He was incensed but also found it delicious. Tom was grateful I'd saved his life. Sheriff Hasbro had his culprit.

Love Song to David Bowie

I was standing in a crowd in a park in Hamburg, Germany, in a huge crowd, in front of a giant spider. I hate spiders. Especially huge ones. But I had my reasons to be in the crowd in the park in Hamburg in front of the giant spider.

A guy came on the stage with a pink guitar and spiked hair; the screaming guitar solo wailed as a couple of dancers and drummers descended from the spider on long webs.

And then his voice, David Bowie's voice, came through the speakers delivering a weird monologue. The jaws of the spider opened, and Bowie began to descend. In a pink suit. Sitting in a chair singing into an old telephone, like a 1930s phone, coming out of the spider's mouth, and I was transfixed and in awe and in love with the idea of a man who said, "OK, we're going to build a giant spider, I'm going to put on a pink suit, sit in a chair, and descend on webs. Also give me an old phone. Why? Because this is my job, and I get to do this sorta of thing."

I was seventeen, and I was halfway around the world, and I was half a football field, albeit a European football field, from the single most flamboyant and fearless man in the world.

I can't definitively say what the first Bowie song I ever heard was. Rush's *Spirit of the Radio* and Queen's *Radio Gaga* are love songs to a time when the radio was my only outlet to the outside world. Queen sang:

I'd sit alone and watch your light
my only friend through teenage nights
and everything I had to know
I heard it on my radio

When I was a kid in rural West Virginia, I could only hear music. I couldn't see it. I didn't even know you could buy it.

My parents weren't fans of Rock 'n' Roll.

When I asked the little old librarian at our library if she could get *Rolling Stone* magazine, she gasped and called my parents, the principal at the junior high, and the Nazarene pastor.

I had the radio and my imagination. I didn't know what a single Rock 'n' Roll star looked like.

The Beatles had broken up, Elvis had died in 1977. They didn't grace magazine covers anymore. I was maybe eleven years old when I really started listening to the radio on my own, and I just assumed Rock 'n' Roll stars looked like the people I knew in Halfdollar-- preachers, teachers, auto mechanics, coal miners, and choir leaders. Imagine my surprise the first time I saw a poster of the band Kiss. Nobody in my town dressed like Kiss. Not in public, anyway.

My eighth grade history teacher- sweet-tempered, demure Mrs. Metcalf- came to school one Halloween decked out in a rented set of full-on Iron Maiden, heavy-metal leathers, with thigh-high boots, spiked bracelets, and a spiked collar. Years later, and for no reason at all, it occurred to me that Mrs. Metcalf didn't rent those clothes. She owned them. God bless and keep you, Mrs. Metcalf.

I would lie in my bedroom at night with the radio turned low and listen to the top forty station. Hearing a song you liked was pure chance. Maybe the DJ would play it, maybe not. Sometimes you could call in and request a song, but not very often. You waited, and you hoped you could press 'Record' on the cassette recorder in time to catch most of your favorite tune.

I would turn on the radio low, hit 'Record,' and steal forty-five minutes of random hits from a broadcast while I slept.

And somewhere in that mix I started to hear *Let's Dance*. *China Girl*. *Blue Jean*. *Modern Love*. Then *Space Oddity*. Maybe *Heroes*, but that was such a long song they didn't play it often. Then I heard *Rebel Rebel*. *Ziggy Stardust*. The DJ said they were by a guy named David Bowie. David Bowie seemed like a normal enough name, probably a nice chap you could bring home to meet the folks…

And then…

And then…

And then…

And then MTV reared its ugly, devil-worshiper-spawning, drug-taking, heavy-drinking-inducing, ruination of Gen X, the world was going to Hell, AND I WAS NOT UNDER ANY CIRCUMSTANCES EVER ALLOWED TO WATCH MTV, head. But I did watch and for the first time in my whole life I SAW what rock music looked like. What these heroes of my radio and illicit cassette tapes looked like when they played music and shot videos, and holy cow the world was on fire!

These were the days when Springsteen was ascending, Tom Petty was the coolest thing in the world, The Stones were the Stones, The Who, Pat Benatar, Rush, Joan Jett… but those were just normal folks with drums and guitars. Many of those guys did look like the guys in Halfdollar. At least like the coal miners and mechanics. And the Talking Heads looked like the bankers in town.

The first video I ever remember seeing was Tom Petty's *You Got Lucky, Babe*. Tom and the Heartbreakers roll up to this bar in the middle of the desert on futuristic Mad Max motorcycles, and then they go in and play video games while singing *You Got Lucky*. It made no sense. The song had nothing to do with the video, and yet it was beautiful.

At some point, the VJ said, "Coming up next hour is David Bowie's *Ashes to Ashes*." I was finally going to see David Bowie. I had never seen Bowie.

Ashes to Ashes came on and… Okay, it's sepia tone, and Bowie is walking on a beach, in a French clown costume, and there are other people in weird costumes, and then it's black and white, and Bowie's out of the clown costume and sitting in the seat of a space ship, but wait, he's not in a space ship; he's in a 1960s era sitcom kitchen, and there is a perfectly normal lady cooking at the stove, and Bowie is singing:

Ashes to Ashes funk to funky
We all know Major Tom's a junky
Strung out in Heaven's high
hitting an all time low

Then the clown is back on the beach.

I knew Major Tom. Major Tom is the guy in Bowie's *Space Oddity* who drifts off into deep space when something goes wrong and he wants ground control to tell his wife he loves her very much, but now he's in a whole new song, and he's a junky! I guess he eventually dropped out of orbit and landed in June Beaver's kitchen, and she doesn't seem to know, or mind. Nothing like that ever happened in Halfdollar. If anything even half that artsy had occurred in 1981, in Halfdollar, the librarian would certainly have been on the phone with the Nazarene minister.

Time went on. We got rides to the mall, we went to the record store and bought albums, we subscribed to *Rolling Stone* and had it sent to Fern Dale's house 'cause Fern Dale's parents were cool. We got our driver's licenses and saw more of the world. I saw Aerosmith and Guns 'n' Roses in Wheeling, West Virginia, and Steven Tyler spit on me from stage. We saw the Replacements, Rush, Springsteen, REM...

Our worlds expanded. Skeeter found Neil Young. Fern Dale was a fan of the Violent Femmes and the punk scene. Toad Gilky, bless his heart, leaned toward Hall & Oats and Tears for Fears.

But it was always Bowie above and beyond for me. One of the things that set him apart was that he was an enigma. Springsteen is always Springsteen. But you never knew which Bowie you were going to get-- Ziggy Stardust Bowie in his big, high-heeled, glittered, 1970s space boots, jamming good with Willy and the Spider's from Mars? The totally coked-out Thin White Duke Bowie? Diamond Dogs? Heroes Bowie? Let's Dance? You just never knew where he was going next.

This story is obviously a love song to Bowie. I won't be the first person to tell you that Bowie changed their life. He's a hero in many communities because of his shapeshifting, his androgyny, his personas. Thousands, millions of people, and artists will tell you that watching Bowie, listening to Bowie, allowed them to have the courage to be who they truly are. Because Bowie was himself on a world stage, regular people could be themselves in their smaller worlds. I think that is wonderful.

But that's not exactly what Bowie did for me. I had no idea who I was. I didn't know what I wanted to do, or who I wanted to be. That was Bowie's magic to me. When I heard Bowie sing, when I saw him on TV, when I saw him descending from a giant spider's mouth in a pink suit, I realized that I wanted to be on stage, not because I could get on stage and be who I always wanted to be, but so I could get on stage and be *whoever* I wanted to be.

And yeah, I'm wearing a t-shirt, jeans, and a ball cap. I can't sing. No Spiders from Mars, no giant spider; honestly, I hope there's no spiders up here at all, but inside, in my mind, I'm wearing glittery, silver, high-heeled space boots.

Washing Machine Rodeo

I didn't play football in high school. My mother wouldn't let me because I was just a skinny little kid. I would not have been a good quarterback, or a linesman, but I think I could have been a decent receiver, and I know I could have been a great cornerback. That's the guy that runs down the field with the receiver and tries to prevent him from catching the ball. By my junior year I was finally tall enough to block most guys in high school, I was big enough to grab hold and slow a receiver down long enough for some bigger guy to plow into him, and I was fast. I have always been able to run. To be a cornerback, you have to be able to run fast and swat the ball out of the sky. Run fast and disrupt things. I think I could have been good at that.

"Mom," I would plead, "let me play cornerback. All I gotta do is run down the field and swat the ball out of the sky."

"You'll get hurt."

"I'll hardly ever get hit."

"Those big boys will hurt you."

"I'll mostly be up against receivers. They're tall, but not that big. And they will be trying even harder to not get hit. Their job is to not get hit."

"No."

So, I didn't play football.

One of the benefits of not playing cornerback on the football team was that I didn't have to all the time explain what a cornerback was. "No, not quarterback. Cornerback." Another benefit was that I didn't have to go to football practice all the time. Football players practice a lot. Spring, summer, and fall.

One of the drawbacks to not playing cornerback was that since I didn't have football practice all the time, my parents expected me to get a job.

Skeeter and I wanted jobs, at least that summer. We wanted to save enough money to buy a couple of new scopes for our hunting rifles. The trouble was, there were few jobs to come by.

Hank had new kids working for him at the Chinese restaurant. Then, we made the mistake of mentioning to our fathers that we were, in fact, actively looking for work. The problem with mentioning to your father that you were looking for a job is that fathers invariably know a guy who needs something done, and that something is usually so miserable that only a convict or teenager in need of cash can be cajoled into doing it. In this case, Skeet's dad happened to know a farmer who needed help putting up hay.

Putting up hay is a miserable job. A tractor drives through a field scooping up the loose grass, runs it through a device that turns it into bales, and then drops the bales into the field. Somebody has to walk through the field and pick up the hay bales and toss them to another guy who is riding on a trailer behind a tractor. It sounds innocent enough, but the bales weigh forty or fifty pounds, and you have to do the job in the spring or summer, with the hot sun beating down. The hay is scratchy and dusty, so you have to wear long sleeves, gloves, long pants, and a bandana around your neck so you don't cut yourself to pieces. It is hot, sweaty, itchy work that results in watery eyes, pounds of dust stuck to the back of your throat, and a thousand tiny cuts on your wrists and forearms. Plus, the job gets progressively harder as the hay on the wagon stacks up. As the pile gets higher you have to throw the bales higher and higher as the day gets hotter. The farmer keeps saying things like, "Don't be so dern slow. We gotta get this done. This ain't the only thing we got to do today." I would be thinking, "Yes, it is the only thing I have to do today." All for a couple dollars an hour.

The people who need hay put up are very often farmers. Farmers are people who think that the day begins at, or before dawn, and that a good day is a day when one has completed twelve or more hours honest work. Honest work, to them, is hard work. Hard, sweaty, itchy work that often involves your own blood. Skeet and I were more interested in soft work. Not necessarily dishonest work, but certainly work of questionable moral fiber.

Skeet and I were not keen on putting up hay, so we deferred the offer from Skeet's dad and looked for other things to do. Furthermore, while working for a farmer the previous summer, we had recalibrated the baler so it produced bales the size of a briefcase. They were much easier to toss around. The farmer didn't think it was funny. Farmers weren't enthusiastic about hiring us.

One summer afternoon, we were driving Toad Gilky home. Toad lived way out of town at the very end of a dirt road. The road to the Gilky's house was an old logging road that actively hated travelers. After you crossed the rickety bridge over Skitter creek, there was a flat straight-away of about two hundred yards, then there was a cut-back curve before the road ascended steeply to the Gilky homestead on Pity Me Mountain. On both sides of the road there were deep ditches that were becoming overgrown with weeds and saplings. Toad's dad was looking for someone to clear the ditches but that job was almost as bad as putting up hay. The three of us had been building our summer around not being home, nor at each other's houses, when any of our fathers might deem it the appropriate time for us to throw hay or clear ditches.

Toad and I sat in the cab of the truck with Skeet as he prepared to turn off the paved road and onto the Gilky's road. Just before the turn there was a wide gravel spot where people set up roadside sales in hopes of making a few extra bucks. We saw an old fella with the tailgate down, selling odds and ends. One of the odds was a set of longhorn cow horns mounted for display.

"Those bull horns would look good on the front of your truck," Toad said to Skeet.

"They certainly would," Skeet acknowledged, "but I'm trying to save what money I can to buy a new scope for my rifle."

Skeet made the turn and bounced down the dirt road toward the Gilky's. One of the best things about being seventeen years old is that you are an idiot, and thus, it is perfectly reasonable for you to drive way too fast down a rutted and pitted dirt road in a pickup truck. Skeet hit fifth gear by the time we got to the bridge, and we were bouncing and laughing like mad in the cab as Skeet slid into the turn to make the ascent. The truck was down in first gear and digging hard by the time we got to the dead end where the Gilky's house was.

"Look at that," Toad said as we approached the dead end, "somebody left a washing machine at the end of our road."

Another advantage to being seventeen is that you figure everything on God's green earth is there for your amusement, if you can just cipher out how to use it. The law of the jungle clearly states that if you dump something at the end of a dirt road, that something belongs to the first person who can conjure a use for it.

Skeet pulled to a stop, and the three of us gathered around the washing machine. We studied it for several moments and then Skeet asked, "What could we do with that?"

"Wash clothes?" Toad asked uncertainly, hoping that was the wrong answer.

"I've got a big chain in the back of my truck," Skeet said.

"We're going to have to go back and get those bull horns," I added.

It took a while to configure, but the result was as follows:

We were back down at the bridge. The washing machine was laying on its front side, the chain wrapped around the washing machine and attached to the tow bar on the back of Skeeter's truck. We had mounted the bull horns to the front of the washing machine. We were going to have a washing machine rodeo. A quick game of rock, paper, scissors determined that Skeet would drive for the first round, Toad would ride in the back of the truck as chief observer and timer, and I would take the first ride on the washing machine.

Skeet and Toad got into their respective places, and I straddled the washing machine. This being a rodeo, I was only allowed to hold on with one hand. We had bolted the cow horns to the washer, and then run a loop of rope around them for a handhold.

I waved at Toad, Toad banged on the side of the truck, and Skeet hit the gas. The chain jerked taut, and the washing machine shot off like a bull loosed from the pens.

It was an amazing ride. Every time the machine hit a bump it bounced into the air. It swung back and forth on the end of the chain, and then it slammed back into the ground, which generally caused it to bounce higher, which increased the sway, and the more it swayed and bounced, the less balanced I became, which caused the machine to tilt left or right, which required me to tilt right or left to combat the whole thing from tipping over. But I made it from the bridge to the turn without falling off or touching my other hand to the machine.

"Great," said Skeet. "This time, I'm going to see what happens if I get up to five miles an hour."

After a few more test runs we determined that while the machine did a fine job of bouncing and skidding and swaying and twisting, we could still add one more element to the ride.

"Look," said Skeet, "if we take the back off, we can sit on top of the drum. That will be more like sitting on a bull."

"And," I added, "we could put a generator in the back of your truck and run an extension cord down the chain and actually turn the washer on. We can set it to one of those settings where the drum goes back and forth real fast. That'll add a whole 'nother axis of rotation."

"My dad has a generator," Toad said.

We took a saw and cut the back off the washer but when we plugged it in we discovered it wouldn't run if it wasn't in the upright position. We bypassed that flaw with some simple rerouting of wires only to find out that the darn thing wouldn't agitate if the lid was open. That was fixed by removing that sensor altogether.

The chain was about thirty feet long, and the orange extension cord connecting the washer to the generator snaked along it. Toad sat in the washer, legs around the drum. He gave me the thumbs up, which was my signal to start the generator. Toad had to reach under the console to switch the knob to the agitate stage once the generator started. I thumped the top of the truck cab, and Skeet took off. His goal was to get to at least twenty-five miles an hour before slamming on the brakes.

It is safe to say that we should have strapped the generator down. We had tied and fastened and taped the two ends of the cord in place at the washer connection and at the generator connection so that they would not come unplugged, but we had failed to secure the generator.

Toad and the washing machine bounced about six feet off the ground when we hit the first bump, and the generator bounced about four feet up out of the bed of the truck, which put it about eight feet above the road and thus even with Toad's nose. I grabbed the handle on the generator to stop it from falling out of the truck, but that generator was twenty-five pounds heavier than I was. It pulled me right out of the truck before slamming into the ground. It slid for a few feet, hit a bump, and went airborne. I went with it. The generator bounced its way down the road toward the oncoming washer. The generator hit the bumps a few seconds before the washer did, so Toad and I were not bouncing in sync. I would fly up when he was down and as I came down, he would fly up.

It was clear that very soon the generator was going to smack into the washer, with me and Toad along for the ride.

The generator was still purring away, but smoke and fluids were now emerging from portions of the generator that had not formerly been part of the exhaust system.

My options were to let go of the generator, which was traveling about twenty-five miles an hour, before it hit the washer, or wait to be knocked off by the impact with the washer. This is another good thing about being seventeen. You have options. The world is wide open. I let go and crashed into the dirt road. I watched the generator soar into the air.

Toad saw the generator coming. The washer had entered the spin cycle. Skeeter was trying to hit fifty miles per hour, oblivious to our plight. I was scraping gravel out of my eyes.

I realized that the generator wasn't going to smack the washer. It was going to broadside Toad himself. Toad was going to have smoke and fluids emerging from portions of his anatomy that had not formerly been part of his exhaust system.

Toad managed to dive into the drum of the washer like a rodeo clown avoiding a bull. The generator sideswiped the washer, which sent the washer careening out over the ditch. The chain was pulled tight, and it shredded the weeds and the saplings in the ditch before hitting a rock and bouncing all the way across the road and into the other ditch, slicing through all the flora on that side. Skeet hit the brakes.

I collected myself off the road, and Toad climbed somewhat unsteadily out of the washer. The washer was a mess, completely unrideable.

We got in the truck and dragged the washer back up to Toad's. We unchained it from the truck and did what we figured you would do to a horse or bull that was too lame to live. We shot it. Several times.

We had not heard Toad's dad pull up in his car. He walked up behind us and said, "What have you got there?"

"Dead washing machine."

Mr. Gilky rubbed his chin and said, "That washing machine was your mother's birthday present. I had it delivered up here from the hardware store."

Such a thing had never occurred to us.

Then he said, "Did I see my generator laying by the side of the road back before the turn?"

"Maybe?" Toad answered.

I limped into my house later and Mom asked what I had been doing.

"Playing football."

"See?" she said.

We spent the rest of the summer putting up hay to raise money to buy Mrs. Gilky a new washing machine and Mr. Gilky a new generator. And he didn't even give us credit for clearing the brush from his ditches.

The Nickel

My friend Charolais Fester had a tough life. She was the last child and only daughter of Angus Fester. Charolais was the only girl, and her home wasn't good for a girl. The only other good person in her house was her mother, Helen.

Charolais and Skeeter fell in love in second grade, and they never stopped. It was a serious relationship by the time we were seniors.

The summer before our senior year, Helen, Charolais's mother, had had enough. She packed up a few things and left Angus Fester. Charolais went with her. They moved from Halfdollar, to Sioux Falls, South Dakota. Helen picked Sioux Falls because it was farther than she had ever been, and she figured if Angus ever got it into his head to look for her and Charolais, he'd get bored, too drunk, or simply forget where he was going by the time he got halfway across Ohio. Charolais liked the choice of Sioux Falls because she was a fan of Siouxsie and the Banshees.

Charolais had had enough of the cold after her first winter in South Dakota. Charolais was a worker. She'd had a job at the movie theater, and one at the ice cream store, and she had saved up $300. She told her mom, "I love you, Mom. And I thank you for taking me away, but I have to try the world on my own for now, at least for a while."

Her mom smiled and said, "I ain't got much, honey, but what I have is yours." Mrs. Fester took $100 out of the cookie jar and made Charolais take it.

The next morning, Charolais's mom drove her to the Greyhound station. There was a big board with the names of all the destinations Greyhound served. Mrs. Fester said, "Where you gonna go?" Mrs. Fester hadn't asked yet because she understood that sometimes a destination was secondary to going.

Charolais said, "Somewhere warm."

On the wall was a poster for Myrtle Beach. Lots of West Virginians travel to Myrtle Beach every year. It's a familiar destination, so popular that some in our state have suggested making

Myrtle Beach the capital of West Virginia. But rumor has it that Myrtle Beach is already the capital of Kentucky, so that might be tricky.

Greyhound was running a special. One way to Myrtle Beach, $39.95. Charolais laid two twenties on the counter and walked away with the ticket in her hand.

It was thirty-two hours on the bus through Kansas City, St. Louis, Paducah, Nashville, Cookeville, Knoxville, Ashville, Greenville, and Florence. She got off the bus in Myrtle Beach and walked to the pier.

Charolais had never been to Myrtle Beach, had never set out on her own, but she wasn't scared. After you've lived in West Virginia and South Dakota, there isn't much South Carolina can throw at you that you can't handle.

The air was warm and breezy. She'd never seen the ocean, and it was something to see. She stood there looking at the happy people, and the sand, and the pelicans, and the sunlight on the seagulls and the porpoises, and she smelled the salty air.

Charolais'd packed up some emotional baggage in her life, but the vastness of the sea has a way of pulling hard things free. She knew that somewhere over there was Europe and Africa, and that there was nothing in between her and them except a few sailing ships and cargo vessels.

She took a hotel room for $25 that first night and had $335 left.

She called her mom collect from a payphone. Her mom said, "How you doin'?"

Charolais said she'd be alright.

"Yer all alone," her mother said.

"No, I'm not. I just don't know nobody yet."

Charolais got a job at an amusement park. She walked up to the manager and asked for an application, and the manager smiled and said, "How tall are you?"

Charolais hated that question, but maybe there was a safety issue, so she answered, "Four foot ten."

The manager giggled and said, "I got the perfect job for you."

She led Charolais past the line waiting for the rollercoaster, and they stopped in front of a painting of a mouse that sorta resembled a mouse with which this amusement park had no affiliation. Above the mouse were the words, "You must be taller than this to ride this ride."

"Look, lady," Charolais said to the manager, "I guess you think it's funny, me being short, but I don't need this job enough to get made fun of."

The manager said, "I ain't makin' fun of you. I'm sure you've had your disappointments because you're short. There's things life deals us we can't do nuthin' about, and they can make us bitter, or they can make us sweet. Kids get excited to be in this place. They wait in that line for a long time to ride this ride. Their folks ain't bringin' them to this amusement park 'cause they're flush with money. They scrape together what they can and do their best for their kids. That kid gets up to the front of the line, her folks wantin' her to have a good time. That kid gets all the way up here, then she can't ride the ride 'cause she's shorter than a mouse some insurance company made us paint on the wall? Ruins everybody's day. I wanna see how you deal with that."

Charolais backed up to the mouse and found out that she, a full grown, independent woman, was just tall enough to ride the ride. She took the job.

Charolais had to stand on her tiptoes to see if kids were too short. If a kid was just a little too short, Charolais would say, "Let's try one more thing. We'll stand back-to-back. If you are taller than me, I'll let you ride." Somehow Charolais was always just shorter than the earnest kids and just taller than the brats.

Then, one day she looked up and there was Skeeter and I standing in her line. She smiled, and she and Skeeter hugged and stuff.

The job at the amusement park didn't make ends meet so Charolais worked at a restaurant as well. She waited tables and called Bingo on the pier. She had a shift that night. Skeet and I tagged along.

Bingo isn't a complicated game. But the people playing Bingo were complicated people.

There you are, at Myrtle Beach. Sun, sand, ocean, beaches, bars, fishing, boating, body surfing, live music, carnival rides, arcades, outlet malls…thousands of fun and exciting things to do if you enjoy that version of Hell. And you choose Bingo? What sort of person plans a vacation to their idea of paradise and spends their time playing Bingo?

Skeet and I had a reason to play. Charolais was calling the game. She was Skeet's girlfriend, so the only way for him to spend time with her was to go to the restaurant where she worked and play Bingo while she called. But who else was looking at a Bingo card with their back to the beautiful ocean? I'll tell you who. Grandmas and Grandpas had been parked there by families with other things to do. At twenty-five cents a card, Bingo was the cheapest elder care ever developed. And the sunburned. People so red and blistered they couldn't move enough to do anything but play Bingo. Young parents who were too new to parenting to realize that Bingo wasn't going to be a good game for two or three year old toddlers. And drunks. Most people playing seemed to fall into at least two of the above categories. As far as I could tell, Skeet, myself, and the toddlers were the only sober people playing Bingo on the dock while Charolais called out numbers and letters.

Charolais's job was harder than I'd thought.

"G-46," she called.

"Bingo," said an old man.

"You can't have a bingo yet, sir" Charolais explained. "That's the first number I've called this game."

I thought of Lillian Crimm and her famous one-ball bingos.

"N-37," Charolais said.

"And 37 what?" came a drunk voice.

"What?" Charolais asked back.

"You said, 'And 37.'"

"Oh," Charolais said, "I'm sorry, but I said N-37."

"Yeah," came the voice, "and 37 what?"

"Sir," explained Charolais, "we're playing Bingo. It's a context thing. If I say N and then any numbers including 31-45, look at your card. I'm not saying 'and 37.'"

"And 37 what?" asked the same voice.

"You already called N 37," said several people impatiently.

"Bingo!" called another voice.

"You can't have a bingo," Charolais explained patiently. "I've only called two numbers."

"You said N-37 five times," said the voice. "I stacked five chips on top of each other. Five in a row is a bingo!"

Charolais reached into the basket and drew a new ball. "I-16"

"I-16 goes to Savannah, not Myrtle Beach," someone explained.

"Bingo!"

These weren't people who *could* play Bingo. These were people who merely *thought* they could play Bingo. And they were wrong.

We three went elsewhere to get something to eat when Charolais's Bingo shift was over. The restaurant we went to had a stage with a band playing. A long-haired dude in a bowler cap was playing guitar and singing Jimmy Buffett songs and other covers.

Charolais hushed us. She said, "Oh, I think this guy was playing at the restaurant where I work, a few weeks back. Most nights, there's a band playing covers and mostly, I tune them out. Same cover songs, again and again. But that night I heard a song that started, like:

> She walked into a Greyhound station in Syracuse, New York,
> laid $40 on the counter and set her suitcase on the floor.
> The man said, "Can I help you?"
> And she said, "All I want to know is, I have $40,
> how far south will that much go?"
> He said, "Little lady, it looks like you're in luck
> 'cause you can ride to South Carolina
> for under forty bucks.

"Which was funny," Charolais continued, "'cause that's exactly how I got here. I had forty bucks, and there was a special. At first I hated the song. 'Cause, you know, I hate being called 'little lady.' But that was silly. The song wasn't about me.

"Then I did that thing where you play it back in your head, play back what had drawn your attention to the song in the first place. And it was the woman laying $40 on the counter to go to Myrtle

Beach. I paused waiting tables for a minute and listened to the singer sing..."

The singer interrupted her reminiscence. He said to the crowd: "One night, I dreamt about a young woman walking into a bus station and buying a ticket to someplace south, so I wrote this song…"

"This is the song!" Charolais said. "Don't say nuthin' 'til it's over. She turned her chair and faced the band, her big brown eyes wide and a smile on her face. The singer sang:

She walked into the Greyhound station in Syracuse, New York,
Laid $40 on the counter and set her suitcase on the floor.
The man said, "Can I help you?"
And she said, "All I want to know is I have $40.
How far south will that much go?"
He said, "Little lady, it looks like you're in luck
'cause you can ride to South Carolina
for under forty bucks."

And he pointed to a poster that said, "Special of the Week.
$39.95 one way to Myrtle Beach
So she bought herself a ticket and turned to walk away
And she heard the man behind the ticket counter say,
"Ma'am, you forgot your change. This five cents belongs to you."
And she said, "When you're as broke as I am, what's a nickel gonna do?"
And he said "This nickel ain't worth nothin' for all that it'll buy
But with it you can stand up straight and look folks in the eye.
And you'll never be a loser if you never do lose hope."

The song went on to describe how the tough young lady from Syracuse made it work out, and how she hung onto that nickel through all that life threw her way.

When the song was over, Charolais turned back to me and Skeet and said, "The ticket guy in the South Dakota bus station didn't give me my nickel back. Bastard must have pocketed it. Anyway," she went on, "when I heard the song that first time, it made me smile." Then, she chuckled and said, "And I reached into my pocket to see if I had a nickel. I didn't. But I had a ten-dollar bill that was all mine. I walked toward the table where a very pretty lady was selling CDs to ask her if there was one with that Nickel song on it. There was a cardboard sign that read, 'CDs $9.95' And I laughed. If I bought a CD, I'd get a nickel back. Dumb to spend $9.95 to get a nickel."

"But my manager met me halfway to the merch table and told me to get back to work. I had customers waiting and dinners to be served. So, I didn't buy the CD. Probably for the best. I was, am, broke and need that ten bucks. Just a stupid song," she trailed off. After a short silence she told us she had to go to the bathroom.

Skeet looked at me when she was gone. He tapped the table like he was thinking. Sometimes he did think. And sometimes he thought well. He got up without a word.

Charolais came back to the table, and a CD, wrapped in cellophane, was resting on her paper placemat. Centered on the cover of the CD was a nickel.

I told them I was going to take a walk.

Christmas Artificial Trees

In my family we don't call it, 'Trimming the tree.' We say, 'Crimming the tree.'

There is no authentic Christmas tree. Traditionally, a Christmas tree is some sort of conifer-- Fir, Pine, Hemlock, Juniper, Yew, Cedar, Cypress, Spruce, Sequoia if you've got the room, or PVC. But even that's not true.

The species of tree is just one of the choices you need to make. You also have to choose cut, live, cut your own, and my favorite, "JUST PICK ONE!"

Farmer Daedalus, famous for his Halloween corn mazes, was like many farmers; he had a lot of side hustles. One of his side businesses was a Christmas tree farm located on his farm outside of Halfdollar. It went out of business when he, uh, bought the farm. Died, is what I'm getting at. His family moved away. Nobody tended the farm anymore, but they still owned the land, and the trees were still there.

Skeeter and I sort of knew Farmer Daedalus's youngest son, Icarus, who had moved to Alaska to work the fishing boats. If your name is Icarus, it is only natural that you would move to the Land of the Midnight Sun. Most people called him Chris, but his friends called him Ick. We wrote him a letter asking him if we could sell the trees. He wrote a letter back that said, "Skeet and Bil, Sure. Ick."

We drove out to the farm in October, cleared the dirt road that led to the trees, repainted the sign out by the paved road, and mowed the overgrown grasses between the trees. We put up signs around town stating Daedalus Christmas Tree Farm would be open for business beginning the day after Thanksgiving.

Sheriff Hasbro stopped by the house to ask us if we had permission to sell Daedalus's trees. "Yes, Sir," I said. "We wrote Ick; he was in our Scout Troop when we first started, so we kind of know him. Anyway, we wrote Ick and asked him if we could sell the trees. He wrote back and said 'Sure.'"

"Can I see the letter," Hasbro asked.

"Sure," I said and went to get the letter. Sheriff Hasbro opened it and read it.

"This says," he said, "'Skeet and Bil, Sure. Ick.'"

"Yep."

"It would be better if it said something like, 'I give permission for Skeet and Bil to sell the Christmas trees on the Daedalus farm,'" said Sheriff Hasbro, "but Ick was never very verbose, so I guess it's okay."

It didn't go well the first year. There just weren't that many people who wanted to come out and cut their own trees.

We figured out why about a week after Christmas. A store over in Rainelle had had a big sale on artificial Christmas trees, and they were a hit. Kind of. A lot of people bought them, but a lot of people weren't satisfied with them. A week after Christmas, there were many artificial Christmas trees by the curb.

Skeet, Fern Dale, and I got in Skeet's pick-up truck and picked them all up.

"They're not artificial Christmas trees," I said. "They're actual Christmas trees; they're just artificial trees. So really, they are Christmas artificial trees."

"Do enlighten us," Fern Dale said.

I said, "The only requirement for an authentic Christmas tree is that it be some sort of conifer-- Fir, Pine, Hemlock, Juniper, Yew, Cedar, Cypress, Spruce, Sequoia if you've got the room, or PVC. But even that's not true. Some of the earliest Christmas trees were discs of wood, descending in size and stacked on top of each other, to represent a real tree. The Germans, way back in like the 19th century were worried about deforestation, so they invented the first Christmas artificial trees by gluing goose feathers to sticks and dying the feathers green."

"I guess they weren't too worried about de-goosation," Fern Dale said.

"And then," I continued, "the Aldis Toilet Brush Factory created the kind of Christmas artificial trees we are accustomed to today, around the time of the Second World War. Some smart toilet brush factory worker realized the bristles on a toilet brush looked very much like the needles on a conifer. So, the Aldis Toilet Brush

Factory made the first of what we think of as artificial Christmas trees from exactly the same bristles they made the toilet brushes from, only dyed green.

"You can even trace Christmas artificial trees all the way back to the Wise Men because Christmas artificial trees are made from polymers, or many mers, and we all know the Wise Men brought gold, frankincense, and mer. So, a real tree isn't any more an authentic Christmas tree than a Christmas artificial tree because Christmas artificial trees have been around as long, if not longer than, what you might describe as a Christmas real tree."

"I'm not sure that's the myrrh the Wise Men brought," Fern Dale chuckled.

We collected several dozen Christmas artificial trees in the back of Skeeter's truck and drove them out to the Daedalus farm and put them in a barn. Then we drove to the high school and picked up a roll of football artificial turf that had been peeled off the football field so new football artificial turf could be laid down.

We drove the turf to Daedalus farm and put the turf by the barn.

We wrote Ick Daedalus and asked if it was okay to make a few modifications to the farm so we could sell Christmas artificial trees the next year.

We got a letter back that said, "Dear Skeeter and Bil and Fern Dale, Yes. Ick."

We returned to the Daedalus farm the following spring and unrolled the football artificial turf out by the road.

"What's this for?" Fern Dale asked.

"Christmas artificial trees grow better on artificial turf than on actual turf," Skeeter said.

We took some of the branches and tops of the Christmas artificial trees and stuck them through the turf and into the ground. Fern Dale painted a big sign out by the road that said "Daedalus Christmas Tree Farm. Now Growing Christmas Actual Trees and Christmas Artificial Trees."

Fern Dale added: "The Amazon Forest of Dry County. The Artificial Lungs of the World."

Sheriff Hasbro rolled up and said, "I supposed you have a letter from Ick agreeing to you rolling out Astro turf and selling Christmas artificial trees that says, 'Dear Skeeter and Bil, Sure, Ick?'"

"Actually," Skeet said, "it says, 'Dear Skeeter and Bil and Fern Dale, Yes. Ick.'"

"Good enough for me," Hasbro said.

Every week or so, we would go out to the tree farm and add branches to the Christmas artificial trees we had planted, so that it looked like they were growing. Christmas actual trees take seven years to mature so, while you can watch them grow, it isn't very exciting. Our Christmas artificial trees grew rapidly. It was a hit. People drove by every couple of weeks to see how much the trees had grown. Folks picnicked in the shade of our Christmas artificial tree orchard in the summer. One couple got engaged under one of the trees and then bought that tree. The tree lasted longer than the marriage.

Our orchard made the paper and the TV news. Families began showing up in October to inquire if they could prepurchase specific trees. We offered a sort of Build a Bear deal where you could come out and assemble your own tree. We offered rental packages. You could bring the tree back and replant it after Christmas so you didn't have to store it. We had rent-to-buy options.

By Thanksgiving, we had sold almost every Christmas artificial tree on the lot.

Me and Skeet were out tending the few trees we had left early in December when Lilian Crimm drove up in her Chevy Chevette. Lilian Crimm, who wasn't dead yet, despite what you read in the Church Organ story, was one of those ladies who covered all her furniture in plastic. She had plastic runners on all her carpets. She had a clear plastic sheet draped over the tablecloth on her Formica table. Her raincoat and boots were plastic. She wore a plastic rain bonnet to protect her plastic wig. She was the first person in town to have a credit card. She loved plastic.

"I want one of your Christmas artificial trees," she announced once she had gotten out of her car. "But I want a big one. And I want you boys to assemble it for me."

"Yes ma'am," we said. We carried a few tree segments from the barn and assembled them.

"Taller," Lilian said, "and I want you to put the lights on it."

"We don't offer that service, ma'am. We don't have any lights."

"Well, I need lights," Lilian said and then considered on it for a solid minute. Finally, she said, "I want you to reenforce it. Make it a triple trunk."

"Triple trunk?"

"Lash three trunks together. I have some things to pick up on the way home."

"We'll have to charge you for the triple trunk."

"Price is no matter for the world's most splendid plastic tree."

We lashed three trunks together and assembled, at the behest of Lilian Crimm, a twenty-foot, triple trunk Christmas artificial tree.

"Now," she said, "tie it to the top of my car."

It wasn't easy, but we secured the twenty-foot, triple trunk, Christmas artificial tree to the top of Lilian Crimm's Chevy Chevette and, as per her directions, it stuck out a good ten feet in front of her car.

"Get in," she commanded. "I'll need you boys to carry it into the house. I understand that's not a service you offer, but I'll compensate you for it."

We got in the car. I got in the front, and Skeet got in the back. The seats were covered in plastic. We had to wear our seatbelts sinched tight not so much for safety, but so we didn't slide into the footwells.

Lilian Crimm had grown up poor in the coal camps of West Virginia during the Depression and World War II and thus had consumed less calcium in her entire live than Skeet and I had had by the time we were three. She had once been an average-sized human but was now the sort of old lady, who, when she drove, looked out through the bottom of the steering wheel and could only see things that were twenty degrees above the dashboard. Skeet and I held on for dear life as she drove down Saturday Sunday Road.

Saturday Sunday Road is the one lane road on which Daedalus Farm is located. It's a solid seven miles from the farm to town. It's a perilous road under normal circumstances. It's extremely curvy, with drop-offs on alternating sides. It is very difficult to see if a car is coming toward you. It is even more difficult to see oncoming traffic if the only traffic you can see is the birds in the tops of the trees and airplanes on approach to Dulles. But at least she drove slow.

We rounded one curve, and there was a split-rail fence on the driver's side of the car. Mrs. Crimm was headed straight for it.

"Mrs. Crimm, you're…" I said.

"Hush boy," was all she said.

The tip of her Christmas artificial tree, sticking ten feet in front of the car, snagged the end of the Christmas lights strung along the fence. Lilian Crimm drove straight on until she had a tight hold on the lights, and then she straightened to follow the road. The lights came off the fence and were scooped up by the tree. She got fifty yards of extension cord to boot.

She drove like that all the way home. By the time we got to her house, eight fences, two church nativity scenes, and the gutter of one house built too close to the road had been divested of their lights.

When she was finally parked in her driveway she said, "When you take the tree off the car, spin it around a few times to even out the lights. Then, carry it into the living room, stand it up, and plug it in."

And that's why we call it 'Crimming the tree.'

Book Reports

One spring evening Fern Dale asked me if I wanted to ride over to Beckley to get a burger with her. It was a long way to go for a burger, but I was seventeen, and Fern Dale was beautiful. In the back seat she had a set of walkie-talkies.

I asked her what they were for.

"I've got an idea," she said. Fern Dale was like Skeeter when it came to ideas. You just had to hold on and hope for the best. Except Fern Dale's plans were thought out all the way to the end, including an exit or extraction plan.

We pulled into the Wendy's parking lot, and low and behold, Skeeter's truck was there. Fern Dale pulled in next to the passenger side of his truck, and Charolais stuck her head out to say, "Hey Fernny."

Charolais was in from South Dakota. It was her spring break.

Fern Dale handed Charolais one of the walkie-talkies and told her and Skeeter to go to the Burger King next door and get in the drive-through line. Fern Dale told them that we would get in line at the Wendy's. Fern Dale told Skeet to time it so she and he pulled up to the speakers at the same time.

We watched Skeet and Charolais pull away, and then Fern Dale backed her Volvo out and got into position in the drive-through line. I guess everybody knew what was going on but me.

Fern Dale took the walkie-talkie and held it up to the Wendy's drive-through speaker. Skeet held his walkie out to the Burger King speaker.

Fern Dale was an electronics genius. We had a full recording studio at our high school, audio and visual. A guy from our town had done sound for the Grateful Dead for years and years and then returned home to Halfdollar to retire. Retirement bored him, so he donated a bunch of money to the school to build the recording studio. That act of benevolence credential him to teach. He was a great teacher. He only taught you what you wanted to know. It's a rare skill. Fern Dale wanted to know everything, so she learned recording, splicing, wiring, the works.

She figured out how to make walkie-talkies receive and transmit without depressing and releasing the button.

"They work like phones," she said.

I turned the walkie-talkie over in my hand, examining it. "That'd be crazy," I said, "if we could carry phones around wherever we went. You should invent a Xerox machine hooked up to a telephone so people can send documents over the phone lines."

Skeeter held his walkie-talkie up to the Burger King microphone, and the Wendy's lady heard: "Would you like to try our Whopper Special?"

Wendy's said: "I'm sorry sir, we don't serve Whoppers."

Burger King guy: "Yes, we serve Whoppers."

Wendy's: "No, we don't serve Whoppers. Would you like a Dave's Double?"

Burger King: "Dave's not here. And I don't think he's working a double."

Wendy's: "So, that's one Dave's Double?"

Burger King: "I said Dave's not here!"

Wendy's: "We don't have root beer. And you don't have to scream."

Burger King: "So, ice cream?"

Wendy's: "We just have Frostys."

Burger King: "Look, lady, if you want a Frosty, you gotta go to Wendy's."

Wendy's: "This is Wendy's."

Burger King: "Well, Wendy, Dave's not here, but I'll tell him you stopped by."

We pulled away, laughing, and headed to the Burger Carte.

Our high school English teacher, Mrs. Short, would give us extra credit for doing book reports on books not assigned in class. We had to fill out a one-page form she had mimeographed. You had to list the title, the author, whether the book was fiction or non-fiction, give a brief summary, write a review, and, because the books had to come from our school library, include the Dewey Decimal number on the book.

While I assume her intent was for us to actually read the books we reported on, it was never clearly stated in the instructions that reading the books was mandatory.

I went one step further. Instead of reporting on actual books, I filled out the forms wholly from my own imagination. Because I was making books up, I had to avoid well-known authors, figuring my English teacher would be familiar with the works of famous writers.

I also had to make the books sound boring and maudlin so that my teacher would not be tempted to read them. It would have been a grave mistake to create a book so interesting that she might want to curl up with my fictional work of fiction.

I'd turn in a report something like:

The Sunset Swing Set by Archibald Kinkade, Fiction, Dewey Decimal number Fic Kin. (Our library filed fiction with the alphabetical system rather than by Cutter number.)

Summary: In *The Sunset Swing Set,* Roger Templeton falls in love with Mary Cartwright when they are still in high school. They plan to get married, but WWII breaks out and he is drafted into the Navy. The book explores their lives, hers in the States, his in the Pacific, shifting between points of view. The reader learns what life was like for people in the Navy and for people living at home with limited supplies and rations. They both survive the war and are reunited. They get married and spend their evenings sitting on the swing set watching the sunset and discussing how lucky they are to have survived and to have each other.

Review: While the book was interesting and gave a lot of information about life during the war, it was too much of a love story for my tastes. However, I think if someone was looking for a good romance book, this book wouldn't be good for them either because the book never fully commits to either theme.

I almost always concluded with a statement about why the book wasn't worth reading, no matter what your tastes were. My English teacher thought I had the absolute worst ability to pick decent books. Mrs. Short suggested a few books she thought I might enjoy, but I told her I mostly selected books that hadn't been checked out of the library for years and years because I felt sorry for those books, like they were serving a life sentence in solitary confinement. (In those days, you could look in the back of a library book to see when it was last checked out, and by whom.)

Mrs. Short thought that was sweet.

I turned in dozens of book reports the year I had her as a teacher. I needed the extra credit. Most of those were books I invented on the bus ride to school. Would it have been easier to just read real books? Probably. But in the long run, it was great practice for making things up.

Our school days began like many other peoples. We arrived at the school by bus or by car and went to our first period classrooms. The bell would ring, and shortly after that our principal, a man named Dr. Hundfoos, would begin the morning announcements. Dr. Hundfoos was not an elegant public speaker. He seldom simply spoke the announcements. He read, laboriously, announcements that someone else had written.

Some people get to use a microphone because they have interesting things to say that lots of people want to hear.

Some people ascend to a position where they think it is necessary to use a microphone to re-enforce their importance.

The reason Dr. Hundfoos read the announcements, instead of saying the announcements, is because Dr. Hundfoos rarely had anything interesting to say and seldom had a creative thought.

Dr. Hundfoos could have been a Third World dictator, petty despot, or at least the warden of a corrupt prison if he hadn't had the misfortune of going into public school administration.

He always began the announcements by saying: "This is Dr. Hundfoos, principal of Halfdollar High School," just in case we'd forgotten who he was since his last announcement. He always concluded with: "This has been Dr. Hundfoos, principal of Halfdollar High School," just in case we'd forgotten who he was during his announcements.

One bright day, he came on the loudspeaker and said: "This is Dr. Hundfoos, principal of Halfdollar High School. There has been a terrible accident on the road in front of the school. Nobody look out the windows! This has been Dr. Hundfoos, principal of Halfdollar High School." The entire building shifted in that direction.

Skeeter, Fern Dale, and I were sitting at the lunch table one day when Skeeter said, "I really don't think Dr. Hundfoos ever reads the announcements before he goes on air. It's clear from his stumbling and rereading that he never proofreads or pre-reads anything before he goes on air."

"So?"

"So? So, if we could get into the office, we could slip anything into the announcement basket, and he'd read it to the whole school without knowing he was being duped," Skeet said.

Fern Dale said, "I work in the office most days for my service hours. Skeeter's right; Hundfoos never reads anything over before he goes on air. Type something up, and I'll slip in the basket tomorrow morning. We'll see what happens. Something clean."

We eagerly awaited the announcements the next morning. We heard: "This is Dr. Hundfoos, principal of Halfdollar High School…(there were some basic and sundry announcements and then we heard)… And finally, (rustling of paper) uh, tryouts for the Halfdollar water polo team will be held at the Halfdollar city swimming pool at 4:30 this afternoon. Life jackets will be supplied, but you must bring your own horse. This has been Dr. Hundfoos, principal of Halfdollar High School."

One truly incredible aspect of Dr. Hundfoos's personality was that if he heard himself say something, he believed it. He believed anything he heard himself say. He knew in his heart he wouldn't say anything incorrect, and thus if he said anything at all, it must be true. That trait was a Godsend to us students, who started writing his scripts. Having announced that there would be water polo tryouts, Dr. Hundfoos believed in the water polo tryouts as if he had instituted them himself.

Only one teacher on staff liked Dr. Hundfoos. Mrs. Doberman clearly had a crush on Dr. Hundfoos. Fern Dale overheard Mrs. Doberman trying to convince Dr. Hundfoos that the water polo announcement might be fake.

"So, what do we do about it?" I asked Fern Dale at lunch.

"I'm not sure what to do," Fern Dale said.

"Follow me," Skeet said. We followed him down to the payphone on the wall beside the office. He dropped in a dime and dialed a number. The phone rang in the office. Skeeter was standing in the hall, holding the receiver of the pay phone, looking through the picture window into the office and at the secretary who answered the phone. She said, "Halfdollar High School. How may I direct your call?"

"Hey, Jean," said Skeeter. "This is Tommy, down at the pool." Tommy Cofield managed the pool. "Can I talk to Hundfoos?"

Skeet winked at us. We saw Hundfoos pick up the receiver.

"Principal Hundfoos here, principal of Halfdollar High School."

"Hey Hundfoos, this is Tommy from down at the pool calling you back. What can I do for you?"

"I called you?" Hundfoos asked.

"You just said so."

"So I did," Dr. Hundfoos mused.

"Anyway," Skeeter said, "I have a message on my desk, says, 'Dr. Hundfoos, principal of Halfdollar High School, called to inquire about the water polo tryouts.'"

"Well," said Hundfoos, "then I guess I must have called. Does the note say what I wanted to know?"

Fern Dale and I were laughing. We were standing beside the open door of the office and could thus hear both sides of the conversation.

"The message," Skeet repeated, "says you wanted to know about water polo tryouts."

"Right, right. Then I guess I want to know about the water polo tryouts," Dr. Hundfoos said confidently.

Skeet said, "Well, we're having an issue with the water hydrator down at the pool. Can't get the water wet enough to keep the horses buoyant. If we can't float the horses, the kids can't try out."

"Oh, that's too bad. I made the announcement about the tryouts earlier today. The students will be so disappointed. What should I tell them?"

Skeeter was about to lose it.

Fern Dale put her hand on Skeet's arm and whispered, "I'll take care of it; you hang up before you laugh."

Skeet got a hold of himself and said, "Hey, Hundfoos, we got an emergency down here. I gotta go. The pool's on fire."

"How can the pool be on fire?" asked Hundfoos.

"I told you," Skeet explained, "the hydrator isn't working." And he hung up.

Fern Dale was one of those people who just radiated competence and authority, even at seventeen. No one ever thought she was up to anything because she seemed exactly like the kind of person who was never up to anything, and thus she could get away with almost anything. She walked into the office, went behind the desk, fed a piece of paper into the typewriter, clicked a few keys, pulled the sheet from the roller, and handed it to Dr. Hundfoos. She said, "Mr. Tommy at the pool told me to type this up for you. About the water polo tryouts."

"He did? When?"

"I just got off the phone with him," Fern Dale said.

"But… how? There's a fire at the pool."

"Pools are made of water," Fern Dale said, snapping her gum. She shook the paper in front of Hundfoos.

"But the hydrator isn't working," he said.

"Tommy got it going. Water's wet now. Fire's out. But it's touch and go." Fern Dale shook the paper in front of Hundfoos. "You need to make this announcement."

Dr. Hundfoos took the paper and without pre-reading it, walked to the public address system where he picked up the mic. Shortly, the public address system crackled to life, and we heard, "This is Dr. Hundfoos, principal of Halfdollar High School. We aren't positive the water polo tryouts are happening today. The hydrator at the pool is acting up, and the water may not be wet enough to provide buoyancy for the horses. If you brought your horse to school, you may store it in your locker overnight. This has been Dr. Hundfoos, principal of Halfdollar High School."

We limited our doctored announcements, doling them out judiciously. We tried to limit them to once a week. Everyone looked forward to them. The drama teacher especially. He would marvel after an announcement and say, "Lord, that's good. I wonder who writes his stuff?"

And that was a problem. Once other kids figured out what was going on, they wanted to produce their own announcements. Fern Dale kept a tight watch on the announcement bin in the office.

The teachers figured out what was going on, but petty despots are seldom respected by their troops. The teachers thought it was hilarious.

We often timed the announcements so that we could be in certain classes, or locations, to observe specific people's reactions. Teachers would occasionally say out loud, "I wish he'd make an announcement about…" and if it was good material those suggestions found their way into a script.

The announcements were getting routine after a few weeks. We were going to quit for a while. We'd run out of good ideas. I thought we turned in the last one. But one day, I heard Dr. Hundfoos saying, "Dr. Dewey Decimal, inventor of both the decimal and the Dewey Decimal system, will be visiting our school for an assembly on Friday, thanks to a grant from the Librarian of Congress. All students will go to the gym after lunch on Friday for the assembly. This has been Dr. Hundfoos, principal of Halfdollar High School."

That reminded me of my book reports. I feared Mrs. Short, my English teacher, was on to me. I guess I had slipped up and made a book sound too interesting. She came to me and said she couldn't find it in the library. When I told her someone else must have checked it out, she said the librarian had no record of the book being checked out, so she said she looked in the card catalog and there was no card for the book. I asked her if she looked up the title card, the subject card, or the author card. She said she looked up the author card but didn't think about looking up the others. I suggested maybe the author card was missing. And then I asked her which book she was looking for.

I went to the library as soon as I could. Our card catalog cards were a mix of styles since the catalog had been there for decades. Many of the cards were three-by-five index cards with a hole punched through the bottom. I dug through my backpack and found the book report Mrs. Short had been referring to. I grabbed a couple of index cards off the librarian's desk, went to the typewriter, and painstakingly manufactured subject and title cards for a spurious book called *Flounder and Pete*. It's a book allegedly about (and allegedly a book) a kid nicknamed Flounder whose best friend is a flounder named Pete. Who would want to read that?

Having created the cards, I pulled the proper drawers from the catalog. A card catalog drawer was fifteen inches long, six inches wide, and four inches high. The cards were placed in the drawer alphabetically from front to back. Each card had a hole punched in its bottom middle through which ran a metal rod that kept the cards from falling out if the drawer tipped.

To remove that rod, you unscrewed it and pulled it out. It was 16 inches long. Pulling it out was easy. It's like taking a curtain off the rod. But once you'd removed that rod you left open the possibility of two hundred index cards spilling free.

I was in a hurry. Fearing my English teacher may at any moment enter the library, I took the subject drawer for the proper alphabetic section and unscrewed the rod. Not realizing that I only had to pull the rod out far enough to insert my card in the line-up, I jerked the rod completely free of the drawer, like a mad mechanic pulling a dipstick for nefarious purposes.

Two hundred heretofore alphabetized subject cards sprung free. I was like the flower girl at a librarian's theme wedding.

I had to skip my next two classes while I reorganized the cards so that I could finally slip a handcrafted card on the subject of *Fish Friends* between the cards concerning *Fish Environments* and *Fish Gills*.

I tore the bottom of the title card and jammed it into place, instead of fooling with the rod, which is what I should have done with the other.

I made it to English class as the bell rang. Mrs. Short opened the class by saying, "I have a suspicion that some of you have been taking advantage of my extra credit assignment. I think some of you are making up books, rather than reading actual books. For example," she held up a book report form. "There is no book called *Fahrenheit 452: A Hot Sequel*."

That wasn't one of my books. Were others making up books, too? Making up books was MY idea. That's theft of my intellectual property! I didn't say a word, though.

Mrs. Short picked up a thick file folder. "In this folder, I have copies of each book report you students have turned in. After the assembly Friday, with the mysterious Dr. Dewey Decimal, I'll be sequestering myself in the library discovering which, if any, of these books actually exist. I'll stay all weekend if I have to."

All of this took place on Wednesday. The assembly was Friday. I had two nights.

A mild panic swept through the classroom.

Kids were discussing what they were going to do as we left class.

Some kids debated stealing all the books in the library or moving all the books to different shelves to sew confusion, or burning the school down… but I didn't think anyone would actually go that far. Besides, those plans, except for arson, didn't solve the problem of the card catalog. Missing books was one thing. The card catalog cards were the key to the deception. I needed proof that the books had existed, even if they were missing now. Who would go through all the trouble of making three card catalog cards for every fake book they'd ever never read?

I went through my backpack and locker and found every book report that I could. I spent that night in my bedroom typing up subject, author, and title cards for books called insipid things like *The Divine Bovine, The Teacher in the Patriotic Bathing Suit, Egg Babies, Mayhem Dressed as an Eight Point Buck, Punching the*

Lard, Christmas Artificial Trees, and *The Ojai Mountain Lion*. Who would want to read drivel like that?

But I couldn't just make the cards. I had to weather them, bend them, mark them up, smear them, and otherwise make it look like they weren't all created on the same day.

"What's in the oven?" my mother asked.

"Oh, I'm browning some card catalog cards."

She didn't bat an eye. Last of five children. She'd learned not to ask.

I went to school as usual on Thursday.

Thursday night I snuck out of my house and rode my bike to the school. I went around back to the library. My plan was to stash my bike behind the dumpster. To my surprise, Skeeter's bike was already there. I looked closely at the library windows and could make out a flashlight bobbing around inside.

I slid open a window I'd left unlocked earlier and quietly called Skeet's name.

"You, too?" he whispered back.

"Naturally. It was my idea, after all. You're not stealing books or reshelving are you? Or starting a fire?"

"It wasn't your idea to fake books. It was mine. And I'm not reshelving. Librarians don't like you to reshelve. There are signs all over the place about it. And only fascists burn books."

Fern Dale stepped up beside me at the window and I jumped about a foot when she poked my shoulder.

"Good," she said. "There's three of us. One for author, one for subject, one for title cards." Fern Dale and I climbed through the window. I said to Fern Dale, "I'm surprised you made up bogus book reports."

"I didn't. But I figured you morons had. And I figured you'd be breaking into the library to insert fake cards in the card catalog."

"You didn't think we'd burn the school down?"

"You're morons, but not stupid."

"So why are you here?"

Fern Dale pulled a Ziploc bag of homemade card catalog cards from her pocket. "I bet you guys made phony cards for all the books you made up, right?"

"Yep," I said proudly, shaking my own baggie of bogus cards.

"Well," Fern Dale said, "if the only books missing, or the majority of books missing, from the whole library are the books people did fake reports on, but only the books you two cite have card catalog cards, that'll look suspicious. So, I made up extra counterfeit cards so more books than yours come up present in the catalog but absent on the shelves."

"Genius," I said. And kinda sweet.

She winked at me.

The three of us set to work filling the card catalog with apocryphal cards, feverishly pulling rods, and placing ringers to pollute the catalog and confuse the system.

Nice? No.

Necessary? Yes.

"Better than burning down the library," Skeet said.

"I think I know how you got caught," said Fern Dale, looking at some of Skeeter's homemade cards. "*Fahrenheit 452: A Hot Sequel*? That was you, huh? *1985*? *The Greater Gatsby*? *Revenge of the Mocking Bird*? *The Crepes of Wrath*? *Moby*... oh, I'm not even finishing that."

Skeet chuckled. "I was running out of ideas."

"Did you ever consider just reading a real book?" Fern Dale asked.

We finished with just enough time to bike home, sneak into our houses, eat breakfast, and get back to school.

The day passed uneventfully. After lunch the whole school went into the gym, which was set up with a podium and patriotic bunting for the visit of the esteemed Dr. Dewey Decimal. Dr. Hundfoos gave a few brief remarks, and then we all waited. And waited. And waited.

Dr. Dewey Decimal never did show up. He never sent word. We sat restlessly in the hot gym waiting for the man who had invented the library shelving system and the decimal, to appear.

An hour and a half we waited.

Finally, Dr. Hundfoos dismissed us. He couldn't believe Dr. Dewey Decimal hadn't shown up. It seemed to Dr. Hundfoos that the inventor of the decimal would be more precise and organized, that he wouldn't abandon a gym full of kids and teachers. Dr. Hundfoos himself had said that Dr. Decimal was coming. And Dr. Hundfoos believed every word out of his own mouth.

Mrs. Short spent the rest of the afternoon, and most of Saturday, in the library. Unfortunately for us, and her, Alicia Snitch volunteered to help her.

We found out Monday that Alicia and Mrs. Short had combed through the entire card catalog and double checked the shelves for every volume chronicled therein. Sure enough, there were a bunch of cards for books that weren't on the shelves, or otherwise accounted for. Many of those books bore the titles of books we had done reports on. There were also many books on which reports had been done that had no evidence of ever having existed. Nary a card to be found.

The kids who had no proof were definitely in trouble, but Skeet and I at least had some cover.

Mrs. Short had not planned on telling Dr. Hundfoos. Mrs. short was the sort of teacher who dished out her own punishments. Hundfoos would have given us detention or something we could endure and then forget. Mrs. Short liked to tell us she was disappointed in us, which stung a lot more, and hung with you forever.

Alicia, however, decided it was her duty as God's own handmaiden to inform Dr. Hundfoos that a bunch of books were missing from the library.

Having anticipated something like this, Fern Dale had a ready-made announcement she'd already dropped into the bin.

"This is Dr. Hundfoos, principal of Halfdollar High School. I have some upsetting news. It would seem that while we were waiting for Dr. Dewey Decimal, Dr. Dewey Decimal pulled a fast one. He slipped into our library and stole several dozen books from the shelves while we were in the gym. It is a sad crime to rob a high school of books, but Dr. Dewey Decimal does not appear to be as upstanding a citizen as he would seem. I have already called Sheriff Hasbro to discuss this matter. This has been Dr. Hundfoos, principal of Halfdollar High School."

Skeet and I found reasons to join Fern Dale in the office.

When Dr. Hundfoos put the mic down and turned around, he bumped into Sheriff Hasbro's belly.

"You call for me?" Hasbro asked.

"Did I?" Hundfoos said, confused.

"You just said you did."

"So I did. I guess I must have then."

"What's this about Dr. Dewey Decimal stealing books from your library?" Hasbro asked.

"Well, he, uh, got us all in the gym on Friday, and then he robbed the library."

"Melvil Dewey robbed your library?" The Sheriff was smiling.

"No. Dr. Dewey Decimal robbed our library." Dr. Hundfoos was frothing.

"Melvil Dewey died in 1931."

"I don't care about any Melvil Dewey!" Hundfoos sputtered. "What I care about is that Dr. Dewey Decimal robbed our library."

"You sure?"

"I just said it, didn't I?"

"How do you know the books were stolen?"

"Because they're gone."

"And the librarian has no record of them being checked out?"

"Correct."

"So, aside from the fact that the books aren't present, how do you know they're stolen?"

"Mrs. Short began to suspect some of her students were making up books to do book reports on," Dr. Hundfoos explained.

Hasbro glanced at us, raised an eyebrow.

"As part of the assignment," Dr. Hundfoos continued, "the students had to write down the Dewey Decimal code of the books they did reports on. Mrs. Short and Alicia Snitch inventoried the entire library. Alicia reported to me."

"Figures," Hasbro said softly. Then more audibly, "But did you ever wonder why Dr. Dewey Decimal would come all the way to Halfdollar to steal books?"

"Maybe," Hundfoos tried, "they were rare books."

"Oh," I whispered, "they were rare all right."

Sheriff Hasbro gave Dr. Hundfoos a long look, then turned to look at me, Fern Dale, and Skeet. He made a face of mild disgust at us for having interrupted his day, I suspect. He came our way. He put a cigarette between his lips, half smiled, turned to Hundfoos, and said, "I'll look into it. See if I can't figure out who's behind all of this." Hasbro turned to face us but continued addressing Dr. Hundfoos, "My guess is that someone has gone to a lot of work to get out of a little work. All we have to do is figure out who would go to all that trouble."

Hasbro did nothing about it. Adding bogus cards to the card catalog was not listed as a crime anywhere in the law volumes of Dry County. Not until then, anyway.

Mrs. Short failed almost everybody who did fake book reports, but she admired mine and Skeet's efforts, so he and I got Cs. "For creative writing and effort, not reading," she explained. She almost hit us when we asked if there was anything we could do for extra credit. We were not given any credit for having to comb through the card catalog and pull out all the bogus cards.

Fern Dale got an A, all on her own.

Skeet, Fern Dale, and I were in the lunchroom several days later. Dr. Hundfoos was there as well. The PA system crackled to life.

"This is Dr. Hundfoos, principal of Halfdollar High School...." It was clearly Hundfoos's voice.

Everybody turned to look at Dr. Hundfoos. He was staring at the loudspeaker. Utterly bewildered. He touched his chest and face as if reassuring himself he was standing in the cafeteria and not in the office making an announcement.

"Fern Dale," Skeet marveled. "You're a genius. You recorded everything he ever said, didn't you? Spliced what you wanted, and now you're somehow playing it back, remotely?"

Fern Dale shushed us.

"This is Dr. Hundfoos, principal of Halfdollar High School. There's been a terrible accident. I'm being rushed to the hospital. Please keep me in your prayers. This has been Dr. Hundfoos, principal of Halfdollar High School."

We watched Hundfoos slump into a chair, still checking himself.

"Gotta be hard for a guy who believes everything he hears himself say to hear himself say he's on the way to the hospital," Skeet said, shaking his head.

Fern Dale walked over and knelt in front of Dr. Hundfoos. "Principal?" she asked. "Are you okay?"

"I don't know. I feel okay, but you just heard me say I've been in an accident. I might be on the way to the hospital."

"Well," Fern Dale suggested, "maybe you ought to get in your car and drive up to the hospital to see how you're doing."

And he did.

Bored Gourd

Skeeter grew a giant pumpkin in 1988. It weighed 480 pounds and won all the prizes at the county and state fairs.

His girlfriend, Charolais, had moved to South Dakota the year before, and Skeeter was a mess. They were still a couple, but they were half a country apart. He wrote her a letter in the fall of 1987 and said, "I don't know what to do without you." A week later he got a letter back from her. It contained a package of giant pumpkin seeds. Her note said, "Do something constructive. Grow a giant pumpkin. Gargantuan fruits are a balm for the brokenhearted."

Skeet smiled. He went to the library and read up, in real books, on growing giant produce. Turns out you need fertilizer rich in potassium, phosphates, and nitrogen. A lot of fertilizer, to grow a giant pumpkin.

Skeet showed up at my house with shovels and burlap bags in the middle of the night. He handed me a shovel and said, "Come on." I didn't ask questions. No use ruining the surprise. We broke into the Halfdollar Baptist church.

"What are we doing here?" I asked.

"Stealing bat guano," he said, crossing himself as we walked by the altar.

"Why?" I asked. Nodding a quick prayer at the cross. Well, more of a 'What's up?'

"Bat guano is rich in potassium, phosphates, and nitrogen," he said.

I took a breath. "Why?"

"I'm growing a giant pumpkin. They need fertilizer. Lots of it. Charolais said I needed to do something constructive."

"When she said 'constructive' do you think she meant breaking into the Baptist church to steal guano?" I asked.

He shrugged. "She knows I think outside the box."

I tried again: "Why are we *breaking* into the church at all? Don't you think the pastor would be absolutely happy to let us into the church to shovel guano out of his attic?"

"Maybe," Skeet acknowledged, "but that ain't our style. Besides, he's probably still mad about the whole baptismal thing and us punching a hole in the ceiling of his sanctuary."

"I'm sure he's forgiven us for that by now. That was ten years ago."

"That pastor ain't really the forgivin' type."

"You could tell him you're being constructive."

"He wouldn't buy it."

"Well," I acquiesced as we ascended the stairs, "I guess if we're gonna take crap from the Baptists, we ain't gonna ask for it."

"That's the spirit," Skeet said.

So, we did. We took several hundred pounds of fertilizer. We carried the bat guano, bag by bag, through the late-night streets of Halfdollar and dumped it in a huge hole Skeeter had dug in his backyard. Then we covered it with dirt.

"Now what?" I asked.

"We wait until spring," he said, staring at the plot.

"Do we wait here?" I asked, leaning on my shovel, "Or can we wait inside?"

"Inside would probably be okay."

"You feeling better about Charolais going away? Now that you're being constructive?"

"Absolutely."

Whereas growing giant pumpkins is indeed a balm for the broken hearted, waiting for buried bat guano to fertilize the dirt beneath the empty giant pumpkin patch over the long winter months does little to soothe the soul. Skeeter sulked until late March. He'd gone as far as Charleston to visit the big library there to learn about growing giant pumpkins. He knew to file the seeds to make it easier for the leaves to emerge, to soak the seeds in warm water to make them softer, he knew it took seven to ten days for the seeds to germinate, and he knew it could take 150 days for the pumpkins to mature. In mid-April, four days before the projected last frost, Skeeter planted his pumpkin seeds straight into the ground.

We waited and watched. The first leaves emerged, and the vines grew, and the flowers bloomed, and fruit began to form and grow.

All the while, Skeet watered the ground and fed the plants and fended off the bugs.

You're supposed to pick the pumpkin you think has the best chance and pluck the others from the vine so the vine can concentrate all its energy on just one pumpkin. But Skeet couldn't do it. Charolais had had a tough life and was the most compassionate person we knew. Some people in town wrote her off because her father and brothers were such miserable people, which is why she and her mom had moved. Charolais hated it when potential went ignored or neglected. She gave every good thing a chance. Skeet said, "Charolais would say, 'You got no idea which of these pumpkins is going to be the best. You let 'em all have their chance.'" So, Skeet let them all grow.

Grow they did. One particular pumpkin outdid all its kin. It was as big as a volleyball in no time at all, and Skeeter gently lifted it off the ground and placed a padded palette beneath it so that once the pumpkin matured, it could be more easily moved. "Gotta think ahead," he said. Soon, it was as big as a beach ball and then as big as the Blob.

Skeet put a lawn chair beneath a beach umbrella out in his pumpkin patch, and he sat and sipped lemonade all day long while he watched his pumpkin grow.

Skeeter's yard was bordered by one of Angus Fester's cow pastures. Angus was Charolais's father and our sworn enemy since childhood. A bull, almost as mean as Angus himself, lived in the pasture. That bull stood in the field and watched the pumpkin grow as well. It's difficult to know exactly what goes on in the head of a bull, but that bull did not seem to like that pumpkin. He eyed that pumpkin day and night. He would slowly draw closer, sniffing and drooling, and turning his head so one big bull eye could gander at the orange mass growing in the grass. Then the bull would startle and run off, only to creep forward again.

"What," you may ask, "was Skeeter doing in the pumpkin patch beneath his umbrella?"

It's difficult to know exactly what goes on in the head of Skeeter. He was watching his pumpkin grow. Giant pumpkins can grow as much as forty pounds a day. You can actually watch them grow.

Fern Dale came over one day and asked Skeet, "How's it going?"

Skeet said, "I think my pumpkin is bored."

"I think you may be projecting your feelings on the pumpkin," Fern Dale said.

"Oh, I'm not bored," Skeet said. "I'm watching my pumpkin grow. It's fascinating."

"If it is fascinating to watch the pumpkin grow, don't you think the pumpkin would be fascinated with its own growing?" Fern Dale asked.

"I'm not sure the pumpkin has the capacity for fascination," Skeet replied.

"So, it can be bored, but not fascinated?" Fern Dale asked.

"Like a baby," Skeet argued. "People are fascinated watching a baby grow, but do you think the baby knows it's growing?"

We all thought on that for a bit. And then Fern Dale said, "So you have a bored gourd?"

From then on, the giant pumpkin was called the Bored Gourd.

The bull in the field was growing more and more agitated by the giant thing growing on the other side of the barbed wire fence. Maybe he could see the pumpkin growing. Maybe he could hear it. Maybe it squeaked as it stretched and grew, giving off a high-pitched howl that drove cattle mad. A bull whistle.

The Bored Gourd got so big it started to list, to tilt, and was in danger of toppling off its padded pallet. Skeeter pondered this, walking around the pumpkin, studying it, wondering how to prop it up. He said, "When you grow giant tomatoes it's a common practice to sling them up in a bra to support them."

"I doubt they make a bra big enough for this," I said.

Skeet agreed.

Skeet and his dad figured out a way to brace the Bored Gourd with a series of treated two by twelves and a hammock. The hammock supported the gourd but didn't inhibit its growth. The

Bored Gourd swung lazily back and forth in its hammock while amassing weight.

The bull was not pleased with these developments. He snorted and stamped his hoof.

"I'm worried about that bull," Skeet said from beneath his umbrella. "There's only that barbed wire fence separating him from the Bored Gourd."

"That bull probably hates the pumpkin 'cause it's us growing it," I said. "Every Fester 'cept for Mrs. and Charolais hate everything about us. Probably extends to Angus's bovines as well."

Word got around about the Bored Gourd. A reporter dropped by. He wrote an agricultural column for the local weekly paper, *The Halfdollar Two Bits*.

When the reporter asked, "Son, why are you growing a giant pumpkin?"

Skeeter considered for a minute and said, "Well, my girlfriend moved to South Dakota, so, you know..."

The reporter didn't know. Not everybody combats grief and heartbreak by growing giant produce. The reporter changed tack and asked, "How'd you do it?"

Skeeter took a breath and said, "There are those who say it starts with the seed. And then there are those who say it starts with the manure. I'm a manure man myself. You need to lay a bed of fertilizer rich in phosphates, potassium, and nitrogen. Bat guano works real good."

The reporter asked how to spell 'guano.' "Is that your secret ingredient? Aren't you reluctant to give that information away?"

"Naw," Skeet said, "growing a giant pumpkin does my heart good. I hope everybody does it. But I'm going out to be with my girl in South Dakota soon, and I doubt she'll want much to do with guano."

The reporter wrote an agricultural column. He didn't want a love story. Didn't know what to do with it. He went back to something he knew he could use. "How much guano did you use?"

"Couple, several hundred pounds."

"Where'd you'd get hundreds of pounds of bat guano?" asked the reporter.

Skeet closed his eyes, put his tented hands in front of his face, and said, "I went to the Lord."

One day, Skeet, myself, and Fern Dale were out in the pumpkin patch watching the Bored Gourd swing in its hammock in a gentle late autumn breeze when Angus Fester's bull snapped. He just couldn't tolerate the Bored Gourd anymore, swinging as it was in a hammock. The bull grunted, which drew our attention, and then charged. Before Skeeter or I could stand up, the enraged bovine tore through the barbed wire fence and lowered his horns toward the Bored Gourd. Fern Dale reacted much quicker than we had. Fern Dale picked up a six-foot length of two by twelve and held it horizontally between the bull and the Bored Gourd, bracing one end on a tree. She held steady, a matadoras risking her life to save the Bored Gourd, armed with a board instead of a sword. The bull hit the board full force, his horns piercing the treated lumber. That stopped the bull. He looked at the three of us; Skeet and I had finally managed to get out of our chairs. The stunned bull eyed us each, then turned and walked back to his pasture swinging his head trying to shake free the six-foot-two by twelve stuck on his horns. We quickly repaired the fence as best as possible.

"That was close," Skeet said. "I don't know why that stupid bovine hates the Bored Gourd."

Angus Fester showed up a little later in his truck, enraged, and holding a six-foot-two by twelve with two holes blasted through it. Sheriff Hasbro pulled up soon after.

Fester said, "Sheriff, thanks for coming. These kids hit my prize bull with a two by twelve! This here board was stuck to his horns."

Sheriff Hasbro hated Angus Fester for myriad reasons. But he was an honest sheriff and asked us, "Did you hit the bull with a two by twelve?"

"No, Sir," said Fern Dale, "the bull hit the two by twelve. I doubt I could swing a two by twelve hard enough to pierce it on a bull's horns, but I guarantee a bull could hit a two by twelve hard enough to pierce it. That bull burst through the fence over there to attack

Skeeter's pumpkin, so I held up the wood, and the bull ran into the board."

"Why did the bull charge the gourd?" Hasbro asked.

"Who knows the ins and out of bovid contemplation?" Fern Dale asked. She added, "We call the pumpkin the Bored Gourd."

"So," Sheriff Hasbro said, "let me get this straight: The bull broke through the barbed wire fence to gore the Bored Gourd, but you held up a big board and instead of goring the Bored Gourd, the bull gored the board?"

"Couldn't have said it better myself," Fern Dale said.

Hasbro turned to Fester and said, "Seems pretty simple to me, Fester. Shore up that fence and see to it your bull doesn't harm the Bored Gourd. Skeeter's finally doing something constructive."

A few weeks later we loaded the Bored Gourd on a flatbed truck Mr. Barth rented and drove the pumpkin to the county and state fairs, where it won all the prizes a giant pumpkin could win. The 4-H kids and the FFA kids griped about a boy from the big city of Halfdollar winning all the prizes.

And then we did what you do with a giant pumpkin. The Viking funeral equivalent for giant produce is launch it from a catapult. The pastor of the Halfdollar Baptist church was not a man with a sense of humor, nor a man who took delight in trivial things, but he did love to launch pumpkins. Every year, he hosted a Pumpkin Chuckin' festival at his little church.

The congregation of the Halfdollar Baptist church had decided they needed to tear the church building down because the decades-long bat infestation in the attic had done irreparable damage. They were going to rebuild in a different spot.

The church had a tall and sturdy steeple. Because the church was coming down anyway, the pastor built a trebuchet on the steeple.

A trebuchet is similar to a catapult except that a catapult gets its power by pulling back the beam with, to put it simply, a big rubber band. The potential energy in the rubber band converts to kinetic energy when you release the rubber band, which flings the beam, and anything on it, forward. A trebuchet works by putting a beam, in this case a telephone pole, on a pivot. On the one end of the pivot is a sling into which you put the projectile you want to hurl. The sling gives you extra power. On the other end of the pole is a counterweight. You lift the counterweight as far above the projectile as possible. When you let the weight loose, gravity pulls the weight down, and the other end lifts, launching your projectile. The heavier the counterweight, and the higher you lift it, the more force you generate at the other end.

The Baptist pastor built a powerful trebuchet on the steeple and launched produce into the hillside by the church.

He raised the counterweight, and we rolled the Bored Gourd into the sling. "Son," he said to Skeeter, "I'm glad you finally quit foolin' around and did something constructive with your time."

He dropped the counterweight.

The whole town was there. I was standing beside Fern Dale. Charolais had come to visit and see the Bored Gourd she had inspired. She and Skeet held hands.

The counterweight dropped and the Bored Gourd lifted into the air.

The Bored Gourd was many things: a giant pumpkin, a thorn in the side of an angry bull, a balm for the brokenhearted. It was all those things. But it was not flight worthy. It went up, a little, and then it came down, and, as if returning to that which had given it life, the Bored Gourd crashed through the roof of the Halfdollar Baptist church. We heard it crash through the ceiling and into the sanctuary where it landed as a pile of smashed pumpkin pieces amongst the bat guano that had nurtured it.

Dust, debris, pumpkin parts, and bat guano flew from the roof and fell on the crowd.

The four walls of the church collapsed, one by one.

The crowd was silent but obviously suppressing laughter.

The Baptist pastor turned to look at me, and then at Skeeter. And he mumbled, "Boys, boys, boys…" He looked at the dust and filth on his sleeves and said, "Tainted and stained. Stained and tainted…."

Skeeter turned to the crowd and addressed them solemnly, saying, "Unto God we commend the soul of our departed pumpkin, and therefore commit this gourd to the guano. Earth to Earth, ashes to ashes, dust to dust in the sure and certain hope of resurrection and eternal life…"

The crowd cheered in a manner not often heard at a funeral.

Skeeter, Fern Dale, and I had graduated from high school earlier that year. He moved to South Dakota to go to college with Charolais. I went to my college. Fern Dale went to her college.

When we came home for summer break the next year me and Skeet and Charolais and Fern Dale drove by the former sight of the church. The building was gone. But in the field where the church once stood were a hundred or more bat boxes. And beneath the bat boxes were hundreds of girthful vines growing giant pumpkins.

Skeeter smiled and saluted the Bored Gourd's mighty brood.

Silent Letters

Small town parades are tricky affairs. There's only one high school, so there's only one marching band. The Boy Scouts, Girl Scouts, 4-Hers, and FFA kids are all invited to make floats, but most of the Scouts, 4-Hers, and FFA kids are in the marching band, so they march in the band in their Scout uniforms, 4-H shirts and FFA jackets, with their prize calves, goats, and chickens tethered to the drum corps.

In front of the band is the VFW Honor Guard, and behind the band is the United Methodist Men, the Baptist Men's Coalition, who also comprise the Lions, Kiwanis, and Rotary clubs; then there is the county's only hearse, three old John Deere tractors (not antique, just old), Olen Gwinn's vintage Model T, Handy's ambulance, and the one fire truck pulling a wagon with Sheriff Hasbro dressed as Santa.

All the other adults are either Scout leaders, FFA leaders, 4-H leaders, or at the churches preparing the after-parade meal. Thus, there is no one to actually watch the parade.

The entire town turns out to march down Main Street in front of no one, play songs for no one, wave at no one, and throw candy to no one.

Since everyone is at the parade, there is no chance the fire truck will get called to an emergency because if anyone's house does catch fire, they won't know until they get home, and then it won't really be an emergency anymore.

It ain't exactly Macy's Thanksgiving Day Parade.

If you held the parade on election day you'd have 100% voter turnout- but only once because everybody'd vote to never have the parade again. But small towns aren't democracies. They are usually puppet patriarchies fronting for not-so-secret matriarchies.

Mrs. Crankberry was the single meanest woman I ever met. She was the Chairwoman down at the church for the Committee of Little Old Ladies Who Want to be Angry About Something.

In 1966 or 67, Mrs. Crankberry visited her sister who had long ago married and moved to Porterdale, Georgia. It was Christmas time, and in that town folks had made big plywood Christmas decorations- trees, stars, manger scenes, snowmen- and hung them from power poles and lamp posts. Mrs. Crankberry thought it was lovely and took photos so that when she got back to Halfdollar she could have someone make similar decorations. Which she did. And then she convinced the Town Council to hang the decorations down Main Street. She decided the ornaments were so precious that a parade should be organized to celebrate the decorations. And also to celebrate Christmas, of course.

Ben Smathers was born dirt poor in 1898. He lied about his age and joined the US Army so long ago that he served as one of the last drummer boys in the US military before fighting in the trenches of WWI. When that war ended, he and a fifer got another guy to carry a flag, and they marched in the victory parade through Paris dressed as the famous Colonial trio.

After the war, he went to New Orleans and became a drummer in the burgeoning jazz scene and then toured with the big names and big bands all over the world until the Japanese bombed Pearl Harbor. Ben Smathers lied about his age again, this time in the other direction, so he could rejoin the US Army infantry. When that war was over, he got a fifer and a flag bearer and marched in the Paris victory parade.

After that war he went back to jazz, eventually retiring to the family farm in Halfdollar.

Ben had served as an enlisted man in the War to End all Wars, and the one after that. He knew an officious busy body when he met one. He always addressed Mrs. Crankberry as the Lieutenant Colonel in honor of all the stalled out, miserable, SOB officers- his words- he had had the misfortune to serve under.

She hated him right back.

And when but at Christmas do hatred and grudges most rear their ugly
heads?

In those days Halfdollar's population was much larger because the coal and timber industries were still thriving, thus there were plenty of people to both watch and participate in the parade. So many people wanted in, you had to submit an application and be juried. Naturally, the jury was Mrs. Crankberry.

Ben Smathers's favorite Christmas song was *Little Drummer Boy*.

Mrs. Crankberry's least favorite Christmas song was *We Three Kings*, but *Little Drummer Boy* was a close second.

She rejected Ben Smathers's request to play *Little Drummer Boy* in the parade.

Ben Smathers fought at Belleau Woods, then in North Africa, Italy, stormed the beaches on D-Day, and fought through the Battle of the Bulge. He played drums in two victory parades in Paris after two world wars. He had eight campaign medals from two world wars, three Purple Hearts, a Silver Star with Oak Clusters, and various and sundry medals from foreign powers for thanks and valor. He wasn't nearly as easy to beat as his drum. He'd survived far worse than Lt. Colonel Crankberry.

The whole town turned out to either watch or march in the parade. Those watching saw Mrs. Crankberry come around the corner of Main Street as the parade began. Some anonymous person had donated a banner to be carried at the front of the parade. It read, 'The Mrs. Frank R. Crankberry Christmas Parade. In Honor of Her Life.' She acknowledged that the banner was so lovely that it should be carried in front of her, at the very front of the parade.

She was followed by the marching band, the majorettes, the goats and calves and lambs, the Methodist and Baptist men, the hearse, three John Deere tractors, a Model T, the fire truck, and Sheriff Hasbro dressed as Santa.

There are only three viable parading blocks in Halfdollar. Mrs. Crankberry almost immediately stepped out of the parade so she could stand beneath one of her newly minted plywood decorations hanging from a power pole and watch the parade go by. Hands clasped to her chest, tears in her eyes, she watched with deep pleasure until after Sheriff Hasbro rounded the corner dressed as Santa. She bowed her head as if in prayer.

And then we heard it. *Ba rum pa pa pum.*

The band had stopped playing as soon as they had crossed the finish line of the parade. They were stripping their uniforms and tending their goats and calves and lambs. Their drums lay stacked silently behind the school bus.

And yet there was no mistaking the sound of the snare.

Around the corner came Ben Smathers, dressed in his Dough Boy uniform, eyes front, marching, and keeping time with *Little Drummer Boy*.

Mrs. Crankberry frowned.

She stepped into the street, fists at her sides, and strode toward Ben Smathers, who kept his eyes forward. He marched and drummed on, pounding out the song.

She stepped into his path.

He did a left face, a right face, a right face, a left face, around her and continued his march.

Sheriff Hasbro sauntered over in his Santa suit. Mrs. Crankberry said, "Sheriff Hasbro, I'm in charge of this parade, and that man has no right to be marching in it. I demand you stop him."

"Ma'am," Santa Hasbro said, "you were in charge of the previous parade. He's not marching in your parade."

"Then he needs to be arrested for parading without a permit."

"But he's not."

"What do you mean?"

"Ben came into my office and applied for his own parade permit when you rejected him from your parade. Scheduled to start fifteen seconds after the last float in your parade rolled out of the staging area," explained Santa Hasbro.

"And you issued the permit?"

"Waived the $10 filing fee, too."

Mrs. Crankberry did not like that.

Ben had marched the three blocks, turned, and was now walking back toward his house.

Mrs. Crankberry sneered. "Ben Smathers! Yer messin' up my Christmas parade! In honor of all these fine decorations I had made!"

Ben stopped. He said, "If you think a Christmas parade should honor anything but Jesus, maybe you need to take a refresher course."

"Those decorations are fine things, Ben Smathers. Not that you would know anything about fine things, playing in those jazz bands, banging that drum all your life, growing up poor like you did. No, you wouldn't know fine things."

Ben Smathers smiled. Nodded. Looked Mrs. Crankberry in the eyes and said, "Lt. Colonel Crankberry, the finest things I ever knew are buried in the fields of France, and Italy, and Africa, and Belgium, and Germany. Some of them haven't celebrated Christmas for almost fifty years. Every Christmas I take out this drum, and I play for them.

"They were poor boys, too. They gave their finest things for countries and for kings. And now they lay before the King. To honor them, I play my drum for them. I have no gift to bring that's fit, except to play my drum."

Mrs. Crankberry looked almost like she had been affected by his words. Almost.

He turned to go. Stopped. Turned back. Smiled. "It's okay if, deep down, you're moved by my gesture. After all, the ass and lamb kept time, too."

Toad Gilky was working on his Eagle Scout project down at the county maintenance building. He was also fulfilling community service hours he'd been given for some unlawful infraction. The judge was his Scoutmaster, so he allowed Toad to do his Eagle and court mandated service hours concurrently.

It had been seventeen or eighteen years since Mrs. Crankberry had had the big decorations made. She had died long ago, and it wasn't my fault. No one had done much in the way of upkeep of the decorations. Toad was refurbishing the signs. He was a competent carpenter and a decent painter. But only from a distance. He did most of the scenery for the school plays, so he was good at making things look good in dim light and thirty feet away.

Mrs. Crankberry had been dead for a long time, but Halfdollar still hung the decorations after Thanksgiving, and we still held the parade. Both parades. Mrs. Crankberry's and Ben Smathers's, who was still alive and still marched with his drum every year.

Skeeter and I went down to the county building to help Toad. We weren't working off any community service hours, but Sheriff Hasbro said it was alright if we helped Toad because we probably owed some service hours for something.

Toad had the decorations laid out, and he'd already painted a bunch of them. Some of them were so damaged Toad had to make new ones. He'd used stencils and spray paint to do the lettering.

Unfortunately, neither stencils nor spray paint have Spell Check.

"Toad, you spelled Christmas wrong," Skeeter said.

"Whada ya mean?" said Toad.

"There's a T in Christmas."

"No there's not. Listen, 'Chrismas.' There's no T," Toad argued. "It rhymes with Swiss Miss."

"Yes, there is a T. It's a silent letter," Skeet insisted.

"What's a silent letter?"

"Seriously, Toad? A silent letter is like the K and W in 'Know.' Or the W in 'Sword.' It's a letter in a word that doesn't make any sound. It's a letter you don't say. It's silent."

"All the letters are silent if you don't say 'em!" Toad contended.

"Well," Skeet surrendered, "there's a T in Christmas."

I went to college about an hour from Halfdollar. I rented a single-wide trailer to live in. The trailer was in the floodplain, so the landlord had put it up on eight twenty-foot telephone poles. Like you see at the beach but not as classy.

The trailer had spent its entire life on the floodplain and had lived through several floods but had only recently been put up on the telephone poles. The floor was rotten in several places as a result. There was a two-foot hole clean through the floor in the living room.

"What's the rent?" I asked the landlord.

"Two fifty a month."

"There's a gaping hole in the floor."

"Okay, two hundred a month, and I'll put a carpet over the hole."

"Deal."

The landlord had a sense of humor. The carpet was round, with a red circle in the middle, a white circle around that, and another red circle on the outside edge.

There was an exterior door on each of the long sides of the trailer. Going up to each door was a rickety wood staircase. At the top of each staircase was a three-by-five plywood landing. I had an artist friend paint a 3D painting on the back landing, the sort of thing chalk artists draw on the sidewalk so it looks like you are about to fall into the sewer or subway system.

Sometimes friends would come over and drink beer. Not me. Baptist friends. My space was a safe space where people could be themselves. When they asked for the bathroom, I would point toward the backdoor. They would open it and be about to take a step when they would see the 3D painting, think they were about to plummet, and fall back into the room. Hilarious.

I was dating a girl from town named Marie. College towns always have a tension between the college folks and the townies. Marie was both. It added some spice to the relationship.

Marie was from a rural West Virginia town much like Halfdollar, but she belonged to a Christian denomination that didn't celebrate holidays.

Marie's mom told me, "We celebrate the birth of Jesus every day, not just on December 25th."

I said, "That's probably not an awful theological stance, but I wouldn't want Walmart to get hold of the idea of celebrating Christmas every day."

I didn't get along well with Marie's mom.

Marie grew up watching her friends from other denominations celebrate, decorate, and exchange gifts for Christmas. She really wanted to decorate for Christmas.

"You can decorate my trailer," I told her. "Knock yourself out."

"Oh," she said, "that would be fantastic. But we can't buy the tree or decorations in town because somebody'll call my mom or pastor and rat me out."

"I know where we can get a tree," I winked. "What kind of tree do you want? Fir, Pine, Hemlock, Juniper, Yew, Cedar, Cyprus, Sequoia if you've got the space, or a PVC Christmas artificial tree?"

"What are you talking about?" she asked.

"Inside joke," I muttered, then said, "Let's drive over to Halfdollar and buy the stuff there. You don't have any people over there, so no one will tell your mom."

People say, "We grew up poor, but we never knew it." Now you know it because someone builds a Dollar General in your town.

"We're not poor. Wait… what's that? Oh. Snap. I guess we are poor."

We got back to the trailer at night, and in the darkness hauled the decorations and tree up to the living room. Marie was decorating the interior of the trailer, putting up the cardboard fireplace, hanging the stockings, and stringing lights. I was on the couch doing nothing, practicing for being married.

The trailer started rocking as someone pounded up the stairs. The front door flew open and Marie's mom glared in at us. "Marie! What are you doing?"

Marie was defiant. "I'm decorating for Christmas! I'm eighteen years old. I can decorate for Christmas if I want to!"

I gotta say, it's pretty embarrassing when your girlfriend's mom walks in and catches you decorating for Christmas.

Marie's mom shouted back, "But Marie! We don't decorate!"

"Mom! I'm an adult! I can do what I want."

Marie's mom was flabbergasted. She began staggering around the trailer looking at the decorations, aghast. All she wanted was out of there, and when she came to a door, she flung it open to escape.

It was the back door. She expected to see the landing, the steps, but instead, she was confronted with a 3D drawing of the gaping hole. She stumbled backward, stepped on the center of the target carpet, and slowly started sinking down through the hole in the floor.

"Don't struggle!" I yelled.

"Put your arms out to the side!" Marie suggested.

"It's not quicksand," Marie's mom shouted back.

Marie's mom sank to her bosom, and then she stopped descending. She was like Great Stuff. She form-fit the hole. No amount of pulling by me and Marie freed her. We had to call the volunteer fire department.

The firemen put a ladder up under Marie's mom and had to use a razor blade to cut away the carpet. There was some struggling, and some effort toward modesty, but one of the firemen casually remarked, "Looks like she's decorating for something."

Marie and I were grounded from seeing each other for two weeks after that. We got back together a few days before Christmas. We drove over to Halfdollar for the parade. I pulled some strings in town and, as one of her Christmas presents, she got to ride one of the Christmas floats as a Christmas queen. She was elated.

Charolais was in town, so Skeet, Charolais, Toad and I were the only spectators at the parade.

Skeet looked up at the Christmas decorations hanging from the light poles.

Skeet said, "Toad, you spelled Christmas wrong."

"I put the T in it," he said shortly.

"You put it in the wrong place. It goes in the middle, after the first 's'."

The rest of us looked up at the decorations. Several of them read, 'Merry Chrismast.'

Toad stared, then proclaimed, "Well, if the letter is silent, it doesn't matter where it goes!"

Skunks

I worked at a series of camps during the summers while I was in college. One summer I worked at Camp Horseshoe, just outside of St. George, West Virginia. That's just outside of Parsons if that clears anything up for you.

Skeeter, Wally, Uncle Deebo, and I all worked at the camp. The four of us were counselors and lived in the same cabin. The cabin was big. It had two wings for the campers, each with probably twenty-five bunk beds, and then a little room in the back where the four of us counselors lived. We also slept on two bunk beds.

There was a big foyer with benches and coat hooks for taking off boots and hanging up rain gear just inside the front door of the cabin. On either side of the foyer were the wings the kids lived in. If you went straight through the foyer, you entered our little space, which was just big enough to accommodate our two bunks, one on each side of the door. There was a screen door at the back of our room so we could come in and out of our quarters without disturbing the kids.

Skeet and I had one bunk; Wally and Uncle Deebo the other. Skeet slept on bottom, me on top. Wally slept on the bottom, Uncle Deebo on top.

One day Wally cut his finger badly enough that we had to drive him over the mountain to get stitches. The doctor put him on pain killers, and he came back to camp a little woozy. We were helping him up the stairs to the back door of the cabin. Well, we weren't really helping him. The stairs were uneven, and Wally was woozy, so it was fun to watch him try to negotiate the steps. He fell. He had just enough awareness to know that one hand was damaged, so he put that hand behind his back and reached out with his good hand. He broke two fingers when he landed. Bent them all the way back to his wrist. It's an interesting thing to witness if it's happening to someone else. "Ohhh, can the human body do that? Yikes. Not successfully."

We had to take him back to the doctor. The doctor put his fingers in a splint and put him on more pain killers. This time we helped him up the stairs when we got back because we were nice guys, and because it was almost supper, and we didn't want to miss that.

We got Wally situated in his bunk, ate supper, managed to get the campers into their bunks, and then went to bed ourselves.

I don't know how long I had been asleep when I heard Skeeter whispering my name. "Bil, Bil, wake up. But don't move."

This is a difficult way in which to be awakened because your body fills with adrenaline, and you want to jump into action but you also know that if you jump into action, you may die. I brought myself slowly out of my slumber and lay still in my bed. I whispered, "I'm awake. What's up?"

"There's a skunk in the cabin. Shut the door," Skeet whispered.

I knew what he meant. There was that door that led out of our little room and into the common area. If the skunk went in there, it was going to go into one of the wings, and a kid was going to see it. Each wing bunked about fifty teenagers. If a kid screamed, the skunk was going to go off. We left the door open at night so we could hear the noises from the kids that we were going to ignore. I understood why Skeeter wanted me to close the door. He wanted to contain the threat. He wanted to keep the skunk from wandering into the realm of one hundred teenage boys. I wasn't sure I wanted to contain the threat. I thought, "Out there is one hundred teen-aged boys. They haven't bathed in a week. How much worse could it smell?" But I saw his point. We were contractually obligated to look after the well-being of those children.

I sat up in my bed, got on my knees, reached out, and pushed the dividing door shut. It shut with a *snick*. Then, I lay back on the bed.

The skunk didn't seem to notice, but Uncle Deebo had awakened at some point.

He asked, "There's a skunk in the cabin?"

Skeeter said, "Yes."

Uncle Deebo was the last of seventeen children. I don't want to call him dumb, but I think his older siblings had claimed all the intelligence genes. Uncle Deebo was a farm kid, a country boy, but he had no common sense.

"Will it bite?" Uncle Deebo asked softly.

That's the wrong question. If a bear wanders into your cabin, you don't ask, "Does it stink?" If a mountain lion walks in, you don't ask, "Will I get fleas?" I wanted to thump Uncle Deebo, but then the skunk would have sprayed.

"What now?" Uncle Deebo asked.

"Wait it out," Skeet advised. "And whisper!"

"How did it get in here?" Uncle Deebo asked.

"It must have come in through the screen door. Hopefully, it'll go out the screen door."

But it didn't. In fact, the screen door went *fump-fump*, and a second skunk came in.

"Now there's two of them," Uncle Deebo noted helpfully.

"Thanks for the heads up," I muttered.

He asked, "If one goes off, will the other one go off, too?"

"Yes," Skeeter said. "They're like hornets. If you make one mad, you make all of them mad."

"They can swarm," I added.

By this time, Skeeter and I were laughing. But it was a quiet laugh, like you do in school, or in church, or at a funeral.

I was in the top bunk. One reason I was in the top bunk is because I knew I would be living in that cabin for eight weeks, and I figured a bear was bound to wander in sooner or later. I figured the bear was most likely to bite the person on the bottom bunk. Bears are basically lazy. They're like water. They're going to take the course of least resistance. They're going to eat the guy in the bottom bunk. I could get free of the cabin while that was happening. I figured a bear would be a hazard to just one of us, and so long as that one wasn't me, I wasn't worried.

But a skunk? Skunks are equal opportunity hazards. If you get sprayed by a skunk the stink sticks with you and everything you own for days and days. If Skeeter got eaten by a bear I would be devastated, but I would probably be over it by morning. It would take weeks to get over being sprayed by a skunk.

Skeeter got ahold of himself and asked, "Bil, did you brush your teeth?"

I thought I knew where he was going with this, so I said, "No."

Uncle Deebo said, "I brushed my teeth. Why does that matter?"

"Skunks are scavengers, like bears," Skeet explained. "They are attracted to scents like toothpaste. They love toothpaste."

I was gripping the edge of my bunk trying not to convulse with laughter. Tears were rolling into my ears.

"I'll be okay," Uncle Deebo said. "I'm on the top bunk. They can't get to me."

"Why do you think people call skunks polecats?" Skeet asked.

Uncle Deebo took a deep breath, like he didn't intend to exhale for the rest of his life.

Mine and Skeet's bunk was rocking from laughter, at about 1.8 on the Richter scale.

We were taunting poor Uncle Deebo, but we were doomed anyway. Let our tombstones read, "They Went Down Taunting."

The skunks' claws clacked on the wooden floor.

The screen door went *fump-fump* and a third skunk wandered in.

Wally had thus far slept through the whole thing. Wally was a good camp counselor because he was one of those guys who woke up in the morning happy. He loved to watch the sunrise, which was a good complement to my counseling style. I was better at night. In fact, I couldn't swear to you that the sun did rise because I'd only ever seen it set.

Wally always woke up singing songs about happy birds and trees going *chirp*, *chirp*, *chirp*. He shouted, "GOOD MORNING," as he sprang from bed every day.

Wally woke up in the midst of the skunk invasion and, in his drug-addled state, thought it was morning. He shouted, "GOOD MORNIG" and leapt from the bed. He landed in the middle of a triangle of skunks.

The three skunks froze in their tracks and looked at Wally. Wally saw the skunks and, with the sublime innocence of a drunk, cooed, "Kitty cats." He knelt and scratched one of the skunks behind its ears, muttering and murmuring sweet sounds the whole time. The skunk didn't know what to make of it, but it wasn't entirely unpleasant. The skunk moved closer. Wally picked the skunk up and stood. He turned toward Uncle Deebo, extended his arms, and said, "Look Uncle Deebo, a kitty cat."

The skunk crawled off Wally's hands and onto Uncle Deebo's chest.

Uncle Deebo screamed.

The skunk bit him.

All three skunks sprayed.

Skeeter and I lay there, choking, gagging, coughing, and laughing. Then, from the ether, there came a voice saying, "Boys, boys, boys. When a man does things purely for his own enjoyment, and not for the benefit of others, or the glory of God, he will be tainted and stained, that others may know."

Tunaball

A twenty-one-year-old man can look only so long at a double-bitted axe handle and a stack of tuna fish cans before he concludes he should hit a can of tuna fish with the double-bitted axe handle. Does he realize that he could package those cans of fish up and send them to some famine-ridden country to feed the needy? Yes, he acknowledges that such an act would increase the Greater Good and would satisfy many tenants of the Boy Scout Code. But he also realizes that it would be fun to hit a full can of tuna fish as hard as he could with a hickory, double-bitted axe handle. "I will hit just one can, for the benefit of Science," he says nobly to himself. "The rest of the cans I will send to the starving masses, for the benefit of Humanity." Thus, having resolved the issue, he smacks a can of tuna fish as hard as he can with the double-bitted axe handle. It feels so good, so right, he allows himself one more can. And so, a game, a pastime, a veritable agreeable activity, has its genesis.

I worked at Philmont Scout Ranch in Cimarron, New Mexico, the summer I was twenty-one years old. I worked at a backcountry campsite called Pueblano. Myself and five other staff members emulated a late 19th century logging camp. During the day we showed scouts how loggers climbed trees, cut timber, and made railroad ties. During the evenings we played a game called Tunaball.

The name of the game is a little misgiving since there was no ball involved. We had adopted the name tunaball since the game, to some extent, resembled baseball, but it was more fun than baseball. There was a pitcher, a batter, and fielders, but the fielders were little more than active bystanders. I realize that 'active bystander' is somewhat of an oxymoron, but mostly the fielders just stood there waiting for their chance to bat. There is no base running in tunaball, no catching fly balls, no thwarting stolen bases; there weren't bases. At the conception of the game there wasn't any declared object of the game beyond creatively diminishing our stock of tuna fish. Come to think of it, there wasn't even a pitcher in the earliest days of our pastime. There was just inspiration.

Each week a truck would come up our lonely road and deliver supplies: Toilet paper, spaghetti noodles, onions, peanut butter, regular butter, bread, oatmeal, coffee, milk, juice, and for some odd reason, cases of tuna fish. Each week, we received twelve cans of tuna fish. Three of my fellow staff members were borderline to serious vegans. They would not eat tuna. The rest of us just didn't like the stuff. After two months at camp our stock of tuna began to rival that of the Atlantic Ocean. Except, unlike the ocean, all our tuna was dead. We did not have room to store the tuna. We tried to send the stuff back down the mountain, but the delivery guy refused our pleas. The memory of our mothers talking about starving children prevented us from throwing the stuff away.

There were two main goals in tunaball. First, the batter tried to hit the can of tuna in such a way that the axe handle left a perfect impression of itself in the can. Second, the batter, the pitcher, and the fielders tried hard to not get hit by the can or tuna splatter when the can eventually exploded. And the can *always* eventually exploded. Your average can of tuna has far greater structural integrity than you might imagine. A single can of tuna will withstand numerous whacks from an axe handle, but you'd be amazed at how much area six ounces of tuna will cover when it does finally explode.

After two or three evenings of tunaball, our yard had a thick sheen of shredded, broadcast tuna lying about half an inch thick, in a pattern that started at home base and expanded in a one-dimensional, topographic cone for more than ten yards along what would have been the first and third baselines, had such lines existed in tunaball. There was a great delta of tuna laying ankle deep in our yard. We had to suspend the evening games due to the smell.

Philmont is bear country. And mountain lion country. It wasn't long before we had a brand-new fan base clamoring for us to play tunaball.

Fortunately, before the bears and lions became a real problem, the rain started. We got hit with a torrential summer thunderstorm that lasted for six days and dropped buckets of hail and an ocean of water. The creek beside the cabin overflowed its banks and tried out for river status. Our foot bridge was washed away, and a 150-year-old Douglas spruce was felled and washed miles downstream. We could barely leave the cabin. We were informed by CB radio that the road connecting us to base camp had suffered so much damage that it would be at least a week, maybe ten days, before we could be resupplied. We already hadn't been resupplied for six days. Our stocks were getting low. Broadcasting all that excess tuna didn't seem like a very good idea now.

Our campsite was located 8080 feet above sea level. Who would have guessed that we were going to be threatened by flood? Fire, avalanche, bear attack, lightning strike--these were the sort of natural disasters we had anticipated. Who hordes caches of tuna in case of a lightning strike? You just don't hear people say, "Yeah, I was struck by lightning. Fortunately, I'd had the foresight to stockpile enough food and water to survive the ordeal."

Eventually the rain stopped, the creek receded, and the sun came out. Seven to ten days later I stepped out the front door of our cabin to discover that a crop of tuna was sprouting like wildflowers in the front lawn. Hundreds, thousands of tiny tuna heads were emerging from the wet ground and gasping for saltwater to fill their tiny gills.

I got to work right away. I grabbed a shovel and started building a system of dikes around the parameters of the tuna crop. I then diverted the creek to flood and irrigate the field. I ran into the kitchen and got all the salt I could find to salinate the water. Before long, and 8080 feet up in the New Mexico Rockies, I had created one of the finest tuna paddies ever made by the hand of man.

I had earned my Agriculture, Gardening, Pet Care, and Oceanography merit badges. With that combined knowledge, I felt certain that I could sustain my tuna paddy and raise a healthy school of fish. There were even a few stray dolphins growing in the field.

The fish grew rapidly, and soon the tuna paddy wasn't big enough to contain the fish. They kept jumping the banks of the paddy to get free. Some made it into the creek and swam off, but others landed in the yard, and I'd have to run out and throw them back into the tuna paddy before they expired. I was worried about the tuna getting loose. I was afraid to release the tuna into the wild since they had no natural predators in the area. I was afraid they'd overrun the mountain streams. I didn't want to be responsible for some sort of tuna plague, equal to the prolific and destructive introduction of Japanese beetles, kudzu, and news about Paris Hilton. (How old is this story???)

Turns out, I needn't have worried. Bears and mountain lions and raccoons and skunks and 'possums came out of the hills in droves. I think the local wildlife were a little confused by the tuna. Those predators and omnivores thought tuna's natural habitat was a Ziplock bag in the pocket of a backpack. But that didn't stop them. The olfactory memory of those creatures recalled the scent. Maybe your average bear couldn't pick a tuna fish out of a line-up, but he can smell a tuna fish in a solid steel box three miles away.

Bears and raccoons and skunks and 'possums, all being omnivores, didn't have any qualms about diving into my tuna paddy and eating their fill. But the mountain lions and coyotes and foxes, being more strictly carnivorous, paused before feasting on the tuna. I think the problem for the lions and the coyotes and the foxes was that they were vain creatures, proud of their carnivore heritage and reputations. And they'd heard somewhere, somehow, something about tuna fish salad. They knew salad was made from vegetables, and they didn't eat vegetables. The lions and the coyotes and the foxes got together and mulled over the idea that the tuna fish might be vegetables instead of fish. It was finally decided that since fruit salad is salad but not made out of vegetables, and Caesar salad is salad but not made from Caesar, and hamburger isn't really ham, and that the label 'Organic' doesn't mean anything at all, that humans simply couldn't be trusted to name food, and so the lions and coyotes and the foxes ate the tuna in my field.

It was a slaughter. I had to do something to give the tuna a fighting chance. I determined I would burst the dike and set them free. I was just about to release the tuna when, much to my surprise, two helicopters landed in our yard. A guy from the Department of Natural Resources, followed by a guy from the

EPA, jumped out of one of the helicopters. A couple of businessmen in suits jumped out of the other chopper.

The DNR and EPA guys asked me a bunch of questions about my tuna paddy, where it came from, how I got the salt in the water, and where my permits were. Then they ran a bunch of tests on the water and the fish.

The DNR and EPA guys quarantined the whole area. Turns out that the mercury content in those fish was so high that my little Rocky Mountain tuna crop posed an environmental hazard.

The businessmen who got out of the other helicopter were also doing tests and soundings. They set up a small drill and drilled into the core of the tuna patty, did some thermo-geographical mapping, surveyed the surrounding area, and took a few infrared scans.

The government fellas concluded their tests and informed me that they needed to close me down. They said I had no permit for a fish farm, that the paddy was an ecological hazard, that I had no right to plant it in the first place, and that they suspected that maybe I had not planted the fish at all but that they had occurred naturally as a result of a prehistoric deposit of tuna eggs left in the silt of the bottom of the sea some eight million years previous and were thus an endangered species. They wanted to declare the place a museum as soon as they condemned the region and spent millions of tax dollars to reclaim the site.

The businessmen, on the other hand, had concluded that the site was ready for an oil well: An Omega 3 oil well. The government guys tried to argue with the businessmen until the businessmen reached into their pockets and pulled out the lawyers and senators that they keep in there. My whole tuna paddy was declared a Nationally Protected Natural Resource Area critical to National Security and Defense.

The government guys and businessmen forced us all to leave and, as far as I know, no civilian has been there since.

Tunaball has subsequently been banned in sixty-four countries.

All I can say is, I hope tuna aren't perennial.

Montina the Divine Bovine

A few years back Skeeter and I drove cross-country to Swan Lake in Flathead County, Montana. We were going black bear hunting. But don't worry, we didn't kill any bears because we didn't even see any bears. I like to think we won because the bear forfeited. I think the truth of the matter is that we were in a minivan, and no self-respecting bear wants to get killed by a guy in a minivan.

We drove maybe two-thirds of the way across the country without a single problem. We got off the interstate and had about fifty miles to go on a two-lane road when an RV thundered up behind us, tailgating. The RV was pushing hard and made several abortive attempts to pass us. The problem was that that stretch of Montana road, with a cliff wall on one side and a sheer drop off on the other, wasn't engineered for an RV to pass a minivan.

The guys in the RV seemed to think that was our fault. They were leaning out the windows of the RV screaming at us. They only seemed to know about five words, but they could use those five words in sort of a tonal swear language, aided by hand gestures which got their point across.

"Nice," Skeet said, sarcastically. "He's driving that thing like a summer assault vehicle."

The driver saw his opening and took it at full throttle.

One of the passengers leaned out the window and expressed his general displeasure with Skeet's driving.

For the next thirty-five miles I had to listen to an enraged Skeeter not finish a sentence about what he was going to do if ever he encountered those fellas again.

"If I ever…"

"The next time I…"

"Let's just say for example…"

"I mean, suppose we…"

"If we had a…"

And so on, until we pulled into the campground forty minutes later. We checked in at the office and then drove over to our assigned site. I looked across the field as we were unloading the gear and, low and behold, there was that same RV and those same three fellas still speaking their five-word tonal swear language. They had a cooler out. I judged them to be about a quarter way through the contents of that cooler. I didn't say anything. I had spent the last thirty-five miles of my life listening to Skeeter not adequately articulate what he was going to do to those guys if he ever saw them again. I figured I'd just wait until Skeet noticed them.

We set up the tent. Made supper. Ate supper. I couldn't take it anymore. I said, "Skeet, aren't you going to cause those guys some trouble?"

Skeet glanced their way. They were halfway through the cooler by that point. He sized them up, nodded, shook his head, shrugged, then said, "Bil, those seem like the kind of guys who can cause themselves trouble. Let's just sit here and see what happens."

Their campsite was bordered by a barbed wire fence. On the other side of the fence was a herd of cows. When they were about three quarters through that cooler, they decided to jump the barbed wire fence. They crept drunkenly- wait a sec, no one has ever crept drunkenly- they drunkenly crept toward the cows. We watched as they made several attempts at cow tipping.

On the off chance you haven't heard of cow tipping, it is said that cows sleep standing up, with their knees locked, and thus if you sneak up beside a sleeping cow and give it a solid push, it will cause the cow to tip over. It's fun for everybody. Except the cow.

Cow tipping is an ancient sport which dates back to the rural Greek dairy farmer Tipratise. He would get drunk and tip cows. Tipratise's intoxicated cow tipping is from whence we derived the word 'tipsy.'

The three fellas tipped several cows and then they noticed, standing all by itself on a knoll, like on the back of an old nickel, a lone buffalo. We watched in awe and wonder as one of the guys stepped up beside the buffalo.

Ever heard of buffalo tipping?

No, of course you haven't. And you haven't heard of buffalo tipping for the very same reason that you have never heard of moose tipping, or elk tipping, or elephant tipping, or even alligator rolling. These are all bad ideas, which means that some man out there somewhere has tried them. And he died a heinous death. His wife told people he ran off with a younger woman rather than facing the embarrassment of admitting her husband died alligator rolling.

I believe that when you tip a cow, the cow gets about halfway to the ground, wakes up, says something like, "What the…," and then hits the ground.

The buffalo was bigger than any cow in that field. It didn't tip. It just woke up, snorted, scraped the ground, and charged.

Those three fellas ran across that field and jumped that barbed wire fence with enough grace and agility to qualify for the International Inebriated Olympics, if only there were such a thing.

Skeet said, "Give them a minute to catch their breaths. Then it is time to cause them some trouble."

When they had caught their breath, Skeet and I wandered over and introduced ourselves, making no mention of the events we had just witnessed. The fellows offered us a beer, and we five now sat around a blazing campfire, sharing small talk. One of the three asked, "So, what are you guys doing out here?"

Skeet said, "Oh, we're doing research for our doctoral thesises."

One guy asked, "What are you studying?"

I gotta tell you, I was just as interested as those guys to find out what we were studying.

Skeet said, "We are studying, uh, Supernatural Bovine Theology."

"Say what?" said one of the three.

"To put it simply," Skeet said, "we are studying the great Bovine Creation Myth."

"Say what?" said the same one of the three.

"The Bovine Creation Myth."

The three looked confused.

"You've never heard of the Bovine Creation Myth? The great cow goddess Montina?" asked Skeet.

"I've never heard of Montina," said one of the three.

"Sure you have," I said. "They named this whole state after her."

Skeeter then launched into the doctrine and dogma of the great cow goddess Montina:

In the beginning was the Herd. And the Herd was good. But the Great Cow Goddess, Montina, was alone. So, she created the universe: the stars, the galaxies, the constellations, the comets, and meteors. But still she was lonely, so she created the solar systems. She created our solar system with the Sun and the Earth. But she wanted more. She wanted company. She created the first two cows, Botox and Bowtie.

Montina put Botox and Bowtie in the Pasture of Eden, here on Earth, and gave them dominion over all the fields and grasses but warned them not to drink from the Pond of Life.

"Now," Skeet interrupted himself, "just to avoid confusion, Botox and Bowtie were both cows, that is to say, females. In this aspect, the story differs from the Adam and Eve account. You see, there's no bull in this story." Skeet winked at me, assuring me that he knew that while this statement could easily set off conservative Christians, the story he was telling was so ridiculously improbable that everyone would instantly understand that he was joking-making a simple pun at the expense of this particular audience in the campsite. He then continued the story of Montina:

After a while Botox and Bowtie got a little bored and decided to take a walk down to the Pond of Life.

"Hold up," said one of the three, "even if this is true, why are you studying it here? At this campground?"

"That's simple." I said, "Our theory is that this land, right here, might be the original location of the Pasture of Eden."

"Oh," said the three, nodding.

"Anyway," continued Skeet:

Botox and Bowtie wandered down to the Pond of Life. They weren't going to drink from the Pond, mind you. They were just going to check it out. At the Pond of Life was a frog. Now this was no ordinary frog. This was a bullfrog. And this was one smooth-talking, sweet-mooing, devilishly handsome bullfrog. That frog looked up at Botox and Bowtie and said, "Kiss me, and I'll turn into a bull prince." And they kissed him. There was a flash of light, a puff of smoke, and voilà, that bullfrog turned into a beefy, handsome bull prince.

"Hey," said one of the three, "I think I *have* heard this story!"
"It's an old story," I said.
Skeet went on:

That ol' bull showed them cows a few things they would have never thought up on their own, and before long they were both with calf. Montina caught wind of the situation and came looking for Botox and Bowtie. But the two cows hid. Montina called for them, and at last Botox and Bowtie showed themselves.

"Why were you hiding?" asked Montina.

"We were naked and ashamed," answered Botox and Bowtie.

"You're not naked," said Montina, "You're cows!"

Montina figured out what had happened, and she expelled Botox and Bowtie from the Pasture of Eden. From that point on, explained Montina, cows would be ruled over by men with big hats and pointy boots. They would stand in fields and chew cud all day long.

"Wow," said one of the three when Skeet had finished, "I've never heard that story before. Is it for real?"

"Well," I said, "that's what we are out here trying to prove. This herd of cows right here is supposed to be the sacred remnant of the original herd of Botox and Bowtie."

The fellas were starting to look a little worried.

"Are they," began one, "like, you know, protected by federal law or something? Like is it a crime to mess with them?"

"Good Lord," I said, aghast, "they are protected by a force far greater than the Law. They are protected by Montina. It is not a crime to mess with them; it is a sin."

"Why do you ask?" said Skeet.

"No reason," said one of the three.

"You didn't, did you? Mess with them?" I asked, worry in my voice. "You didn't mess with the cows, did you?"

"Well," said one of the three, "we might have gone out into the field."

"Did you mess with the cows?"

"We might have touched them."

Skeet gave a low whistle. "It isn't cool to mess with the sacred herd. You didn't try to tip them, did you?"

"We might have…"

Skeet whistled.

I said, "Well, at least there was no Bluff-a-lo in the field."

"Oh yeah, there's a buffalo out there," said one.

"Not a buffalo," I said, "a Bluff-a-lo."

"What's a Bluff-a-lo?" asked one.

"The Bluff-a-lo," I explained, "is the ghost spirit that Montina sends to protect the cows. You should never even approach the Bluff-a-lo. Wait," I paused. "You didn't try to tip the Bluff-a-lo did you?"

"We might have," came a soft, weak answer.

"What happens if you touch him?" asked one.

"You will have the wrath of Montina brought upon you and yours for seven generations."

"Uh-oh," said all three at once.

"The Bluff-a-lo," I said, "is a great believer in the doctrine of an eye for an eye and a hoof for a hoof. If you tried to tip the Bluff-a-lo he will try to tip you. And you don't want to be tipped by a Bluff-a-lo. That's like getting tipped by a school bus."

"Well," said Skeet, "we might save you from serious trouble if we act quickly."

"Say what?" asked one of the three.

"He'll wait until you least expect it and then he will try to knock you over," Skeet said. "The best recourse is for you guys to go into the Prone Defense."

Let me pause here and point out that the Prone Defense is really no defense at all. You rarely hear a football or basketball coach shout to his or her players, "Go Prone! Go Prone! Lie Down!" Prone Defense is more an instinctual self-defense mechanism than an active attempt to thwart an enemy. But those fellas were drunk. They'd go right to sleep if they lay down for any reason, and that was exactly what Skeet and I needed them to do.

I said, "You fellas need to climb into that camper, get in your beds, and lie still. Play dead."

They jumped up to go.

Skeet halted them. "Wait a sec. Listen close. That Bluff-a-lo is coming. I can feel it in my bones. He wants you. Get in your camper. Lock the door. Shut the windows. Close the blinds. Lie down! And DON'T GET UP! No matter what you hear, or feel, or smell, lie still. Don't whisper, don't get up, don't look out the windows. Stay prone and silent. You may hear some snuffling, you might feel some bumping on your camper, but whatever you hear or feel, just stay still. We'll be out here keeping watch. If he comes, we'll do what we can for you."

They ran fast into their camper. The door shut. The blinds closed. The lights went out.

Skeet and I headed back to our campsite. We waited about thirty minutes. By that time we could hear solid snores coming from the camper.

Skeet and I went over the plan one last time, and then we got the hydraulic jack out of our van. It is a dandy of a jack. It extends about four feet in no time at all. Jack in hand, we crept soberly toward our new friends' camper. I mooed a few times, just to see how alert our pals were. They snored on.

We found a heavy chunk of firewood and placed it midway between the front and rear wheels on the driver's side of the camper. We put the jack on the piece of firewood and started working the jack as fast as possible. It does not take long, with a hydraulic jack, to compromise an RVs center of gravity. As the

RV began to tilt we heard the unmistakable *THUMP* of a drunk man rolling off his bunk. Then we heard him say, "Oh, CRAP! THE BLUFF-A-LO!"

I put my hands on the side of the camper and started to push. We were doing a little camper tipping now- it's harmless. A few hard shoves sent the RV toppling over with a resounding *crash.* It fell over the fence and into the Pasture of Eden.

The screams of the three men inside the camper attracted the attention of the buffalo. The buffalo wasn't keen about the large, white rectangle that had fallen into his field. The buffalo dropped his head and charged.

If there is one thing in this world you can be sure of, it is that the engineers who design RVs never once asked themselves, "How are we going to buffalo-proof the roof of this RV?"

That buffalo went headfirst into that camper like a bullet through a bucket.

That action produced the result Skeet and I were counting on. It was Newton's Third Law in action. A body in motion tends to stay in motion. Which is very similar to Skeeter's First Law: A body being chased by the law tends to stay in motion. The three men were moving now. They were climbing out of the windows and doors that were now on top of that RV, clad only in their underwear, trying to get away.

I screamed, "Bluff-A-Lo! Quick, save yourselves!"

The buffalo was stuck in the RV and was charging back and forth, smashing into everything it could hit.

"Save yourselves!" Skeet shouted.

"What do we do?"

I said, "Take off all your clothes!"

I guess having a Bluff-a-lo ransacking the inside of the RV you are standing on is an emotional time. It is amazing what a man will do when he thinks a mythical buffalo is after him. Those fellas were looking to save themselves anyway they could. Three pairs of underwear flew into the air.

"Dance," I yelled. "Dance the Dance of the Bluff-a-lo." I put my pointer fingers above my ears and jumped around like Kevin Costner in *Dances with Wolves.*

The three naked figures atop the camper followed suit.

Even out in the middle of nowhere Montana it doesn't take long for the authorities to get wind of that sort of situation. We heard the sirens of the Sheriffs' cars, and Skeet and I slipped back to our campsite. We were already in our sleeping bags when the cops arrived. We listened with delight as three very naked, very drunk, very handcuffed men tried to explain to a very humorless Sheriff just why they were dancing the Naked Dance of the Bluff-a-lo on the side of their camper in the middle of the night.

"Nice one," I said to Skeet.

"One of my best," he agreed. "I turned that Summer Assault Vehicle into a Somersault Vehicle."

Raised on Hose Water

Skeeter and I, for various reasons that were mostly out of our control, ended up with some hip young people in New York City. These young people thought it would be fun to take a couple of 40ish, smalltown boys to some establishments we might not experience in Halfdollar, West Virginia.

We ended up in a water bar. You heard me. A water bar. A bar that served nothing but various high-priced, high-end waters from springs, glaciers, rivers, lakes, and other bodies of water from all around the world. They had snow and ice from the tops of famous mountains. There was salinated, desalinated, partially desalinated, and resalinated sea water. The bar also had a wide variety of craft-brewed waters on tap.

The Hipsters order things like heavy water from a Norwegian fjord with crushed April ice from Lake Huron, dusted with the snows of Mt. Kilimanjaro.

I looked around for the ghost of Hemingway.

One kid order revaporated jet contrail from the wing of a 737 passing south bound over the Iberian Peninsula. The waitress asked follow-up questions such as, "Left wing or right wing?" because everything is political these days.

Skeet and I were a bit dumbfounded by all of this, including the point.

The waitress turned to me and eyed me skeptically. She asked, "And what would you like?"

I considered saying something smart-alecky, but it wasn't her fault there was a water bar. She was just trying to make a buck while putting herself through school or auditioning for Broadway shows. She didn't need me making her life hard. I said, "Do you have any West Virginia waters?"

"We have waters from the White Sulphur Springs, the Green Sulphur Springs, and the Berkley Springs."

I didn't want sulphur water. I'd had Berkley Springs water. I asked, "What else would you recommend?"

She said, "How about a glass of re-condensed Old Faithful spray with Lake Baikal ice?"

That pushed me over the line. I couldn't take it anymore. I said, "Do you have any water from West Virginia geysers?"

"Sir," she said calmly, "we don't have any West Virginia geyser water. I don't think there are any geysers in West Virginia. The geothermal conditions aren't suitable. The magma isn't close enough to the surface."

I blinked. I had not expected that response. I said, "Actually, the conditions do exist. You see, just as New York City sits above many levels of a labyrinthine warren of subway tunnels going every which way, West Virginia also sits atop a hive-like complex of coal mine tunnels. These mines are both active and abandoned.

"Sometimes coal mines catch on fire and since the fires have tons and tons of coal to fuel them, it can be very difficult to extinguish the fires. The only thing to do is seal the mine off and hope the fire goes out. But the fires don't always go out. There are mines around the world that have been burning for centuries."

I paused here to scan my audience. It is more difficult to lie in this day and age because people are connected to the Web. There are times when you need to throw out an outlandish fact or two, let people look them up, verify what you are saying on *Wikipedia*, or wherever. The young people I was with were being polite. They were not picking up their phones to check my statements. But their thumbs twitched, impatient to search out the truth. "Go ahead," I encouraged. "Look it up. Search 'Engine coal seam fire.' Or 'Centralia, Pennsylvania.' There has been a massive mine fire burning under Centralia since May of 1962."

They did. They found out I wasn't lying. At least about that. One person said, "It's true there is a fire under Centralia. It's been burning since the 60s when the town folks started a fire at the dump, which fell into a mine and caught the mine on fire. Most of the town is abandoned now."

"There are coal seam fires burning all around the world," said another.

"But," chimed a third, "I don't see anything about West Virginia geysers."

"That," I said, "is because they are very hard to document. They are rare, like St. Elmo's Fire. You don't know where they are going to pop up, or when. They are nothing like Old Faithful. You see, there are times when it rains so hard that the ground is oversaturated, and the creeks and rivers flood. Some of that excess water finds its way into coal seams that are on fire. The water vaporizes, turns to steam. When the steam pressure builds up to a great enough level, the ground explodes, and a geyser is formed for a brief and glorious moment." I stopped talking after that. The crowd was unsure.

The waitress said, politely, "Well, we don't have any West Virginia geyser water."

"Then surprise me," I said to her. "Bring me whatever you think is best."

She turned toward Skeeter. She didn't want to ask him what he wanted. She didn't care. And she certainly didn't want another long geyser story. To her relief, Skeet said, "What would you recommend?"

She took a deep breath and said, "How about a Lake Geneva, Loch Ness cocktail with fresh-harvested Greenland glacier ice, infused with Persian rose water?"

It was loud in the bar. Maybe Skeet actually misunderstood her. Maybe Skeet deliberately misunderstood her. He said, "*Infused* with hose water? Don't *infuse* it with hose water. Bring me a whole glass of hose water, but let the hose run a bit so the water gets cold."

It was no longer loud in the bar. Everybody had heard him. Sound carries over water.

The waitress cleared her throat and said, "Sir, we don't serve hose water. Hose water is extremely bad for you, full of toxins."

Skeet looked at me, looked at the waitress, at the crowd, and said, "Listen, when me and this guy were about twelve years old, we built a fort way off in the woods, like a hideaway, maybe a mile from our houses. In case we robbed a bank or something. We hauled two by fours out there, scraps of plywood, corrugated roofing, even a couch. Built a little cabin." He turned to me and said, "Right?"

"Absolutely," I agreed, even though I knew he was lying. I wanted to see what this had to do with hose water.

Skeet continued: "We had everything we needed, except a water source. And carrying enough water up there was laborious. This was, of course, before bottled water.

"So, me and Bil here got a bright idea. Why not run a hose up to our hideaway? Like I said, it was about a mile away from our houses. My family had a hose, but it wasn't a mile long. Bil's family had a hose, but it wasn't a mile long either. And believe it or not, when we screwed those two hoses together, they still weren't a mile long. But we were close. We only lacked about 5,180 feet of hose. We decided to borrow some of the neighbors' hoses. Operating under the principle that not everyone was going to want to loan us their hoses indefinitely, we decided to borrow them without asking. At night. People are more generous when they don't know you are borrowing their stuff.

"We scoured the whole county and ended up with about three-quarter mile of hose. We were still a quarter mile short but a lot closer than we had been. We screwed all those hoses together, hooked them to a spigot behind another neighbor's barn, and pulled and dragged and tugged them through the brush and bramble toward our hideaway.

"It's hot, heavy work dragging 3,600 feet of hose. That's a lot of lead. We were thirsty for some fresh, cool, hose water by the time we'd stretched that hose as far as it was going to go. Which is how we came to appreciate that we hadn't turned the hose on before we started dragging. We had to walk three quarters of a mile home to turn the hose on, then three quarters of a mile back, to the business end of the hose, to get a drink. It was a long way to go but utterly worth it."

The waitress and the patrons, and the young folks with us, were slack-jawed. They didn't know if they should believe Skeeter or not. I knew they shouldn't, but I wasn't going to say anything about it. I did say something, though. I thought a little scripture would be helpful at this juncture. I said, "Proverbs 9.17. Stolen water is sweet…It's even sweeter through three-quarter mile of stolen hose."

We let the assembled mull on the scripture for a few seconds, and then Skeeter nodded at me, knowing that while he was laying the groundwork, I would have been formulating the next chapter.

"We learned from that experience" I explained. "We learned we never wanted to forget to turn the hose on again, and the simplest way to not forget to turn it on was to never turn it off. We didn't have one of those fancy nozzles, or any nozzle at all, so we just let the water flow when we were up there. We tied an overhand knot in the hose when we went home, which slowed the water to a trickle. But we had a goat up there. A goat we had borrowed from Angus Fester…"

"Borrowed at night," Skeet interjected.

"Goats," I said, "are fantastic at clearing brush and bramble, and we had brush and bramble we needed cleared. When the goat got thirsty he'd walk over and drink the water coming out of the hose."

"You drank from the same hose as a goat?" asked one of the folks.

"The goat didn't mind," Skeet shrugged.

"Skeet and I tied off the hose one night and headed home," I began to conclude. "We got involved in this and that and, before we knew it, a week or more had passed since we had been up to our hideaway.

"It was Saturday, and we were down on the corner in town listening to Angus Fester yell at Sheriff Hasbro. He was saying:

"My goat got stolen and you ain't doin' nuthin' about it!"

Hasbro was giving it right back to Angus Fester: "How can I worry about one goat when a hundred and thirty garden hoses have gone missing?"

"Do you think the crimes are connected?" asked Fester.

"What would a hundred and thirty garden hoses have to do with a goat?" screamed Hasbro.

"And just like that," I said to the crowd at the bar, "a goat fell out of the sky and plopped on the lawn of the church. Everyone who was downtown at the time turned to look at Skeet and me."

Now, I don't want to preach to you, or tell you how to live your life, but let me just say that if a goat falls out of the clear blue sky and plops down, dead, on the lawn of the church, and everyone in town assumes you had something to do with it, you must be living right.

"The autopsy," I went on, "revealed about a foot of undigested, knotted garden hose in the goat's stomach. From there, it wasn't hard to figure out what had happened." I didn't say anything after that.

Everyone stared at me.

"What did happen?" asked the waitress. I could tell she didn't want to ask, but she couldn't help herself. She was asking on behalf of the others, for you, I'm sure.

I shrugged, "Well, 'Autopsy' might be too strong a word. An autopsy was rendered unnecessary given the way the goat exploded on impact." It is satisfying to watch the faces of vegan hipsters when you tell them a goat exploded. "Sherriff Hasbro saw the knotted hose chunk right away. He started walking backyards looking for the hoses and finally found the end of our hose that was connected to my neighbor's spigot. The Sheriff followed the hose three-quarters of a mile into the woods.

"The goat, it would seem, had gotten thirsty during our absence, and he chewed the end of the knotted water hose free, then swallowed it. But that's not what killed him." I stopped again.

"What killed him?" asked the waitress.

"Oh, well, the garden hose, left to run free for a week or so, saturated the ground. The water poured into an old burning coal mine underneath our hideout, where it boiled and turned to steam. The water kept coming in, the steam kept building up, until the pressure was so great that a geyser erupted directly under the goat, which propelled him clear to town where he plopped down onto the church lawn, which, incidentally, is what killed him."

We sat in silence for about fifteen seconds.

"So," Skeet said, "we drank hose water and nothing bad happened to us."

"It didn't do the goat much good," said someone.

"Yeah, but it wasn't so much the drinking from the hose that killed the goat. It was the resulting geyser."

The waitress was no dummy. She didn't believe us. She even smiled a little. She didn't quite know what to say. She wanted to win her argument, press her point that hose water is dangerous. She said, "Hose water contains lead, antimony, bromine, and BPA."

Skeet and I didn't respond.

She pressed harder: "Hose water can damage the liver, the kidneys, and other organs."

No response from us. I was tired of talking. Skeeter had started this. Heck, I was thirsty. Let him finish it.

She continued, "Hose water can damage the endocrine system, cause behavioral problems, and lower intelligence."

Skeet could use that. He said, "All I'm saying is we were raised on hose water. It didn't make us any dumber."

The waitress smiled, said, "With all due respect, you're sorta making my argument for me."

She went away to get our drinks.

Skeet held up his glass when she returned, sipped, and asked, "Romanian hose water?"

She winked. Waited for him to take another sip, and said, "New York City public restroom dirty mop water."

We left a hefty tip.